I0675784

His Incomparable Duchess

By
V.H. Lunden

His Incomparable Duchess

Published by Bright Performance Ltd.

Bright Performance Reg U.S. Trademark

Copyright © 2013 V.H. Lunden.

All rights reserved.

Library of Congress Cataloging-in-Publication

Data available upon request.

ISBN – 978-0982253946

Published in the United States of America

This book may not be reproduced in any form or by any means, electronic or mechanical, including photocopying, recording, or by any information storage or retrieval system now known or hereafter devised, without permission in writing from the copyright holder.

For my saving grace, my lovely mum!

Bloody Hell! What was that awful racket? Half asleep,

Edgar Hamilton, the Eighth Duke of Grangefield, realized the

noise was growing louder and closer. He needed sleep, a

precious commodity on this long voyage from India, particularly

after his son had fallen ill.

Untimely as it was, the door of his cabin banged open.

Before Edgar had the presence of mind to drag a sheet over his

naked body, his son ran into the room.

"Baba," he shouted, breathless; his Indian accent muted

by a bout of coughing. "You must be awake."

Edgar lifted his head off the pillow, trying not to frown

when the boy emitted several more coughs. This morning Sabeer

appeared thinner and weaker, a consequence of his prolonged

illness. His dark skin looked pale, and he shuddered, adjusting to

the cold. Edgar felt sorry for the lad; how much more could he

endure? The list of injustices grew daily, starting with a

tempestuous sea voyage, and now this unkind, English weather. Much worse, and perhaps the precipitator to this whole mad voyage, had been the sudden death of his mother. Yes, it was all too much, and there wasn't a thing he could do about any of it.

The *HMS Alexandra* had carried them on their three-month journey, and at some point during the night it had dropped anchor. Edgar had been away from England for more than a decade, and yet he regarded his impromptu return with both regret and elation.

"Boy, what is the meaning of all this? I explicitly said no interruptions."

Edgar had to remind himself that Sabeer was still suffering from whatever ailed him. From the first day they had set sail, his young body had not been able to adjust to the turbulent seas.

"Baba, I have come on an utmost urgent matter," his child's voice croaked. He was too weak to even lift one of his small brown hands to cover his mouth. He stood before Edgar wearing an overly long, white nightshirt. Edgar dismissed his fatherly concerns, deciding instead to concentrate on the boy's enthusiasm.

"Turn around."

Sabeer looked at him puzzled.

"Turn to the wall," he repeated, "I am naked and I would like to preserve some degree of modesty."

The boy didn't move.

It was at that moment Mr. Jones entered the cabin. His trusted servant, a fellow soldier in the queen's cavalry, and usually a pillar of good manners, had been in hurried pursuit of the boy. The man was out of breath and red-faced with exertion. Just behind him he dragged a haggard-looking female, dressed in clothing that exposed entirely too much cleavage.

"'Ere, stop pulling on me arm, I got two legs and I know how to use 'em," the woman stammered.

"If you stepped a bit faster, miss, I wouldn't 'ave to pull your arm, would I?" Jones muttered.

"What is the meaning of all this, Jones?" Edgar asked.

"You be the duke, then?" the woman interrupted.

Again, Edgar looked to Jones for explanation.

"Your Grace, I went down to the docks, just like you asked. I found this 'ere woman, and I mentioned about needn' a nurse. I told her the boy could be an 'and full, and she said she could nurse anyone." He raised an eyebrow at Sabeer before continuing. "As we were comin' up the ramp, I saw the young master 'ere, runnin' from his cabin; he was supposed to be asleep."

"That be my patient?" the woman asked. "That dark little 'un. The one that's staring at me with his mouth set to catch flies."

Edgar looked from Sabeer to the woman. Indeed, his son stared directly at the woman's ample and protruding bosom. His little eyes had widened, and his mouth hung open.

"Sabeer!"

The boy did an immediate about face, turning to the wall.

"Sorry, Cap'n," Jones said. "The boy, well, he refuses to stay in bed. I think somehow he got wind that Mr. Arnold was boarding the ship. I suspect he wanted to come and tell you the news."

"Baba," Sabeer interrupted, "Mr. Arnold is a most obedient servant, unlike these others." He regarded Jones and the nurse, his neck stretching so his nose pointed to the ceiling.

An ever-vigilant nanny, Jones moved a threatening step toward him. "I should return him to his cabin, Your Grace."

The boy stepped away, coughing, ignoring Jones and turning to ogle the woman.

"His cough has not improved, Jones," Edgar said.

"Been hackin' like that on an off, Your Grace. Refuses to stay in bed and let it heal."

"He's seven, Jones. Don't tell me after tending to the boy for all these years, you haven't learned how to control him?"

"It's his tongue, Your Grace, it's longer then one of mi' old rifles."

As if proving the point, Sabeer pointed his tongue at Jones.

"Baba, it is most disrespectful for this coolie to speak in my presence."

"Sabeer, stop playing at being a Rajah, you're not one," Edgar said.

The boy winced. "Mr. Arnold, he is a most jolly fellow," the boy said, changing the subject.

It was then that Mr. Arnold entered the cabin, which prompted Sabeer to quickly move to greet him. Edgar was relieved to see the boy smiling.

"Hello there, Sabeer," Arnold said, his eyes wrinkling with pleasure.

Sabeer didn't reply; instead, he latched his long arms around the older man's waist, offering him an awkward hug.

Raising his hand in greeting, Edgar acknowledged Arnold. The solicitor responded with a nod, while giving Sabeer a reassuring pat on his head. They had become friends three months ago when Arnold had visited Edgar in India to inform him about his inheritance.

"Good morning, Arnold; it is morning, I gather?"

"Quite early, but yes, it is morning, Your Grace."

"I would be happy to meet with you after I have dressed.

"I regret the formalities will have to wait, Your Grace," Arnold said. "I'm here on a rather urgent matter."

"Baba, that is precisely what I was wanting to tell you. I am thinking this visit must be most important."

Edgar ignored the boy. "What has happened?"

"I have taken the liberty and accepted an invitation on your behalf, Your Grace—to a ball."

Edgar looked at him, surprised.

"The reason for my attendance being?"

The solicitor stared at his boots. "Christmas," he stuttered. "Actually, what I meant to say was, being winter there will only be a few opportunities for you to meet eligible marriage candidates during the short social season, and this happens to be a very important event."

Both Sabeer and Mr. Jones looked at Edgar with curious expressions. "You will marry, Baba?"

"I must marry again, Sabeer. It is part of the terms of the inheritance."

The boy started coughing, and Edgar looked to Jones, who returned a concerned expression.

"I can arrange for a doctor in London, Your Grace," Arnold interjected.

"Baba, this woman you marry, I am thinking she must be pretty," the boy said. "Also, not so pale. She must also be having small ones, not big ones, like that," he pointed to the nurse's chest.

The woman had been watching the proceedings in silence.

"I'll have you know little 'un, I suckled five of me mites on these two Majestics. My late husband swore they be my finest assets."

Sabeer would not be silent. "She should also not be sounding like Mr. Jones."

"'Ere, are you sure he's sick?" the woman said, looking dubious. "Sounds like he needs a good walloping if you ask me."

Edgar looked at the woman with disgust. He picked up a few coins from a nearby stool, tossing them to the end of his cot. "Take those and leave, we won't be needing a nurse after all. Mr. Jones will escort you out."

"Didn't mean to upset, Your Grace, but I'm thinking your boy would be a right handful, though I'm sure I could manage 'im.'"

When Edgar didn't respond, the woman quickly stepped forward and gathered the coins from the bed. She then looked at Jones: "You're a nice looking man. You can come home with me if you like; but I won't be needn' no escort, not on any ship." She had said this offering him a gaped-tooth smile, exiting the cabin.

Edgar directed his next comment to Sabeer, who sat cross-legged on the floor near Mr. Arnold. His nightshirt had pooled about him like a white cloud. "You need to leave as well, you should be in bed."

Sabeer started to fidget. "Baba, I am thinking that we should be returning to India. Every toe on my foot is frozen, and each eyelash on my eyelids is now white like chalk dust. This

England is a very unhappy country, the sun never graces the sky, and ice water is forever falling on the ground like big teardrops."

"Son, I would guess that it is not even four o'clock in the morning, the sun isn't even out yet. As far as English weather is concerned, regardless of the season, rain is a normal occurrence here; I should get used to it if I were you."

Sabeer frowned and coughed, all at the same time. The wrenching sound came from deep in his chest.

"Jones, put him to bed. You have my permission to tie him to the bedposts if you have to."

Jones reached for the boy, but he shuffled away.

Seeing Edgar's frown, Sabeer, again posing like a Rajah, pointed his nose to the ceiling. Then he stood and walked toward the door.

"You got no shoes on, boy," Jones muttered, lifting Sabeer into his arms.

Sabeer didn't have the opportunity to object when another bout of coughing occupied him. He even curled up in Jones' arms, trying to control his shivers.

Edgar realized that after the hot temperatures of India, Sabeer would have a devil of a time adjusting to the weather in England.

After the two had left the room, Edgar turned his full attention to Mr. Arnold.

"According to my brother's most recent letter, he has hired some woman to act as my social advocate and matchmaker. That being the case, perhaps this woman will be able to provide all the necessary introductions; then I won't need to attend any special functions."

"I think it would be in your best interests to attend this particular event, Your Grace," Arnold said.

"And, why is that?"

"This will be the largest fully attended ball outside of the regular season."

"When is it?" the duke asked.

"Day after tomorrow."

"What were you thinking, Arnold, that is hardly enough time? I don't even have anything suitable to wear to a winter ball.

In addition, how in the blazes am I expected to travel to London?"

"I took the liberty of hiring a coach, it is waiting on the dock. In regards to your attire, I am positive that between our resources, Jones and I will be able to find you something suitable to wear."

Edgar looked at him with skepticism.

"If I may add, Your Grace, the sooner we find the future Duchess of Grangefield, the better. There are several loans outstanding on your properties, and it has been difficult to keep the creditors at bay. In addition, your brother recently borrowed funds for repairs on the tenant cottages; and there is your sister to consider."

"My sister?" Edgar said, confused.

"Lady Tiffany has just turned sixteen, and Viscount Hamilton recently asked for a dowry estimate."

Edgar groaned.

Arnold fumbled in his pouch, removing several folded letters. "These will also require your signature. They are the debt extension notices I mentioned during my visit to India, as well as the letter you asked me to write on your behalf to the queen. Her Highness is still in mourning; however, rumor has it, she still reads her correspondence."

Edgar looked up from fastening the buttons on his britches. "Now that's the best news I've heard since you walked in here, Arnold." He grabbed the letters. "Too bad the law has changed in England. The newly enacted Marriage Act doesn't acknowledge an Indian woman as my wife, or Sabeer as my son. However, if the queen grants my request I won't need to get married again."

Mr. Arnold frowned: The man didn't like taking chances—a typical solicitor.

"What about the boy's status, Your Grace?"

"No one knows he's my son except my brother and Mr. Jones. Eventually the rest of the family will be notified. I assume accommodations have been arranged for him at Grangefield Hall?"

Arnold nodded.

"Furthermore, if I must marry out of duty, the woman I choose must accept the boy."

Arnold said nothing, but Edgar knew English society would have a difficult time accepting a half Indian as his son, let alone his heir.

"Who is hosting this bloody ball anyway?" Edgar asked.

"The event is being held at Cavendish House, Your Grace. It is a come-out party for the earl's daughter, Lady Leticia. Although the ball is off-season, I have it on good authority that several distinguished families will be attending."

"So, I am to be trussed up like a prize pig at the fair: Are you leading me to the slaughter, Arnold?"

Arnold didn't respond.

Edgar sighed. "I suppose I should attend, I have nothing to lose. Of course, this whole escapade is pointless. I married the woman I loved, and then she died. Frankly, I do not wish to marry again, particularly when I am being dictated to by the terms of an ill-conceived will."

Edgar then noticed the solicitor's piteous expression.

"Don't start feeling sorry for me just yet: My father never managed to get me married off when he was alive, and with complete confidence I can assure you, even dead he never will."

~ ~ ~

"Oh, dear, no! Not your gloves as well?"

Perhaps vestal virgin white hadn't been such a good idea

after all, Lady Marjorie Tate, Countess of Penmore thought. She

assessed the attire of her newest charge, and then glared with

disapproval at Viscount Rupert Hamilton. Her best friend sipped

his punch, watching the waltzing couples on the dance floor.

For what felt like the hundredth time, Marjorie adjusted

her feathered mask. She couldn't see a darned thing through the

feathers, unless she tilted her head, which then pushed her

spectacles to the tip of her nose. Oh, how she hated attending

balls, particularly the ones that required wearing a mask.

Thank goodness their small group stood at the very back

of the ballroom. The closest person to them was a tall, dark-

haired gentleman, who had his back to them. How odd, the man

wore a powder-blue coat, the attire quite inappropriate for a

winter ball.

She motioned to Tiffany. "Pay attention, dear: Observe that man in the corner. He, too, is wearing entirely the wrong attire for such a formal gathering; however, unlike us, he seems to have found a suitable place to hide."

Marjorie sighed, seeing the dust stains at the elbows of Lady Tiffany's white gloves, which confirmed that this particular debutante had no interest in marriage.

"In order for us to find you a suitor, you will need to stand where you can be seen." Marjorie gestured with her fan.

"Good! Now, make sure to clasp your wrists thus; and, do avoid shaking hands with anyone."

She waited for the girl to object. When she did not, Marjorie continued. "When introduced, simply curtsy, which should suffice under the circumstances."

Although the girl nodded agreement, Marjorie noticed that her lips had compressed into an irritated sliver. It was unfortunate that Lady Tiffany had deigned to arrange her own coiffure. Her black hair was styled in dangling ringlets, and she wore not a smidgen of face powder, which displayed all her freckles—yet another defiant gesture. What was the point of chaperoning this gal if she continued to disregard her instructions?

She noticed Rupert was also frowning at his sister; his expression quite dastardly since his mask covered most of his hare-lip, flattening his mustache tips against his cheeks.

"Tiffany, try to look as if you're enjoying yourself," he said.

"You never listen, Rupert: I told you, I have no interest in marriage."

"Sister, I am fully aware of your marital objections. However, since we are here you, must endure the process. In addition, need I remind you it was your idea to attend this ball?" He turned to glare at Marjorie, and beneath his mask his eye pleaded for help.

Marjorie relied on her no-nonsense tone, the one she reserved for unruly servants.

"Tiffany, dear, we agreed that this would be a trial venture."

"But..."

Rupert interrupted. "If I were you, I'd feel very grateful that Marjorie is providing you with her matchmaking expertise."

"But ..."

Rupert turned his back, focusing his lofty gaze on Marjorie.

"Madame, have you had time to consider our other matrimonial dilemma?"

Marjorie schooled her features, well aware of what Rupert alluded to.

"*He* should be arriving in England any day now," Rupert said.

Marjorie noticed that the man wearing the powder blue had moved closer. A few steps in the wrong direction and they might collide.

She stepped away from him, facing the sea of colorful ball gowns and black evening attire. That evening she felt particularly unfestive. Although a year had passed, and she was officially out of mourning, she had chosen not to wear a vibrant-colored gown. Instead, not wanting to outshine Tiffany, she had chosen a drab gray ensemble. Thankfully, her choice reminded her that being a widow at eight and twenty had other advantages beyond the whims of fashion.

Rupert stepped closer and lowered his voice. "Marjorie, you already know that Edgar has been away from England for almost ten years."

Marjorie felt her jaw loosen.

"I understand this news is not helpful to your matchmaking endeavors. You see, Edgar and my father, the late duke, did not see eye to eye on many issues, including arranged marriages. To escape the old man's nearsighted opinions, Edgar enlisted in the Queen's cavalry, and was later stationed in India."

"But why would his past necessitate a hasty marriage now?" Marjorie whispered.

"My dear, as the heir presumptive, because father failed to marry him off, and Edgar abruptly left England, a scandal ensued. To make matters worse, the woman he left at the altar killed herself."

"Good Lord!" Marjorie exclaimed.

"This prompted father to add a provision to his will," Rupert continued. "It stated that if Edgar inherited the title, he would have to marry an English woman to gain access to the Hamilton fortune."

"So now Edgar Hamilton must find a well-bred, bride of English origin," Marjorie mumbled.

"Exactly right."

Rupert scratched his forehead, prompting Marjorie to tap his arm with her fan to gain his attention.

He stopped scratching, regarding her with an apologetic expression. "Marjorie, if there is no legal marriage within a specified period, the debt collectors will be knocking down our doors. From an operating perspective, other than the duke's title, which Edgar has now inherited, the fortune is vital to the running of Grangefield.

"With access to the fortune I could have kept things going, but father has been dead for almost a year, and Edgar has been otherwise occupied in India."

Marjorie pondered this. "But considering your brother's steadfast disposition on the issue of marriage, how do you propose I accomplish this matchmaking miracle?"

"This is not a point of debate, Marjorie: It is not how, but how soon. Remember, the estate is already in arrears. At this point Edgar simply has little choice in the matter."

She glanced at Tiffany. "Don't slouch, dear."

Surprised, Tiffany immediately straightened her shoulders.

"Rupert, it appears that my energies would be better served here," she nodded toward his sister.

Rupert caught the attention of a passing footman, and divested himself of his empty punch cup.

"I understand from his letters that Edgar resents having the title. There is a strong possibility that he might take matters into his own hands, and find a wife on his own—now *that* would be a disaster. Much worse, he has a stubborn streak—it is a noted family flaw." Rupert said, nodding toward Tiffany, who promptly glared back at him.

"On a positive note, I recall Edgar's looks were far from unappealing; I am confident you will not have any problems finding him a match."

"If he is so devastatingly handsome he won't need my help, will he?" Marjorie said, determined not to get roped into yet another difficult assignment.

"He might be handsome, Marjorie, but Edgar has been away from England for almost a decade. Everything will be new to him, and he will need someone who can properly guide his reentry into polite society, someone like you."

Marjorie sighed. "How old is the duke?"

"I beg your pardon?" Rupert said, surprised.

"I said, how old is your brother? And, please do lower your voice: Have you not noticed, we are not alone?" Using her fan, she gestured toward the man in the powder blue coat.

Rupert glanced over her shoulder, whispering, "He is two years older than me, seven and twenty. Why? Are you agreeing to help?"

"No, I am not. However, if I were to offer my support, I would want to know as much about the duke as possible."

The grand orchestra began to play the melodic chords of a Strauss waltz, and Marjorie realized that she was tapping her foot. Oh, she did so long to dance.

"I'm not undermining your techniques, my dear, but you must understand, this is a very unusual situation; and Edgar needs to be handled very delicately."

"Most delicately," Tiffany chimed in.

"Do continue, my lord, we appear to be all ears," Marjorie muttered.

Rupert ignored his sister. "The last letter I received from Edgar, before he left India, mentioned that he would set sail in late October. Barring any unforeseen circumstances, there's nothing preventing him from coming straight to the ducal seat to claim his title."

Marjorie interrupted: "So he will arrive at Grangefield Hall, then what?"

Rupert's impatient glare reminded her how much he hated being interrupted.

"As I was about to say, my goal is to make Edgar feel at home, that way we can both keep an eye on him."

"Both?" Marjorie blurted, raising her fan to her face. Thank goodness the man wearing the powder blue coat appeared distracted.

"That won't be possible. I just can't stop my activities and go to Grangefield Hall. In addition, must I remind you, all the major come-outs are hosted in London. That said, the actual matchmaking must happen in town."

"Actually, working at Grangefield Hall was Agnes's idea. My wife has threads of genius when she is not suffering from bouts of morning sickness. Agnes rationalized, quite brilliantly might I add, that your presence at the estate would help expedite Edgar's training. It would also provide a discrete location where you could work with my brother uninterrupted."

Marjorie had to admit that the plan did have merit.

"In addition, " Rupert continued, "we have the advantage of introducing you to society as his tutor in social decorum."

"Good Lord!" Marjorie muttered.

"'Good Lord' sums things up quite nicely."

While Rupert beamed with delight, Marjorie had already made up her mind: She would not be participating in this ludicrous plan: Not today, not tomorrow—not ever!

~ ~ ~

Chapter Three

Taking a sip of mulled wine, Edgar pursed his lips and stretched his neck like a distressed barn owl, feeling completely out of place. He was surrounded by a distinguished gathering of people, wearing black evening tailcoats and colorful satin ball gowns. His initial glance confirmed that he was wearing entirely the wrong clothing for this sort of social gathering. Suppressing a groan, he eyeballed his well-starched lawn shirt and powder blue frock coat.

Unfortunately, his current circumstances were more dire than his unsuitable attire. En route to the ball that evening, the coach Mr. Arnold had hired, had suffered a mysterious mishap. One of the wheels had come loose, and the coach had almost veered off the path toward a steep ravine. After inspecting the driving mechanism, Edgar concluded the danger had been deliberate. Thank heavens, Jones had been riding with the driver. Only his quick reflexes had saved them from certain injury, and possibly even death.

Interrupting his anxious thoughts, a well-dressed woman wearing ostrich feathers in her hair, bumped into him.

"I do beg your pardon," he said, bowing.

The woman simply stared at him. She looked frightened, and Edgar wished for the hundredth time he had taken more care with his appearance. Unshaven and unfashionably dressed, he no doubt looked hideous.

Well, there was very little he could do to remedy the situation now. He reminded himself his mission tonight was to find a wife. However, in conflict with his plans, all evening he had remained hidden in an obscure portico avoiding the crowd.

It was at that moment his stomach growled. The noise prompted a wig-wearing footman to politely offer him directions to the supper room.

"Is that you, Edgar Hamilton?" a male voice shouted.

Edgar's cup of mulled wine jostled in his hand. It seemed unimaginable that someone could have recognized him at a crowded party, particularly when he wore a mask of blue sequins and feathers, which covered most of his face.

From the goatee, the exaggerated limp, and the rest of his solicitor's accurate description, Edgar recognized the Duke of Buccleuch. He groaned.

"Buccleuch," Edgar murmured, bowing to acknowledge the older man.

"You remembered! So you've returned to accept the title, have you?" Buccleuch said, eying him through his monocle.

Edgar offered a patient smile.

"By the by, I've not seen Viscount Hamilton in an age. Too busy with his new wife, I suppose. Were you informed about the marriage?" Buccleuch mumbled, glancing about the hallway.

"Yes, I was," Edgar responded, without enthusiasm.

The elderly man ignored him, tilting his punch cup, and consuming the entire contents. "Shame you missed the wedding—grandest affair all season long. Even the Queen graced us with her presence. Too bad she still has that annoying habit of wearing black: Bit of a faux pas at a wedding, don't you think?"

Buccleuch hacked as if he had just ingested a large pinch of snuff. "Young Hamilton married well; a nice enough gal, and from good family stock. Let me think for a moment and I will come up with her name." He took a pose of contemplation, waving his monocle to and fro.

"Agnes, Countess Forester?" Edgar supplied.

"Yes! Yes! Quite right, old boy! I'd wager that you're considering marriage yourself? Wanting an heir and a spare, I suspect. Plenty of pretty young things here tonight: All of 'em waiting to be plucked up and carried off, if you catch my meaning." Buccleuch winked.

Edgar nodded. "If you'll excuse me, Buccleuch, I was just heading toward the supper room."

"You were? Well, I won't keep you."

But the older man didn't move. "I believe we were discussing your marriage prospects."

"Yes, but I'm afraid it will have to wait, I was on my way into supper. Do you mind moving aside?"

"Moving aside? But I did so want to hear about your plans."

"As I said," Edgar stated calmly, "I'm afraid that will have to wait, I'm really quite famished."

Buccleuch shuffled to one side, at the same time raising his monocle to admire someone standing behind Edgar.

This small distraction allowed Edgar to use his advantage and edge to the right. It was then his boot trod on something soft, and then he smelled the scent of lemons. Almost simultaneously, there came a high-pitched feminine yowl.

Amidst a gaggle of shocked gasps, Edgar could only watch helpless. The contents of his punch cup splashed on the woman's face and down the bodice of her dove-gray dress.

"Bad luck, old boy," Buccleuch said. Without looking back, the old fool quickly retreated down the hallway.

Edgar's gaze moved downward. The woman stood no taller than his chest. Her face looked flushed, the same shade of pink as the seashells he'd once seen scattered on the beaches of South East India.

Patting her damp face with a handkerchief, the woman's attention remained focused on the large scarlet patch that covered the bodice of her gown. Her jet-black hair had unraveled from its topknot, cascading in an unruly mass of curls about her face. She had at some point extended her arms, and was flapping them like a wet bird.

When she finally looked at him, Edgar felt a reassuring warmth course in the region of his chest. He realized his jaw now gaped. Drenched in wine, she had been forced to remove her mask and spectacles, giving him the opportunity to drink in her features. Her skin was translucent, her eyes wide and expressive, like those of a startled child. Her lips were crimson, like the finest rubies, and they glistened as she licked them.

"I'm terribly sorry," Edgar blurted, with every ounce of sincerity he could muster. His abdomen had clenched with some unknown emotion: Could this feeling be lust?

She was busy adjusting her spectacles, which she had wiped clean of wine droplets. That was when Edgar noticed the wedding band on her finger: His heart constricted.

"Madame, if you will provide me with the name of your husband, I will send for him."

Edgar heard her whisper a single phrase, he felt positive it sounded like, "Good Lord."

Instinct cautioned him to stop, but he had already reached toward her head. He ignored the collective gasp from their audience, and too late, he touched the woman's black hair, adjusting several strands, unveiling more of her perfect features.

"Unhand me, you brute," she yelped, slapping his wrist away.

As if scalded, he released her hair and stepped back.

"I was just trying to help."

"You are definitely not helping."

She had mumbled this while rubbing her temple, offering up her angelic features, which were now pinched with a pained expression.

"Do you make it a habit of ignoring social dictates—and dressing in such poor taste?"

Edgar suppressed a groan, eyeballing his well-starched lawn shirt and powder blue coat. Then he caught sight of her open-eyed expression. Was she quelling the impulse to scream? Why on earth had he not shaved off his beard?

"I'm afraid I've been away from the London scene for too long," he said.

She moved a step closer to him.

"A pearl of wisdom," she whispered, still speaking to his cravat. "In future, try not to offer a lady assistance without asking first."

Heaven help him this situation was fast turning hellish, Edgar thought.

Regardless, at that moment his angel stood before him covered with red punch drops and jet-black curls, spilling across her face. He might otherwise describe her as indelicate-looking, but in such close proximity Edgar's vital extremities felt both alive and well.

Even those deliciously seductive spectacles of hers seemed to stimulate his arousal. She struggled with them, trying to stop them from sliding down her nose. His imagination took flight: He envisioned her wearing only spectacles, with her legs sheathed in black silk stockings. However, the rest of this image vanished when he felt a sharp poke to his chest.

"Are you paying attention up there?" the woman asked, now standing on tiptoes peering at the folds of his cravat. He could tell by her unhappy expression that she wasn't aware of the sexual tension between them.

"Yes, of course, I am painfully aware of your presence," Edgar muttered. "How could I not hear you, when all of London can?" He raised a hand to stop her comments.

She hastily stepped back.

Did she think he would strike her?

He felt sure apologizing again would not help matters. He opted to reason with her. "Look here, I will of course replace your gown," absently gesturing with his hand, "and anything else that needs replacing."

She continued to stare at his cravat.

"In fact, I will happily replace your entire wardrobe, if you felt it was necessary."

The woman gasped. He was sure he heard her say, "Oh." Then she repeated it several times in succession, at varying degrees of pitch.

"Oh. Oh. Oh."

Her pupils appeared to have grown to the size of perfectly rounded musket balls. Her fists had clenched, and were pressed to her waist.

"I have never met anyone so ignorant of social etiquette," she muttered.

He noticed that her slipper now tapped with fervor, depressing a dent in the plush carpeting.

Their audience stood transfixed, as if sitting in a theater watching a riveting sword fight. However, this did not deter the woman from delivering the rest of her unflattering assessment.

"In addition, sir, your manners are atrocious, and..."

He watched as her attention roamed, no doubt her husband had arrived: Now there would be hell to pay.

The person in question was a young, awkward-looking female. Edgar could only describe the gal as reed-like.

She stood by the supper room doorway. Her hair was black, the same color as his, and styled in severe ringlets, which closely resembled a picture he'd once seen of Medusa's serpents.

"Find your brother and Lady Cavendish," his angel ordered.

Without hesitation, the younger woman propped up her mask, then moved at a hurried pace in the direction of the main ballroom.

"But I can help you," Edgar said, mystified by her reaction: "Surely there is no need to call for Lady Cavendish."

The look she gave him spoke to the contrary.

"As I stated before, you have done quite enough," she muttered.

Then she appeared to sober. "Perhaps you could do something," she said, grasping her hair, and trying without success, to rearrange her coiffure.

"Yes. Anything." He heard himself sounding eager to please.

"Well, I would prefer it if you went away."

"I beg your pardon?"

"I said, go away. Leave!"

She lifted onto tiptoes, whispering, "please-goooooo-awway."

Edgar knew his cheeks had warmed. She had somehow managed to tip his temper. Not even his boor of a father had managed to do that. In reaction, his index finger shot up, pointing at her nose.

"Of course; your wish is my command."

Too late, he had shouted. Thankfully, his tirade was interrupted by the arrival of a footman, wearing a mauve jacket, the colors of the Earl of Cavendish. The man's white wig sat askew, and on his gloved palm he carried a small silver plate.

"Your Grace."

Now glaring at the footman, Edgar plucked up the folded scrap of paper.

Come immediately. Jones.

He and the woman were still standing toe to toe.

One last time, he thought, tipping his face closer to hers and inhaling the scent of lemons. Conscious of their audience, his mouth barely opened as he forced his tone to sound calm.

"Madame, I can assure you, we are far from finished."

Following the footman, he performed a perfect about face, and in three efficient strides, moved in the direction of the main entryway. The hammering of his heart lessened, and the scent of lemons faded.

That was when he heard the woman's voice echo like a battle cry across a barren desert.

"Good Lord!" she stammered, "Was that man really a duke?"

~ ~ ~

It had been two days since the horrific incident at the Cavendish Ball. Even now sitting in one of the small salons designated as her business office at Grangefield Hall, Marjorie relived the events in vivid detail. Both awake and asleep, the masked figure haunted her. Prior to this incident, Marjorie had not had a single nightmare since the death of her husband.

An investigation conducted by Rupert was unsuccessful in revealing the identity of the mystery duke. Many of the servants at the ball, who had been brought to London from other Cavendish estates had now returned; even the note-bearing footman could not be identified.

The Duke of Buccleuch had also proved a useless witness. Buccleuch, who was known for his fondness for imbibing strong spirits, had been discovered passed out under a table in the supper room.

At the time, Marjorie had been in such a state of shock, that Rupert had no option but to squire both her and Tiffany

away in the Grangefield coach. Filled with the boldness of a
rescuer, he took full advantage of the situation, and again begged
her to help him find the Duke of Grangefield a wife. To her
infinite regret, the next day instead of recovering from her ordeal
at Henley House, her London residence, Marjorie set out for
Grangefield Hall to spend the Christmas holidays with the
Hamilton family.

Her thoughts came to reality, when she heard a panicked
voice from outside the corridor shouting her name. She tossed
down the latest edition of the *Agrarian Gazette,* annoyed she had
not finished reading the article on *Prolific Crop Rotation.*

Her passion in life was agriculture, and she was lucky
that her late husband had left her sufficient funds to expand her
hobby. Her fields now yielded sufficient crops to sell to several
villages across Surrey. This pastime had become a valuable
endeavor, helping many poor people in the local area to buy
fresh vegetables at fair market prices. Her goal was to expand
production to the next county by the summer. The payment she

would earn for this new matchmaking assignment with the Duke of Grangefield would certainly ensure that would happen.

"Lady Tate! Lady Tate!" the call came again.

How odd? She had never heard Albert sound so urgent, or for that matter so alert.

Her elderly butler appeared at the door. His gray hair, which on most days lay flat, affixed to his scalp with a liberal application of linseed oil, was now feathered across his forehead.

"Madame, Lord Rupert has requested your presence in the entryway. He asked me to mention that you should hurry."

"Why are you in such a dither, Albert?"

His eyebrows arched.

"Madame, I have been informed that His Grace, the Duke of Grangefield, will be descending on Grangefield Hall."

The word "descending" required Marjorie to glance in his direction. But before she could respond, the swish of trouser fabric indicated that Albert had vacated the room, without so much as the customary bow.

Marjorie decided she needed to take a short walk, she wanted to feel composed before she met the duke for the first time. Leaving the salon, she stopped to embrace the view outside a bank of bay windows. Despite the gloomy sky, the glass panes glistened, reflecting the brilliant snow that blanketed the grounds. A sigh escaped her lips, her breath leaving condensation on the glass, which she guiltily wiped away. A stirring winter scene, what a perfect welcome for this temperamental new duke.

"Descending" indeed! What manner of man could cause such an uproar? Now headed toward the main entryway, she took one final deep breath, ready, at least in spirit, to greet her notorious new student.

***

The Grangefield foyer was a sumptuous vision finished in Italian brown marble. Marjorie compared the entryway to the size of a small field. This morning the entire household occupied most of the space, arranged in formation by rank. The most senior servants wore the forest-green livery of the Duke of

Grangefield. An army of maids occupied the last two rows, followed by several cooks, wearing white aprons.

Rupert watched over the proceedings standing beside his wife, Lady Agnes, and next to her stood the duke's sister. Lady Tiffany wore a lovely plum-colored wool gown. Marjorie noted with interest that the duke's unpredictable sister had made an effort with her appearance.

Marjorie watched Rupert make frenzied hand gestures in an attempt to gain everyone's attention. Failing to do so, he proceeded to direct his comments to Henry, the head butler. Albert stood at attention close to Henry, his head drooping to the left. Considering his venerable years, he more than outranked Henry, but he had graciously agreed to participate in the household as a visiting servant.

"I do believe we are ready," Rupert said, dabbing his perspiring brow with a white handkerchief.

"Yes, your lordship," Henry replied.

Rupert unfurled the handkerchief, waving it to gain Marjorie's attention.

"Marjorie, dear, it will be easier to introduce you if you stood in front with the family."

"Marjorie hesitated: I'm not comfortable being the center of attention, I feel like an intruder as it is. Perhaps I should wait until tomorrow to be formally introduced."

Before she could retreat, Marjorie heard the clatter of pounding horses hooves outside, which only charged the atmosphere in the foyer with tension.

Moving to the window facing the driveway, she watched as a rickety old coach rolled through the tall iron gates. A murmur of anticipation filled the hall, causing a few of the younger maids to fidget. Rupert was the first to react, stepping outside to greet the coach, with a footman in tow.

After a brief bout of indecision, Marjorie moved forward. She bolstered Agnes' arm, offering support. During the first few months of her pregnancy, Agnes had become prone to fainting, and Marjorie knew any unplanned incident might induce one of these spells.

She turned to Albert: "Escort Lady Agnes and Lady Tiffany to the library, and stay with them. They can meet the duke later, after things have settled down."

"But who will attend to you, madame? I can't leave you alone."

"Don't be absurd."

Albert's eyebrows arched, but wisely he didn't argue. Instead, he ushered the two women toward the library.

Now standing at the entryway, Marjorie watched the carriage come to a rumbling halt. Then the door opened with such impact that it almost came unhinged. A wide expanse of broad male back, shrouded by a black cloak materialized, the body filling the doorway. With head lowered, the giant carefully descended to the ground, his boots crunching on the gravel. The sight of him presented a haunting image, so formidable that Marjorie heard her breath hitch.

The man's head was covered by a swarm of curly hair, all of it pitch-black and neatly clipped in a short, Grecian style. He straightened, and Marjorie felt immediately dwarfed in his presence. Was that a small body he carried in his arms?

He turned, his gaze meeting hers. How odd, he blinked in seeming recognition.

Also feeling an odd sense of déjà vu, her eyes focused on the most dangerously handsome face she had ever seen in her life.

Indeed, even drawn with fatigue, Edgar Hamilton, the Eighth Duke of Grangefield, could only be described as both imposing and stunning. His face had to be the most distinct she had ever seen. It was clean-shaven, and his mouth was accented by firm, arched lips. His coal-black eyes were draped with uncommonly long lashes, but the most titillating attribute, was the pronounced cleft in the center of his chin, which gave him a certain dangerous air.

Upon spying her, his look of ducal displeasure changed to a smirk.

"Are you enjoying the view, madame? It would appear that fate has destined we meet again."

Good Lord! She recognized that voice! Then the image of her mysterious phantom appeared, and her skin prickled. She blinked: Too late, now her mouth gaped open.

"You! Good Lord, it's you!" she stuttered, imagining her eyes had widened to the size of tea saucers.

They stared at one another, his expression blazing assurance.

"Where are your spectacles, madame? You appear somewhat naked without them," the duke said; "not that I mind, of course."

She looked up, all the way up, as if she were looking into a cloudy gray sky.

"I...uh...don't wear my spectacles all the time."

He offered her another smirk. "Pity; they do quite enhance your appearance."

What on earth did he mean by that? Marjorie thought. Stepping forward, she forced a smile, glaring at him mid-chest, and recalling with disgust that she had been in this position before.

"I say, hello there, Edgar," Rupert interrupted. "We've all been caught off guard with your unexpected arrival. What are you carrying?"

The duke's smirk disappeared. A brief nod was the only acknowledgement he offered his brother, before directing his next comments to her. "Madame, I advise you to step aside before I trample you into my driveway."

An unconscious movement forced Marjorie to step backward. She stumbled off the path, and into the arms of a surprised footman.

Without courtesy, the duke walked passed her into the foyer, spouting orders to his regiment of servants. "You there! Send someone to the village to fetch the doctor. Which one of you is in charge here?"

Revealing himself, Henry stepped forward, offering a nervous bow.

"Make sure my driver is fed and rested, his name is Mr. Jones. While I'm in residence, he will serve as my valet."

The duke continued delivering his demands:

"Rupert, for heaven's sake, make an effort to be useful. Point me to a room with a clean bed, then send up the housekeeper. Which one of the rooms is ready?"

"Blue, the Blue is ready," Rupert sputtered.

Without pause, the duke entered the hall, forcing Rupert and Marjorie to follow at a safe distance. Even after a ten-year absence, he appeared to know where he was going.

Carrying his bundle, he ignored the gawking crowd of servants. Using long strides, he took the staircase. When he reached the second floor, the handsome Duke of Grangefield vanished out of sight.

~ ~ ~

Chapter Five

Marjorie tried again to will the duke's handsome face from her memory. Unfortunately, this only conjured up the image of his arched lips, and his chin with its very perfect crease.

By the time Marjorie reached the North Wing she felt annoyed with every single Hamilton residing at Grangefield Hall, all of them except Agnes, who only became a Hamilton because she married one.

She sought out the main object of her wrath, whom she found standing alone in one of the deserted passageways. He was staring at a wall of portraits, depicting various members of the Hamilton ancestral line.

Marjorie noticed white sheets covered most of the furnishings; apparently this was a lesser-used part of the Hall. Feeling the need to whisper, she stepped closer to Rupert, lifting up on tiptoes.

"Do you happen to know who that child is? The one the duke carried upstairs."

"Can't say," Rupert whispered back, swaying from heel to toe.

Marjorie didn't have the benefit of her spectacles, so she stepped even closer and squinted. From Rupert's expression, he didn't look angry, definitely a good sign.

"Shouldn't you be sending one of the servants to help him?" she asked.

He didn't respond.

"Rupert, your brother has asked for a doctor to attend to his young friend. While we are waiting for the physician to arrive, the duke must have some refreshments."

Another deafening silence.

"I'm sure that in her delicate condition, Agnes might not be inclined to play hostess," Marjorie said. "Why don't I lend a hand and take care of the details for you?"

Rupert managed an affirmative grunt.

After another bout of silence, Marjorie lost patience and poked him in the arm. "Rupert, what on earth is the matter with you? Do you, or do you not want me to take care of the details regarding the duke's reception?"

He mumbled something about the unpredictability of long lost brothers.

"Rupert, please answer my question."

"I'm afraid we are doomed!" he declared with dramatic flare. He then lifted a hand to his forehead. "Doomed!" he repeated. "Marjorie, there's nothing you can do here. I was counting on your help to find him a wife, but now I realize the task is too great. I know how awful the weather conditions are, but perhaps it would be best if you repacked your belongings and spent Christmas at Tate House."

"Rupert, what are you babbling on about?"

Moving to a covered portrait on the wall, Rupert yanked off the covering.

Marjorie held her breath. Good Lord! The duke had always been stunning-looking! If she was a woman who swooned, she would no doubt do just that.

The portrait was encased in an elegant gold frame. Marjorie easily recognized a younger version of Edgar Hamilton. The depiction had the heir riding on top of a white stallion, his pitch black hair flying in the wind.

"Father had that commissioned for the bride-to-be," Rupert said. "After Edgar left home, he didn't want to see his money wasted, so he had it hung here in the gallery covered with a drape. The cloth offered a reminder of how much he despised Edgar for leaving home without his permission."

Rupert continued to twist the tips of his moustache into sharpened points.

"Marjorie, as you know, Edgar's impending marriage is important to the future of the estate. But if I'm not allowed to guide his reentry into polite society, we will all be ruined. After his deplorable behavior toward you on the driveway today, I am afraid of what will happen when he mingles with other, less-familiar, well-bred women."

Marjorie opened her mouth to say something, but Rupert interrupted.

"I tell you, Marjorie, no one in society will acknowledge him if he behaves like that; he was so brusque; so very uncivil."

Marjorie watched a trickle of moisture slip down Rupert's cheek. No time for weakness, she thought. She reminded herself that now it was in her best interests to find the Duke of Grangefield a wife. If she succeeded, her payment would be a land lease for a sizable plot of Grangefield land, which she would use to grow more crops. From a business perspective, this coup would support several of her agricultural projects.

Marjorie decided to leave Rupert to his regrets. Her decision made, she left the room, now fully prepared to fulfill her matchmaking obligations.

***

Arriving in the foyer, she reached the library and opened one of the double doors. Bounding enthusiasm caused her to almost stumble headlong into Albert. Marjorie righted herself, then beckoned for him to leave his post and join her outside. As anticipated, Albert came to attention like a foot soldier awaiting orders.

"Madame," he intoned.

"Albert, I commend you on your sentry duty, you have done an exemplary job."

"Thank you, madame." His response sounded decidedly unimpressed.

"You were right, the duke has indeed *descended* upon us. He has now adjourned to the Blue Room with his visitor, a young boy, who appears to be very ill. You and I will attend to them until his valet, a Mr. Jones, is ready to assume his duties.

"I suggest you start by arranging for some hot water to be brought up from the kitchen, enough for bathing. A suitable meal should follow; one that includes some clear consommé for the child. The duke appears to have a special fondness for the boy, I presume that is why he has been brought upstairs."

Albert quit the hall and her company, without delivering one of his bland "as you wish, madame" responses.

"Impossible man," Marjorie muttered.

Heading toward the staircase, Marjorie heard the duke's angry voice. He was bellowing a single phrase, and the word that was being repeated was "quack," or more precisely, "you quack!"

Marjorie then heard hurried footsteps.

Fortunately, she glanced up the stairwell, and just missed being hit on the head by a medical bag, which had flown over the railing. The bag landed with a thud on the marble tiles. This was followed by a satisfied male grunt, and then the solid slam of an upstairs door.

Marjorie recognized Dr. Ansel, their excellent village doctor, making his way downstairs. Wanting to investigate, she just missed colliding with the elderly, anxious-looking gentleman. He managed a flustered bow, before continuing his mad dash down the final flight of stairs, and then out the door.

Bemused, Marjorie noticed that Albert, who had used the servant's stairwell, had reached the Blue Room before her. He carried a large tray with a silver warming dome, and was glaring at the blue trim on the door. His tightly compressed lips told Marjorie that he had already formed an opinion of the new duke.

"What happened?" she asked.

"I'm not sure, madame. I did hear His Grace refer to the good doctor as a 'quack,' or more precisely, "you quack.'"

"Yes, I heard it, too. Do you think it's safe to enter?" Marjorie asked.

"It appears we have no choice, madame," Albert replied, with apparent disinterest.

Marjorie tapped on the door, then waited.

No answer.

Feeling brave, she gripped the brass door handle, twisting the knob. The hinge creaked, and then the door opened with a soft squeak.

The Blue Room appeared true to its name, decorated in a navy shade. A four-poster bed occupied most of the room, and in the far corner, a white screen obscured a concealed alcove. The rest of the furniture was sparse, and included an antique maple escritoire, positioned between two large bay windows.

A blast of warm air from the fireplace beckoned Marjorie forward. The knowledge that Albert stood behind her brought some comfort, as she looked for that familiar, foreboding male figure.

The figure in question sat on the edge of the bed, his broad back to her. He didn't turn, but by the shifting of his posture he had sensed their intrusion. He dabbed a cloth across the forehead of a dark-complexioned boy. Marjorie could only gawk, she had never seen anyone with such dark skin.

The boy appeared small in stature, his long, ink-black hair was scattered across a snow-white pillow. His body had been covered from the neck down with a heavy blanket. The duke stopped dabbing, and lifted the boy's arms, using a limbering movement.

"He doesn't look at all foreboding at the moment," Marjorie whispered over her shoulder, catching the aroma of roast beef wafting up from Albert's silver platter.

"If you're referring to the boy, I'm sure you're right, madame," Albert responded.

Marjorie ignored him.

"Hello," she said. "I hope you remember me from earlier on the driveway. We have not been properly introduced: I am Lady Marjorie—Marjorie Tate. I've come to welcome you to Grangefield Hall, and to offer you and your guest some refreshments."

Without taking his eyes off the boy, the duke uttered a sound resembling a lion's growl.

"I remember you quite well, madame. However, if you have returned with that village idiot, don't bother stepping any closer."

Marjorie stiffened. She then cleared her throat and attempted a cordial reply. "Uh ... It would appear that the good doctor has returned to the village." She stepped closer to the bed. "It's only me and Albert here, no one else. We decided to throw caution to the wind, and bring you something to eat: Roast beef with small potatoes and carrots, I believe."

"I'm not hungry. Just put it down, and then get out."

"I'm afraid leaving would be out of the question," Marjorie said. "Florence wouldn't approve, and you wouldn't want me to upset Florence, would you?"

The duke hesitated, turning to regard her. His eyebrows rose, his lips were compressed in a thin line. Good Lord, even angry the man was ridiculously handsome.

The duke's expression changed from silent scrutiny to pure disgust.

"Who in the bloody hell is Florence?" he shouted.

More curiosity, perhaps the duke could be tamed after all.

"Your Grace, I refer to none other than the world renowned Florence Nightingale. As you may know, she is a healer. I consider myself a student of hers; although we have never actually met."

The duke frowned. "Are you by chance from Bedlam, madame? You know, one of those oddballs who has lost their mental faculties?"

Marjorie felt her lips quiver before they compressed with irritation.

"Not to my knowledge, Your Grace. However, I have read a great number of Nurse Nightingale's official papers, and have acquired some competency with the healing arts: I am simply here to help.

"Unfortunately, since you have run off the good doctor, am I to understand that you know what you are doing, and you have already diagnosed this poor boy's condition?"

***

Edgar realized things were looking up. In front of him stood the same delectable nymph he had encountered at that awful ball in London. How she had invaded his ancestral home in Surrey still remained a mystery.

She stood only a toe's-width from the bed, shadowed by the most arrogant-looking servant. The old man ignored his age, doddering behind the woman like an ominous dark shadow, no doubt wanting to protect her.

The woman, Lady Tate she had called herself, had the temerity to nudge him aside. She then pressed the pads of her small fingers against Sabeer's forehead.

"He's cool to the touch, no fever yet," she said. "Albert, go fetch hot bricks for the mattress, then ask Cook to make a compress. Have her use some of those fresh eucalyptus leaves, the ones I brought with me from Henley House. Also, bring lots of drinking water, the boy's fluids need replacing."

Amazed, Edgar watched the aged man immediately look alert. He put down the tray and exited the room in a flash of hunter green.

"Is he one of my servants?" he asked.

"No." That was her only answer.

"How long has the boy been ill?" she asked.

Edgar didn't respond at first.

"Did you hear me, Your Grace?"

He turned to face her like a gladiator facing lions in the Coliseum. Did she presume to take over ministering Sabeer?

"When the boy's cough worsened, and he became delirious, I decided to bring him to Grangefield Hall. He has been unconscious for several hours. I made the mistake of bringing him here, I should have taken him to see a doctor in London."

Edgar felt his chest tighten after hearing the woman mumble "stupid." She had already lifted the boy's wrist to check his pulse.

"Have you ministered to the sick before, madame?"

"My name is Lady Tate," the woman said, with a hint of starchiness. Edgar felt his jaw clench, the damnable woman disapproved of him.

"The answer is no. My knowledge comes from extensive reading. Since you have dismissed the village doctor because you consider him incompetent, we now have no choice but to work together to help the boy. Who is he?"

Other than Sabeer, who never took fault with his far-from-sterling personality, Edgar had never encountered such a brash and domineering person. He felt like raising a finger and wagging it at her nose, but he realized that he needed all the help he could get. So he stood up and stepped aside.

"He's a boy, one who happens to be sick. Until I find out exactly who *you* are, that is all you need to know."

He regarded Sabeer, who looked drained of his bustling vitality. His eyes were closed, causing his long eyelashes to graze his cheekbones: Edgar's chest constricted.

Completely unaware of his anxious state, Lady Tate had begun to add blankets to the bed, her small pixie hands making expedient little tugs, as they smoothed out the linens.

Edgar came to abrupt attention when he watched her hands move toward the boy's clothing. She started unbuttoning his pantaloons.

"Step aside, madame; even unconscious the boy deserves some consideration. Why are you taking off his clothes?"

"They are damp." That was all she said.

As he moved to take over, he grazed the skin on her hand, and felt a curious sensation. This caused him to step back. "If you must help, turn away, I will remove the boy's clothing."

By the time Edgar had stripped Sabeer naked and covered him with a sheet, two servants had arrived with the heated blocks, which they handed to Albert, who settled them under the mattress.

Needing something useful to do, Edgar resumed washing Sabeer's face and shoulders. The footmen bundled the boy up in another layer of blankets, his body was now anchored to the bed like a mummy laid in a sarcophagus.

Albert then instructed the footmen to carry in an iron tub. It was placed behind the white screen and filled with hot water. The servants then left, with Lady Tate trailing behind them. She stopped in the doorway, turning to face him.

"Your Grace; my hope is that you will be less inclined to shout after you are bathed, fed, and rested."

Her parting words rang out like a round of unrelenting cannon fire.

"The boy may need some extra warmth during the night; I recommend you summon a servant to replace the bricks. I can only hope that after a good night's sleep your sullen disposition improves."

Yet again she had rendered him speechless.

Before the door closed, she said. "Should you feel inclined, I will take the liberty of inviting you to join the family for dinner; they convene at precisely six o' clock."

She said this offering him another one of her smug expressions, before turning away. As she exited her skirts swished, and Edgar glimpsed a smattering of her black petticoat; on its own, the large oak door then closed with a quiet thud.

Left alone with Sabeer, the image of Lady Tate vanished. All that remained was a deafening silence, accompanied by Edgar's escalating fears about his future in England. His apprehension began to dissipate when he realized that none of this grandeur meant anything, not without his son fully recovered and standing by his side.

~ ~ ~

Chapter Six

The next morning, Edgar heard loud voices as he was walking passed the conservatory.

"I think you should say something."

"No, Rupert, I think you should broach the subject."

"I insist, Marjorie, you're the perfect person to explain the circumstances."

"I must decline, Rupert. He is your your brother, and proprietary necessitates that you inform him. Besides, why would he listen to me, I'm a perfect stranger?"

Why indeed? Edgar thought, as he continued to eavesdrop outside the partially open door. He was crouched in an awkward pose, his head leaning forward, and his knee bent as if he were receiving a knighthood. He had never eavesdropped before, and the very constriction of the position, combined with an overwhelming sense of guilt were enough to justify his scowl.

From a gap in the door, he observed Rupert standing in front of the fireplace. Marjorie was pacing near the far wall, and two women were sitting on the brown chaise, with their backs to him facing both Rupert and the fireplace.

"I tell you, Marjorie, he knows who you are, I explained everything in my letter," Rupert said.

"That's neither here nor there, Rupert. I simply refuse. Don't you dare look at me with those droopy eyelids, I won't change my mind."

"Well, somebody has to tell him," Rupert muttered, staring at the two women.

"Don't look at us," the women blurted in unison.

No doubt the assembled group were talking about him. The two ladies, Edgar guessed, had to be Agnes, Rupert's new wife, and his sister, Tiffany.

Then there was Lady Tate. Edgar mused, she was a curious little thing. Intellectually speaking, he didn't care a hoot about her, but whenever they occupied the same space, she always commanded a certain response from him.

"Rupert, I won't start my lessons until I fully understand his intentions," Lady Tate said, the sound of her voice elevated.

Edgar tilted his head, attempting to peer further into the room. Unfortunately, his view was obscured by several potted ferns, sitting on tall pedestals.

The cramp in his legs reminded him of his restless night's sleep, lying on a cot at the foot of his son's bed. He had heard the door of the Blue Room open several times during the night, and watched Lady Tate shuffle in, followed by her ancient-looking servant, who carried a lantern. She wore an oversized dressing gown, which shrouded her from head to toe. A mob cap covered her head, and those damned delectable spectacles she wore had been perched on the bridge of her prim and proper nose. On each occasion her routine had been the same; she would touch Sabeer's head, then check the poultice on his chest. Satisfied that Sabeer was responding to her treatment, she would then leave.

Indeed, when it came to the boy, the woman appeared to behave with good intentions. Even more obvious, her frosty disposition was replaced by a genuine sense of caring. Edgar realized he disliked her less, respected her more, and felt astonished that he considered her a reasonable female.

A loud sneeze from his sister forced him to return his attention to the conversation in the conservatory. He reminded himself that when it came to military maneuvers, the most successful strategy remained patience; so he tempered his desire to march through the doors and demand an explanation from his brother.

"Rupert, I have a suggestion," Agnes said.

"I am all ears, my turtle-dove."

Edgar heard Lady Tate groan, and liked her even more.

"Why don't we just have the duke summoned here? That way we can tell him about these plans together," Agnes offered.

"Dearest;" Rupert said with impatience, "this situation is delicate, therefore the circumstances must be handled as if we were dusting off fine china. I'm positive Edgar will not be pleased when he hears what we have planned for him."

Edgar listened to them bicker, until Lady Tate uttered the word "marriage." That loathsome word, in conjunction with the word dukedom, caused Edgar's patience to give out; now he had to know what was going on.

He stood, brushed down his clothing, and then strode into the conservatory, ignoring the gasps and blank stares from each of the occupants.

"Good morning, all. What have we here, some sort of family gathering? I don't remember receiving an invitation."

Edgar ignored their stupefied silence. He noticed a musty smell, and realized it came from the plants. Indeed, the conservatory could best be compared to an overindulged garden.

A shiver drew him toward the fireplace. England had to be the coldest country in the world. Since his arrival it had rained almost every day, and just that morning snow flurries had started.

He stood with his back toward the flames, his hips wide, with his hands clasped behind his back, rubbing them together in the direction of the flames. His attention moved to Lady Tate, who wore one of her exasperated expressions. Why on earth was she wearing another gray-colored gown?

"Do continue your conversation; I hope I am not interrupting," he said, smiling at her. "From what I overheard, all the way from the Breakfast Room, it sounded as if your

discussion required a referee."

Both Rupert and Marjorie paled to the shade of fresh

alabaster. Knowing he needed to forge on with his investigation,

Edgar forced his features to stay placid.

"Brother, do tell, what is the subject of this debate?"

Edgar used the tone of authority he reserved for new military

recruits.

"Debate? Oh, nothing pressing," Rupert stuttered.

His brother had avoided his gaze, and continued to trace

patterns in the carpet with his booted foot. Edgar was then

awarded a view of his brother's round balding scalp, as he sat

down on one of the winged-back chairs, positioned close to the

fireplace.

"Well, I suppose my curiosity can wait, at least for the

moment."

Edgar's focus turned to Marjorie. She had walked toward

the north-facing window. She had pinned her attention on

something fascinating outside. Since Edgar knew that particular window faced the rose garden, and nothing bloomed in winter, he suspected she was attempting to ignore him.

"Rupert, I believe a few introductions are called for," Edgar said. "Of course, there's no need to introduce Tiffany: Good morning, sister."

Tiffany giggled.

"I take it the other ladies are my guests?" Edgar asked.

Rupert cleared his throat. "May I introduce my wife;" he gestured to the vivid, orange-haired woman sitting next to Tiffany on the chaise. "It is with great pleasure I introduce Agnes Hamilton, formerly the Countess of Stockesmere. I believe I notified you of the particulars of our marriage in one of my letters."

"Welcome home, Your Grace. It is so good to meet you at last," Agnes said, managing a strangled smile. Almost as an afterthought, she raised an outstretched hand.

Edgar glanced at it with speculation, before stepping forward the required distance. He settled for grabbing four of

Agnes's five fingers, and shaking them up and down. After noting Agnes's pained expression, he abruptly let go.

"Who is *she*, Rupert?" His chin motioned in Marjorie's direction.

"'She?'" Rupert replied, confused. "But, Edgar, you have already met Lady Marjorie."

"Yes, we have met, but not been officially introduced. Why is she staying at Grangefield Hall?"

A collective gasp came from the vicinity of the brown chaise. With satisfaction, Edgar noticed Marjorie's spine stiffen.

She turned to face him, her hands clasping in front of her waist. Even pinched, her features were exquisite. She had the longest black eyelashes he'd ever seen on a woman, and at that particular moment they were fluttering with defiance. Her mouth had formed into an aggravated moue, which forced her chin to jut forward, and her lips to quiver. At that precise moment those lips looked entirely kissable.

There wasn't any sort of rule that said he had to like her to kiss her, was there?

Thankfully, Rupert bridged the silence.

"Uh ... perhaps I should rectify this lapse in protocol, Edgar, also with great pleasure, that I would like to introduce you to Lady Marjorie Tate. I have retained Marjorie to be your personal social advocate and matchmaker.

"My what?" Edgar said, stupified.

"Your matchmaker: You know the one I mentioned in my letter."

"Rupert, are you telling me *this* is the woman you engaged to represent this family?"

"Yes, of course; who else would I engage?"

Again, Edgar had been rendered speechless, this had to be some sort of record.

"Marjorie is a long-time family friend," Rupert continued. "In fact, she introduced Agnes to me two years ago. She also arranged for our betrothal; and as you might imagine, Agnes and I are very grateful. I am confident that with time you will value her as much as we do."

Not bloody likely, Edgar thought, glaring at Marjorie's rather expressive back. She had again turned to stare out the window, her posture rigid. Edgar envisioned her face splotched red, her small white teeth gnawing against her upper lip: This image caused him to smile.

"Your Grace," Agnes offered; "we have also invited Lady Tate to spend Christmas with us."

"That's right, Edgar," Rupert interrupted. "This will give her ample time to plan your tutorials, and of course, help Agnes with baby preparations. By the way, old chap, if you had not heard, you will become an uncle in the Spring."

Edgar had not heard. Surprised, he stooped down to shake Rupert's hand. "Congratulations!"

Not letting go, Rupert smiled, "Thank you, brother. If I have not said so before, it is so good to have you home."

Marjorie watched them, smiling. Edgar decided that he liked her smile.

"All brotherly love aside, Rupert, in light of recent events, I feel obligated to mention that Lady Tate and I have already met at the Cavendish Ball. I will forego the details, but in a nutshell, that meeting was a catastrophe."

He watched Marjorie's smile disappear. "As the patriarch of this family," he continued, "I believe Lady Tate would not be a suitable choice for the task at hand."

In unison, everyone in the room gasped. Unfazed, Edgar persisted. "Her deportment at the gala remains in question, and frankly, I don't believe she has the demeanor to adequately represent the Duke of Grangefield."

"I say, Edgar, perhaps we should discuss this later, in private," Rupert said.

Edgar bit back a smile. "I repeat, Rupert, unless you can convince me otherwise, at this time I am hesitant to employ Lady Tate under any circumstances."

***

The new duke's audacity held no bounds, Marjorie thought. He had just spoken about her as if she were some low-borne servant. Between caring for the boy, wanting her land lease, and helping the duke find a wife, there were now sufficient reasons for her to continue with this mad project and remain at Grangefield Hall.

Feeling the tension in her shoulders, she forced herself to step toward him. But the impact of his gaze had the effect of calming, not hindering. She sensed something else; not anger precisely, but something that drew her closer.

"Sir," she said, repositioning her spectacles, "I find your remarks demeaning. I do understand your reluctance, but for the time being, with or without your permission, I intend to remain here.

"In fact, nothing short of being struck by lightning, or being set upon by an advancing squadron of the Queen's militia, would force me to leave." Not waiting for his response, she sucked in an unladylike breath, moving another step forward. "Your Grace, for your information, my reputation as a matchmaker is held in high regard. Furthermore, your brother and I have reached an agreement, and I for one, intend to keep my end of the bargain."

"What agreement?" the duke asked.

"You should discuss the particulars with Rupert. Regardless, I am here to improve your social character, at best a monstrous task."

"Whatever the services rendered, I intend to pay your bill, madame," he said.

"With what, Your Grace? From my understanding the estate is not in a position to pay anyone."

With satisfaction, Marjorie watched the duke's handsome features mottle. She also noticed the very pronounced cleft in the center of his chin now quivered. She remembered seeing that same expression the day he had arrived at Grangefield Hall. He had been angry then, apparently he was angry now. Well, so be it, the man was being unreasonable.

The duke, still red-faced, had assumed the stance of a militia guard prepared for combat.

"I *will* pay your bill, madame."

Rupert interjected, "As much as I am delighted that you have agreed to the payment terms, Edgar, I stand by my decision to retain Marjorie. She knows what she is doing and I value her opinions. She also knows London society well enough to be able to work in an expeditious manner, which is what we need."

Marjorie, unawares, had moved closer to the duke. She noticed a faded white scar on one tanned cheek. Drat, even with a disfigurement the man remained impossibly handsome. She avoided the temptation to trace the smooth angles of his face, her fingers clasping behind her back.

"This matter is important to the entire Hamilton family, Your Grace. I would not insist on staying if the outcome was not critical." She stopped to look at him. "I can only promise that when we are not working together, I will endeavor to keep out of your way."

The duke then did something out of character he grinned.

Indeed, she realized that the duke's entire stance suggested a subtle form of mockery. She gawked at him, which proved to be another mistake.

The duke started making a gurgling noise in his chest. Her fears were realized when his mouth opened and emitted a bellow of unrestrained laughter. His deep guffaws echoed like a repeating shotgun being fired in a silent woodland grove.

Marjorie's lips thinned. Besides being tall, imposing, and decidedly arrogant, at that moment the duke appeared far too amused. The duke continued to laugh, now holding his sides. Good Lord, had he played a joke on her?

"What has you so amused, Your Grace?" Marjorie said. "We are attempting to save *your* inheritance."

The duke stopped laughing.

Sensing his understanding, Marjorie continued. "I take it as a member of the peerage, you are familiar with your responsibilities?"

He sobered. "Madame, I am entirely aware of my responsibilities! Should I remind you, it is I who has inherited this title, not you." He pointed to Rupert. "And not you either, brother."

"You are correct, Your Grace," Marjorie said. "However, if you are not married soon, the Hamilton fortune will be placed in a forfeit situation, with the Crown being the

second beneficiary to your father's will." Marjorie lost patience.
"Rupert, explain his rights to him, he appears to be oblivious to
the consequences of his own situation."

"Madame, I assure you I am far from oblivious," the
duke shouted.

Both women on the couch gasped.

Marjorie stepped back.

Rupert looked to his brother. "Look here, Edgar,
regardless of father's feelings toward you, he did expect you to
return home, and he never renounced your inheritance."

The duke grunted in disbelief, but Rupert ignored him.
"As you know, if you do not marry soon, the Crown would
ultimately benefit, and financially, this estate cannot afford any
legal loopholes."

"Rupert, I am fully aware of the circumstances, but I
refuse to discuss the particulars with a stranger—that woman to
be precise," he pointed to Marjorie. "Don't tell me she's the sort
of absurd creature you would want me to marry me?"

More loud gasps. This time both Agnes and Tiffany stared at their slippers.

"I assure you, Your Grace," Marjorie said, "I would rather face becoming destitute then to be married to you."

***

Lady Tate's slender form and ample bosom had somehow garnered his attention. Edgar didn't move, although he could feel his entire body twitching; a new affliction in her presence. He had almost forgotten that she had just shouted at him, and berated him in the presence of his family. To be standing a scant distance away and not weeping, wailing, or wanting to touch him, as most women were apt to do, deserved some sort of a medal. To make matters worse, she had not moved during her entire declaration, and Edgar had become mesmerized by the scent of lemons.

He regarded her luminescent skin and her black hair, wrapped up in that severe style, but glistening in the bright light of the conservatory. She, too, watched him, her dark eyes focused on his; and with disgust, Edgar realized he had become smitten. He stepped aside, grieving as the scent of lemons faded.

This would not do. He needed a distraction, so he searched for Rupert, who had moved to Agnes' side, no doubt for moral support.

"So, what do you say, brother? Was the plan to marry me off, like father attempted to do?"

"No, of course not," Rupert said. "Not like …"

"Well, if she's not here to marry me, perhaps she is here to warm my bed?"

Another collective gasp from the brown chaise, coupled with one from Marjorie.

"You are insufferable, sir," she hissed.

"Yes, I know, Lady Tate. Since you continue to point out the obvious, I'm sure I will not forget it. Rupert, an answer, if you please."

"Marjorie is here to teach you, to tutor you, to advise you in the ways of society. In essence, she is here to teach you how to become accustomed to your position. That is, she is here to instruct you, so you can behave like a ... a... "

"Duke." Marjorie finished, her arms folding at her chest. She was now grinning at him with satisfaction.

"Precisely," Rupert muttered, sobering as he realized what he had just said.

"So you two don't think I can behave like a duke?" Edgar said, astonished.

"Edgar, that's not it at all.

Marjorie can help you form a social alliance with a suitable marriage candidate, and she can do it in an expedient and efficient manner. She is considered an expert at bringing couples together; that is why we need her help."

Edgar settled his gaze on the carpet pattern. Somehow his bungling brother and the woman from Bedlam had decided that the Duke of Grangefield was too inept to find a wife. Even worse, they considered him too stupid to handle himself in society.

Unbeknownst to Rupert and Lady Tate, he had gotten over his clumsiness around women with the help of his late wife. He had loved her, even married her.

Well, the tides had turned. Perhaps he could use this situation to his legal advantage, and by doing so, enchant Lady Tate into his bed? Now, that idea held promise.

While they were all attempting to marry him off, he would work independently to find a remedy to his legal problems, using the British court system to contest his father's will.

Excited that his plan had taken form, he fixed his features into a contemplative pose, directing his gaze toward Lady Tate. She still stood close to him, wearing that absurd cat-like grin, coupled with that "so there" sentiment twinkling in her eyes.

"Rupert, even I have to admit your plan has possibilities," Edgar said. "You're right! Since I have been gone from England for a decade, it would be prudent to follow your advice and take advantage of Lady Tate. Uh … What I meant to say was, I think it would be a good idea to take advantage of Lady Tate's expertise."

Edgar walked toward the open doors. Before he exited the room, he turned to face Marjorie.

His gaze moved to her lips. "Madame, for some maniacal reason, I find the prospect of spending time in your company almost agreeable."

He stepped outside, and was about to close the door when he heard Rupert's sigh of relief. This was followed by the sound of swishing. He imagined the swishing came from Marjorie's skirts, as she collapsed in an unladylike heap onto the brown chaise, between Tiffany and Lady Agnes.

Edgar smiled. It occurred to him that when life offered even the smallest of victories, they were definitely meant to be savored.

~ ~ ~

Chapter Seven

The next morning Marjorie felt dismal. The prospect of spending the next few days with the duke had kept her up all night. In addition, she still had not discovered the identity of the boy in the Blue Room.

Reaching the landing of the second floor, she heard a familiar deafening baritone; the duke was shouting. Arriving at the Breakfast Room, she stood just outside the door, which gave her the advantage of not being noticed. She spied the duke sitting at the head of the long dining table. The breakfast buffet had been set out, complete with dome-covered platters. The familiar smell of kippers made her nose crinkle, but the sight of the duke's angry face caused her to lose her appetite. His cheeks were flushed, and the cleft in his chin quivered. His attention was fixed on Henry, the head butler.

She felt surprise when she noticed the boy, Sabeer, sitting by the duke's side. His chair had been placed level with Edgar's, quite unusual for a servant

Who was he?

But she didn't have time to ponder this when she heard the boy sniffle. That was when she noticed that his eyes were red—had he been crying?

Appalling! There was no justification in the world to upset the boy, particularly when he was sick: Really, this time the duke had gone too far. She decided to make her presence known and entered the room.

"Good morning, Your Grace," she said, with cool frigidity.

Her tone did nothing to extinguish the duke's anger. He ignored her, continuing to regard Henry with a scowl. The boy still sobbed.

"Oh, do stop that blubbering, son."

Son? Good Lord! Was that Indian child his son?

The duke's face registered his blunder, and now he frowned at his breakfast.

Marjorie curbed her own surprise, but Henry looked flabbergasted. "I'm sorry, Your Grace," he stuttered. "I didn't know."

The duke was in no mood for apologies. "Henry, it doesn't matter who the boy is. Whomever I give permission to sit at this table is considered my guest, and they are to be treated accordingly."

"That tone is uncalled for, Your Grace," Marjorie said, reaching the dining table. "You're upsetting the boy, and Henry for that matter."

The duke's face reddened. "I appreciate your observations, madame, but I would prefer that you kept your opinions to yourself, particularly when I am reprimanding one of *my* servants."

She ignored him, walking to her seat. "Henry, I will have just toast this morning," she said, knowing full well her voice sounded clipped.

The butler nodded, bowing at the waist. He didn't wait to be dismissed and left the room.

With no servants about, Marjorie attended to herself, reaching for the teapot. The tea fragrance she recognized as Darjeeling, one of her favorites.

"What did poor Henry do to make you so cross, Your Grace?"

Again, the duke didn't bother to look at her. Instead, he positioned his knife as if he were hacking into a tree trunk, rather than a rasher of fatty bacon. "Madame, as you heard, I had to discipline 'poor Henry.' The arrogant fellow decided that it would be beneath his station to serve breakfast to my son." The duke nodded in Sabeer's direction. "I suppose I shouldn't discuss this in front of the boy, but can you believe the audacity, madame? That servant insisted that the color of Sabeer's skin is too dark; and I should have him eat his meals in the servants' hall."

Marjorie choked on her tea. "Oh my."

"Oh my, indeed," the duke said, rising, and thumping her once on the back. "Are you all right?"

She nodded, extracting a handkerchief from her sleeve to pat her mouth.

The duke reseated himself. "Do stop sniveling, Sabeer, and say hello to Lady Tate. This is the woman who saved your life, she deserves some small gesture of gratitude for her expert nursing."

"Oh, that's not necessary," Marjorie said, glancing at the boy.

Sabeer did look up, his eyes were red and damp. Managing a tentative smile, his head lowered, and he resumed his sniveling.

"May I ask who his mother is?" Marjorie asked.

"Chamine."

That was all the explanation she received.

The boy shivered, and this prompted the duke to adjust the blanket draped about his shoulders.

"He doesn't like England," the duke said. "He's constantly complaining how cold it is."

Marjorie was surprised when the duke stood. He lifted the boy and settled him not-too gently on his lap, sitting down again. The blanket slipped, and the duke proceeded to tie the ends, creating an untidy knot under the boy's chin.

"Even though he's exhausted, he refuses to go to sleep," Edgar muttered.

"Is the boy your heir?"

"If I had a legal marriage license he would be. I married his mother in a Hindu wedding ceremony; no license was issued. Are you offended, Lady Tate?"

"No. Of course not."

"Well, that's a relief," the duke mumbled.

"But this could complicate matters," she said.

"I beg your pardon."

"Having a son, it will complicate matters," she repeated, taking a sip of her tea.

He didn't respond, glaring at her, no doubt waiting for an explanation.

"If society doesn't approve of this situation, it may become difficult to find you a wife."

Marjorie whispered, "I mean, if your son's parentage is questioned."

If possible, the duke became even more red-faced.

"Parentage is questioned?" he shouted.

"Particularly if the boy resides under your roof," she finished.

Tired, Sabeer had collapsed his cheek against Edgar's tweed jacket. Of course, the duke's neatly tied cravat became wrinkled, but that didn't seem to bother him. He continued to speak to the boy in hushed tones, at the same time stroking his back.

"I told you it would be like this. You cannot expect English people to understand why your skin is a different color from theirs. They judge you because they are not aware of the world that exists beyond this small island. My only fear is that there may be times when I won't be there to protect you; and then you will have to defend yourself. Do you understand me?"

The boy's dark head bobbed against Edgar's chest. One last sob rent the air, then like a church locked up for the night, the room became silent.

"Well, Lady Tate, the burden to find an unobjectionable female has fallen upon you. I'm sure there is at least one unique woman in England who won't squirm at the sight of a seven-year-old with dark skin."

He stared down at the boy's head, his tone gentle. "Sabeer, there is much cruelty in the world, be prepared to face the worst, Little One."

The reality of the duke's words were not lost to Marjorie, and she felt consumed with sadness. She suppressed the impulse to dab her eyes with her handkerchief. Until that moment she had never considered the degree to which prejudices existed in her world, and she felt ashamed.

"I will do whatever I can to help you, Your Grace."

Edgar stared at her. "Just be yourself, madame, at least your true self; not the one full of bluster that you have paraded in my presence."

The remark stung. "I will contrive to make an effort, Your Grace."

The duke ignored her sarcasm. "Now, Sabeer, try again; say hello to Lady Tate. I think she might even allow you to call her Marjorie."

The boy's head peaked in Marjorie's direction, his mouth curving into a smile. This anxious expression had been replaced by a set of flashing white teeth, which contrasted with the deep chocolate color of his face and shoulders. He rubbed his runny nose on the blanket.

"Hello again," Marjorie said.

He offered her another infectious smile, and she couldn't help but reciprocate.

"How are you feeling, young man?" she asked.

"Incredibly good, Madame. I am much improved. However, I am finding it most difficult to hold myself straight."

His accent, combined with his unusual-sounding English, threatened to impair her senses.

"Yes, I can see that," Marjorie muttered, her smile staying in place.

Pushing his plate aside, the duke now gazed at her with eagle-like intensity.

"Sabeer, your father is very concerned about your health," Marjorie said.

The boy nodded, yawning at the same time.

"Why is he out of bed, Your Grace?"

"My name is Edgar, madame. I give you leave to use it, that is, when we are not in public."

"Thank you. However, under the circumstances that would not be appropriate: We wouldn't want to form any bad habits before you embrace polite society."

Edgar sighed. "Madame, I have already embraced polite society. As you may recall, I found society to be not so polite."

Marjorie felt sure she paled, remembering their first encounter at the Cavendish Ball.

"Also," the duke continued, "there is no one in the room with us except the boy; I can assure you he won't say a word. I presume you will use good judgement and address me informally when we are alone. Now, let's not discuss this matter further."

Marjorie's compressed smile reflected her displeasure.

The duke continued, "To answer your question, the boy is out of bed because after he awoke this morning, he would not stay in it. As you might imagine, it requires some mastery to control a rambunctious, seven-year-old. Furthermore, it would appear that ancient servant of yours hasn't been able to manage the job either."

The duke gently patted Sabeer's arm, continuing his explanation.

"I suppose the shock of seeing someone so old and white, caused the boy to become agitated. Earlier, I witnessed Sabeer screaming, and attempting to flee his bed, the Ancient in hot pursuit. I had no recourse but to bring him down to breakfast."

"That ... that is absolutely absurd!" Marjorie stuttered. "Albert is as gentle as a lamb."

The duke smiled. "I thought you might not believe me."

"Marjorie frowned. "You amuse yourself rather too often, Your Grace."

"I can assure you, madame, I cannot remember ever amusing myself prior to this moment, other than yesterday in the library, of course. I'm afraid your mere presence brings out the worst in me."

Marjorie was saved from answering when Henry reentered the room, holding a tray. His complexion appeared less florid than during his reprimand. He placed a small plate with a slice of dried toast in front of her, and then bowed at the waist before leaving. Marjorie ignored the duke's sour expression, adding a pat of butter to her toast, followed by a generous topping of orange marmalade.

"If you cannot manage him then ..."

"When he is awake, he is awake, madame," the duke said, agitated. "As you will soon find out, the boy is restless by nature, and won't be cooped up. That is how he became ill in the first place."

Marjorie swallowed a bite of toast. "I don't understand."

The duke adjusted his posture. Marjorie noticed Sabeer had fallen asleep. The boy's head now rested on the duke's chest.

"After his mother died he became attached to me. In fact, prior to the voyage from India he had never traveled by ship before, and became quite anxious. In an attempt to wean him away from me, I gave him his own cabin, which he refused to sleep in.

"Unbeknownst to me, Sabeer continued to sleep outside my door each night, and without even a blanket. When the ship crossed the Channel, and we hit bad weather, a storm caused the inner decks to flood. The boy had fallen asleep in the wet passageways, and as a result caught a severe chill. Since we had no doctor on board, he could not be treated, and then his condition worsened. By the time I arrived in London, he could not leave his bed. You know the rest."

"I'm sure he must adore you."

"That he does, madame: I believe he is the one person in this world who does."

Marjorie's heart constricted, that had to be the saddest statement she had ever heard. She couldn't help herself, she regarded the duke with a piteous look. Thankfully, his attention was focused elsewhere, as if swamped in a fog of memories.

He then turned in her direction, and too late, he noticed her watchful regard.

"I loved my wife, madame, and I love our son. I will do whatever is necessary to protect him."

Without ceremony he stood, lifting the boy in his arms. "Now I shall return him to his bed. Perhaps he will sleep until luncheon. Send up that servant of yours, he can sit with him until he awakens."

To alleviate the awkwardness of the moment, Marjorie launched into the first topic that came to mind.

"Has Sabeer eaten anything?"

"He managed a few sips of milk. I'm afraid at his age he's not very interested in food. To coax him, I think I will instruct one of the cooks to make him something more appetizing—he loves sweets."

After another awkward pause, the duke said, "I got the sense earlier that you sought me out on purpose, madame, was I correct?"

"Well, yes."

"How can I be of assistance, Lady Tate?"

His formality grated her nerves, but Marjorie ignored it.

"Uh ... Edgar, I thought we should start our lessons as soon as possible, time being of the essence. Would it be convenient to set out a schedule?"

"As much as I would love to play the role of student, Rupert and I have estate matters to take care of."

"I understand, Your Grace, however ..."

The duke interrupted. "Don't misunderstand me, madame, I do appreciate your efforts. Indeed, if I must reenter society, I'm confident that both you and Rupert will make a supreme effort on my behalf."

Marjorie thought she had failed. The duke had turned, and was heading toward the door with Sabeer. As she contemplated the beautiful expanse of his broad back, he stopped, again directing his attention to her. "If you have the time, perhaps we could meet briefly this afternoon. I presume one hour each day should be sufficient, for shall we say, the next two weeks?"

She felt too dumbfounded to reply.

He reiterated, "Does that sound agreeable, madame?"

His offer sounded generous, perhaps too generous. Why was he being so accommodating?

"I suppose that will have to do, at least for now," Marjorie said. "However, once we arrive in London, I will need more time."

"Madame, are you implying that the local squire's daughter would not be a suitable match for a duke? I believe the terms of the inheritance stipulate I can marry anyone. Whether the woman comes from the country or town is immaterial."

"You know quite well that your position dictates otherwise. No, you simply cannot marry just anyone, Your Grace ... uh ... Edgar."

He smiled. "Well, when we arrive in town we can renegotiate the schedule, is that also agreeable with you?"

"Your Grace?"

"Edgar," he corrected.

Marjorie ignored him, thinking for the hundredth time how insufferable he could be. "I thought that the boy might also benefit from a few lessons in deportment."

The duke looked surprised.

"Madame, I am certain that the boy could benefit from a great many lessons in deportment; what are you proposing?"

"Well, since I will be instructing you for one hour every day, I could use my free time to tutor the boy. Perhaps I could teach Sabeer a few social pointers, that is until a governess is retained."

"A governess?" His eyebrows shot up. "Madame, have you not noticed he looks and behaves like an Indian? Unlike English children, he may not understand the value of having a governess. At any rate, finding a governess with an open disposition to other cultures will not be easy, particularly in this desolate part of Surrey."

"I have a strong belief that everyone is entitled to an education, Your Grace, even someone who is from India." Marjorie stood up. adjusting her spectacles. "If you will allow it, I could make some inquiries and find someone suitable on your behalf."

She had avoided eye contact with the duke, but curiosity forced her to glance up. His lips had curved. If possible, he looked even more handsome, and even more surprised.

With the child in his arms, wrapped in a blanket, he also looked every bit the doting parent. For a moment Marjorie thought that she could grow to like this new duke.

"Your Grace, did you hear what I said?"

"I did. Forgive me, but I am curious; why do you want to offer your time and talent to help hire a governess?"

"I ... uh ... I'm not sure."

"You're not sure?" he said, smiling a full smile.

Marjorie could only stare at him. She realized that her enthusiasm had disappeared the moment Edgar had risen from the table. For some inane reason she wanted Edgar to stay and keep her company.

"I'm not used to being idle, Your Grace. Although I am here at Rupert's invitation, there is nothing to preclude me from being more useful during my visit."

Edgar glared at her with a skeptic's eye.

"Is that sufficient reason for you?" she said, the edge in her voice apparent.

"It will do, madame."

Marjorie noticed his posture had relaxed. "Can Sabeer read and write?" she asked.

"Not much. The battlefields of India were hardly the place for schoolrooms. In hindsight, I do believe the War Office is considering having schools put in, but that hasn't been approved yet."

Another one of his jokes; she wanted to object at his obtuseness, but he cut her off.

"Sabeer does know his alphabets, and he can do a few sums," the duke said, smiling at her. "Even at seven he insists on doing the household shopping every week. Since bartering is considered an art form amongst Indians, I taught him how to count money, and he has become a proficient bargainer."

"Well, I suppose that's a good start," Marjorie said. "So, will you allow me to tutor him?"

"Yes, of course, but there will be a condition."

"What sort of condition?" Marjorie asked, with surprise.

"I don't know," he said, smiling; "I haven't thought of one yet."

Marjorie found herself gaping at his broad back as he left the room. He was gone, and as usual, he had neglected to offer the customary bow, yet another breach in etiquette.

She closed her mouth, but not before it curved into a broad smile. This was the first time she hadn't felt inclined to shout, rant, or rave in the duke's presence.

Progress, Marjorie thought: Realizing with disgust that her eyebrows had arched with indecision.

Chapter Eight

Marjorie glanced at her father's old watch. Almost one o'clock and she hadn't seen a soul since breakfast. Sitting in her parlor, she had to admit that it felt nice to enjoy a few moments of solitude. In less than two hours she would meet with the duke for their first lesson in courtship: She felt both anxious and thrilled.

From Albert, she had heard that the duke had left the hall soon after breakfast. His mission had been to inspect as much of Grangefield as possible, and to deliver Christmas baskets to his tenants. The baskets were filled with pies, as well as seasonal vegetables collected from Marjorie's fields. She felt a sense of accomplishment at being able to offer such a service, particularly during the holiday season.

The duke's sole traveling companion had been Rupert, who had grumbled about leaving Agnes behind. As was tradition, he had wanted to help his wife decorate the hall for the upcoming yule festivities. Sabeer had also been left behind. The duke had instructed him to stay in bed, even after the boy had voiced

several objections in Hindi.

Seated behind her desk, Marjorie penned the final

touches to her lesson plan. She realized that now there were two

glaring challenges she faced in the upcoming weeks; first, to

devise the perfect strategy to find the duke a duchess befitting his

station, and second, to marry him off as soon as possible.

Unfortunately, she would now have to spend a considerable

amount of time in the duke's company, most of it unsupervised.

His mere presence had a curious effect on her: Why on earth did

she always want to touch him?

She heard a soft knock at the salon door and groaned:

Privacy seemed elusive at Grangefield Hall.

"Come in," she muttered.

The door opened, and Agnes peeked into the room.

"I do hope you don't mind, Marge, but I couldn't wait to

show you our beautiful decorations. Tiffany and I were hoping

you would come and inspect our handiwork. Perhaps we could

bribe you with a cup of Cook's brandy eggnog."

Marjorie chuckled. "That sounds tempting, but I can't spare the time at the moment. I'm scheduled to meet with the duke for his first lesson, and I need this extra time to finish my lesson plan. Do you mind if I take the tour before dinner?"

"No, not at all. What has you so busy?" Agnes asked, stepping into the room with Tiffany at her heels. The pair had become inseparable since Agnes had announced her pregnancy. Marjorie suppressed another groan, realizing that with this interruption she would not have enough time to finish writing her lesson plan.

Today Agnes' gown could best be described as a blast to the senses. The tangerine worsted wool covered her from neck to toe, accentuating her pregnant belly. She took her time lowering herself down onto the settee, rearranging the small cushions. With her hands clasped on her lap, she waited for Marjorie to answer her question.

By contrast, Tiffany looked understated. She had worn a gown of burgundy, bordered with a navy panel. A matching shawl draped about her shoulders, secured with a round pearl broach. It seemed having the duke in residence had both curbed

her rebellious streak and unearthed an elegant wardrobe. She had

entered the room, and seated herself next to Agnes, placing a

large book on the marble-topped stool in front of her.

Marjorie avoided asking about the book, guessing it was

either about ancient history or Greek artifacts, two of Tiffany's

favorite topics of discussion. Without a doubt, the girl had very

unusual interests.

"Good day, Tiffany. How are you feeling, dear?"

"Much better, Lady Tate. "Thankfully, I am almost over

this wretched cold." She sneezed on cue. "Oh! Pardon me," she

said, positioning her crumpled handkerchief over her red nose,

and then blowing with vigor. "I'm so pleased to have Edgar

home," she said between sniffles. "He also managed to arrive

before Christmas; such a treat!"

At seventeen, although tall and gangly, the girl had

marginally attractive features. Like all the Hamiltons, she had

black hair, today styled in a delicate coronet, with a few scattered

curls arranged across her forehead.

"Marjorie, are you paying attention?"

Agnes, not one to be ignored, had opened her sandalwood fan, and was now waving it in front of her face. "I say, it's rather stuffy in here."

Marjorie realized that both women were watching her.

Agnes asked again, "I do hate repeating myself, but what are you doing?"

"I'm customizing my lesson plan on courtship rituals. As I mentioned earlier, this is in preparation for the duke's lesson this afternoon." She looked up. "I'm curious, Agnes, when he was courting you, did Rupert ever mention his lessons?"

"No, I don't believe he did. Are you suggesting my husband needed instructions to ask for my hand?" Agnes asked.

"Not at all. He just needed a few pointers on technique. Men are famous for their awkward proposals. I believe it stems from severe reluctance, and a lack of practice."

The women laughed.

"Agnes, wouldn't you agree, once I finished working with him, Rupert became quite the proficient suitor?"

"Yes, dear; even I have to admit 'his technique,' as you call it, was perfect." In an instant her smile changed to a look of concern. "You do have something else planned for the duke? He is so very dissimilar from my Rupert."

Marjorie sighed. "I agree, the brothers are not at all alike. I fear the duke will have to take several awkward steps at first. Of course, after we arrive in London, working with actual marriage candidates will give him more opportunities to put these skills into practice."

"Does that say courting rituals?" Agnes asked, as she glanced over Marjorie's shoulder.

"Yes. I thought we would work on basic introductions first," Marjorie said. "This particular exercise focuses on improving his approach skills."

"That does sound rather bookish," Tiffany chimed in. "Don't you think structure might be difficult for Edgar to manage? I mean, he doesn't seem to be very good at taking orders. Quite surprising really, considering he served in the military. How on earth will you teach him to take your lead?"

Marjorie realized she did not have a suitable answer. "I agree, the prospect does sound daunting. Even finding that perfect candidate for him to marry is proving to be a gargantuan task."

She noticed their odd expressions.

"Tiffany, dear, don't worry, somehow I will find a way to manage your brother. Perhaps I could enlist your support? You see, I need a brave soul to teach him a few dance lessons. Since you two are roughly the same height, and your skills at dance are exemplary, your help would be much appreciated."

"Oh, yes, Lady Tate, I would be delighted to help."

"Good! That's settled. And, my dear, do call me Marjorie; Lady Tate makes me sound so very ancient."

Tiffany smiled.

"I shall relinquish my one hour with the duke on Christmas Eve," Marjorie continued. "I will also make sure Rupert assists, he can play the pianoforte, which he does very well. I suggest you focus on formal dance steps first. He needs to be ready for the Grand Ball on New Year's Eve."

"Oh, thank you so much, Marjorie."

The girl beamed with pleasure, not in the least bit concerned about managing her gruff brother.

Unfortunately, Marjorie felt just the opposite. She happened to be very concerned about spending any time at all with the handsome Duke of Grangefield.

***

The grandfather clock in the hallway chimed precisely three o' clock. Edgar opened one of the gilt doors leading to the main ballroom.

"Good afternoon, madame."

"Hello, Your Grace," Marjorie replied. "You're right on time. Have you enjoyed your day?"

After closing the heavy door, he crossed the threshold, assessing the cavernous interior. His footsteps echoed as he walked toward her.

Marjorie had worn a green wool gown, which made her look like a miniature fir tree. Too bad the shapeless dress left nothing to stimulate his sexual curiosity. Edgar then noticed her feet, and became instantly entranced. Her white, stocking-covered toes peeped out from under the hem of her gown; she appeared to be shoeless. Delectable, he thought, suppressing the urge to drag her into his arms and thoroughly kiss her.

"You've picked an interesting place for our first lesson, madame," he said.

Lifting her gaze to him, she tipped back the thick-bridged spectacles perched on her nose. They were the same pair he'd found so deliciously seductive at the Cavendish Ball.

"Thank you, Your Grace. I hoped that being in a less frequented section of the hall would discourage unnecessary interruptions. I understand you spent the day reacquainting yourself with the grounds."

Distracted, Edgar admired her petite form. She was slender and curvaceous, with adequate-sized breasts and a trim waist.

Apparently she cared little about face paint or ornate clothing. In fact, she wore no jewelry at all, not even her wedding band.

According to Rupert, she had been married to the elderly, Earl of Penmore for four years. Being just eighteen, he supposed Marjorie had needed the protection, particularly after the unexpected death of her father. The arrangement had to have been mutual since the Earl needed to sire an heir. According to Rupert's version, there was no heir when the Earl had died in a hunting accident.

That event left Marjorie a very wealthy widow. According to Rupert, Lady Tate has become an enterprising female, one who is also sensible when it came to her finances: Not just sensible, but philanthropic. Most of her wealth has been diverted to grow crops for the poor; a very noble pastime.

She interrupted his musings with a polite cough.

"Your Grace," she said.

"Yes, Lady Tate," he said, startled.

"I was inquiring about your inspection of the grounds."

"Oh, yes, you were. My outing was quite revealing."

She continued to focus on the papers in her hand.

"How so, Your Grace?"

She seemed somehow less timid than at their first encounter on the Grangefield driveway. In fact, when she had spoken up to him at breakfast she didn't seem the least bit afraid of him, which he realized held some strange appeal.

He strode forward, placing his arm on the backrest of a Baroque chair, one of two chairs in the room, and the only two pieces of furniture in the cavernous ballroom. "Back to formal address, Lady Tate?" he asked, "I thought I had quashed you of the habit."

He considered sitting, but etiquette demanded he stand.

"I managed to explore three acres of the estate today. There are still two hundred more to go. To be frank, I had not remembered Grangefield to be quite so large, or for that matter, occupied by so many tenants. I suppose that chore compares well with these lessons, I must suffer through the discovery process. To answer your question, I still have a great deal more to learn, and not necessarily in the area of courtship."

He watched her nose wrinkle. Then she moved closer to him, standing between the baroque chairs. The impulse to right her crooked spectacles caused his hand to lift of its own accord, but thank goodness, he had the presence of mind to draw his arms down and clasp his hands.

As a distraction, he looked about. The décor of the ballroom provided the only distraction. The walls had been painted in a peach shade, with decorative, white wallpaper bordering each section. Apparently Lady Tate had insisted that there be adequate lighting, as he noted the many wall sconces and massive ceiling chandelier, all burning new candles.

"Your Grace, do you think you will enjoy your role as lord of the manor? Perhaps it is not so different from the life of a soldier? After all, you will be leading an army of servants and retainers." Lady Tate said, smiling.

"Madame, I'm afraid, from my perspective, the enjoyment is irrelevant. Whether I am a soldier, or a man of property, it appears that I must do my duty. From what I hear, you also have demanding responsibilities, is that not so, Marjorie?"

Marjorie's head lifted in question.

This had to be the first time she had looked at him since he'd entered the room. She seemed to immediately regret her decision, drawing in a quick breath, and returning her attention to the papers in her hand.

"Rupert mentioned that you operate not one, but two large estates," he continued, "almost equal in size to Grangefield; quite an accomplishment for a woman of society. Rupert also mentioned you have several competent estate managers, who help run things in your absence. I must admit I am duly impressed."

"Thank you."

"What, no gloating? No eloquent words supporting women's suffrage? I had imagined you might want to take a moment to boast. I also hear you have award-winning radishes."

"I would be more inclined to boast, Your Grace, if I didn't find my responsibilities as challenging as those you have inherited. I don't envy either of our positions."

"Touché! Shall we consider a truce, Marjorie?"

He brushed some invisible lint off his sleeve. No answer came. "Alright, no truce then. Perhaps we should proceed with the lesson. I believe we are covering introductions today."

An awkward silence followed.

She cleared her throat. "You read the lesson plan I sent along with Albert?"

"I did," Edgar replied, smiling.

Marjorie wrinkled her nose. Albert must have told her how hard he'd laughed while reading her handwritten instructions.

"Since you appear so eager, let's begin," she said, pointing to the study sheets in her hand.

Marjorie sat down, and beckoned for Edgar to take the seat in front of him. She leaned forward while adjusting her spectacles. The act caused her to graze his arm, and for one awkward moment they looked at one another.

She was the first to turn away.

"As this exercise is a role-play, I would like you to interject your personality into this scene. Remember, your behavior must appear authentic, even to me. Are the instructions clear, Your Grace?"

Edgar hesitated, before nodding. "Oh, very clear, my dear, I must be myself; I'm sure accomplishing that shouldn't be too difficult at all."

***

Marjorie's mourning period was officially over. Wearing new clothing felt awkward, and to make matters worse, she had felt utterly idiotic roaming about the ballroom in her stocking-covered feet. The brown boots were new, and they'd hurt her toes, so she'd taken them off.

Much worse, the duke now stared at her as if she were some sort of pariah. These days, whether awake or asleep, he seemed to monopolize her thoughts.

Her physical response to him appalled her. A mere smile, a mere lifting of his eyebrow, even one of those horrid smirks of his, and she felt like melting snow dripping into a large wet puddle.

And, why had he gone and mentioned her radishes? If he continued to give her compliments she would have to start liking him, and that would not do at all.

Focus, she told herself. Forty-five minutes left to go, and she needed to keep her wits about her. Pinning her features into an exaggerated smile, Marjorie tilted back her spectacles and assumed the role of teacher.

"Your Grace, this role-play is set in Ancient Rome. Your character is Anthony, and I will play Cleopatra." Well, at least she had not stuttered, Marjorie thought with relief.

"Should I move about the room as if I were wearing a toga?" Edgar asked.

"I suppose the more improvisation the better." She didn't look at him. "No matter how ludicrous, I suggest you remain in character, and always address me as Cleopatra." She turned a page of her script. "Our first meeting is at Caesar's palace."

She forced herself to sit tall in the chair.

"In this lesson you will learn the best technique for attracting a member of the opposite sex. Before we begin, please take a few moments to acquaint yourself with the dialogue."

Marjorie handed Edgar several handwritten sheets of paper.

"What's this?" the duke asked.

"Your script, of course; were you expecting to make up your lines?" Marjorie asked.

The duke didn't respond. Instead, he began reading.

Marjorie ignored his frown. "Your objective is to secure a second meeting with Cleopatra; at the same time, gaining the lady's attention by relying solely on your charms. If I feel you need help, I will offer pointers."

"Will you hold my hand if I become nervous?" Edgar inquired, offering her a lascivious smile.

Marjorie noticed her hand trembling, and grabbed onto the material of her skirts. Keeping her face deadpan, she looked directly at the duke. "You're confident tone tells me that you are eager to begin, am I correct, Your Grace?"

***

Edgar squelched the desire to laugh. Marjorie looked entirely too serious. It seemed unfair to be having so much fun at her expense. Although he enjoyed the idea of having a personal matchmaker, her methods were, without a doubt, unconventional. At present the only role-play he had in mind was a love scene, where each of them exchanged their lines naked, lying on a very large bed. His discomfort became more acute when Marjorie adjusted in her seat, and her dress molded to her chest, allowing him a full view of the curve of her breasts. He barely managed a nod of assent when she handed him one of the scripted pages, which he placed on his lap, covering the all too obvious bulge in his trousers.

"Role Play No. 1," he read aloud.

Scene: A crowded chamber (in a real situation this might be a ballroom, a recital, or a refreshment room). Anthony enters. He is flanked by Roman soldiers. They are all wearing uniforms, with red cloaks, white pleated skirts, and sandals.

Anthony is here to find a romantic assignation with a delectable and desirable woman. He surveys the room and glimpses Cleopatra surrounded by her friends. He becomes instantly smitten. [Very Important: Before Anthony approaches her, he must make discreet inquiries to discover if she is married, or otherwise promised to another. He should also seek out the hostess for a proper introduction. If the hostess is not available, he may use the following discrete methods to gain Cleopatra's attention: 1. Stare at her, or 2. Offer a well-delivered smile. If mutual interest is attained, his new goal is to never lose eye contact with her].

Edgar wanted to roar with laughter. Instead, he feigned a yawn, and then continued reading.

The suitor should never become discouraged.

Anthony's new objective is to gain Cleopatra's permission to meet again. If the lady is reluctant, Anthony must concede defeat, and the role-play will end.

He watched Marjorie resume her pacing ritual. This time her route took her along the north side of the ballroom. The swishing of her skirts interrupted his concentration, and he assumed her pacing had to do with her nervousness. He wanted

to savor her discomposure, but decided against it. He rustled his

script to gain her attention.

"The instructions seem clear enough," he said. "Shall we

begin?"

Not wanting to begin at all.

~ ~ ~

Chapter Nine

"Madame, don't you think this little exercise of yours borders on the extreme?" the duke asked.

Perhaps the role-play had been a poor choice. Not because it wasn't an effective tool when compared to other lessons in etiquette, but because she now would have to feign a romantic interest to interact with the duke. Good Lord, why on earth did she always want to touch him?

"No, Your Grace, this is one of my standard exercises. Of course, I made a few changes to accommodate your circumstances, but other then that, not extreme at all."

The duke broached no further argument. He stood and walked toward her, holding out his hand as if he were about to engage her in a waltz.

"What are you doing?" she asked.

"Aren't you supposed to be sitting? I wanted to escort you to your chair."

"Oh," she said, lifting her hand toward his. His skin felt cool to the touch. The pressure of his hand on hers was firm but gentle, as he led her forward to one of the baroque chairs.

Once seated he didn't let go right away. "Could we bypass the segment on eye contact?" he said, smiling. "I believe I can be quite convincing when I need to gain a woman's attention." He squeezed her hand.

She pried her hand loose. "All right, we can skip that section, but only if you promise to practice on your own in front of a mirror."

"Perhaps I should be seated as well," he said, "that way we can start with the pleasantries."

Without waiting for Marjorie's reply, he moved his chair closer to hers, sitting so their knees touched.

Another awkward silence passed. Both she and the duke had become tongue-tied, that would not do at all.

In an odd gesture, Edgar placed a hand to his forehead, as if he had a headache. Perhaps he felt out of his element, like a large fish floating in a shallow pond. She recalled other students of hers undergoing similar bouts of discomfort with this

particular exercise.

"I really don't need lessons on how to court a woman, as

you may recall, I was married."

Perspiration had gathered on his forehead. Marjorie

thought she heard him say "ridiculous." He then offered up one

of those famous scowls of his and stood.

"Sit, Your Grace," she said, her tone commanding.

"Don't think, just read."

As if responding to a field commander's order, he sat

down. The fact that he held a captain's rank in the cavalry bared

no significance, when it came to her lessons Marjorie could

command anyone.

She withdrew her father's old watch from her pocket,

the fob falling gently against her palm.

"This exercise lasts ten minutes. To begin, I recommend

you use the introductory questions I supplied as your guide: Do

you have them?"

The duke nodded, leafing through his stack of papers.

Marjorie inhaled, fortifying her patience. "Good! Now introduce yourself as if you have just accepted Cleopatra's hand. The acceptable norm regarding social greetings, allows a suitor to press a light kiss on the woman's outside wrist. Any handholding is permitted only for a brief moment, or the gesture is construed a breach of etiquette."

She ignored his disenchanted expression, watching as he nervously fluttered the loose pages. He didn't wait, and began reading.

"Good day. May I introduce myself? I am Lord Anthony."

Marjorie bit back a smile and responded: "It is so nice to make your acquaintance, Lord Anthony."

The duke took the hint. "I have not been here in some time, it seems there have been significant improvements."

He was leering at her chest. Perhaps he was trying to unbalance her, Marjorie thought.

"Do you come here often?" he continued.

"This happens to be my first visit."

"May I ask your name?"

"Cleopatra."

"Well, it seems whoever named you had something special in mind. Cleopatra sounds unique, and far from boring."

"The name was chosen by my mama. She has always had an avid interest in the Egyptians, a subject that also fascinated my father. My name is a result of him indulging her eccentricities."

"It appears your father had the right of it," the duke responded. "I am a strong proponent of a husband paying lavish attention to his wife's whims, particularly when the wife in question will bear his future heirs."

Marjorie forced her eyelashes to flutter with coquettish enthusiasm.

The duke's lips twitched.

She followed his glance to the watch on her lap. Time was running out, the duke had only seven minutes to reach his objective.

His breathing sounded ragged, more so when she moved closer to him. Not knowing where the thought came from, she suppressed the impulse to lean just a fraction closer and kiss his cheek. What on earth was she thinking? Thankfully, his gaze lingered on his script. She got the impression he wanted to forge on.

"Well, unfortunately, I have to take my leave. It has been a pleasure making your acquaintance, Cleopatra."

Marjorie held her breath. Had he given up? Perhaps she had misjudged his abilities.

"However, before I go, may I make a parting request?"

"By all means, sir."

"I find you both beautiful and captivating, and if I may be so bold, I would very much like to see you again."

Relief, he wasn't giving up. "I'm flattered."

"Does tomorrow at the Augustus Ball sound reasonable? If for some reason I should become waylaid, may I call upon you at home?"

Marjorie smiled at him. None of her students had ever gotten this far in such a short amount of time.

"That would be acceptable, my lord. My father is Gaius
Octavian."

"Is he now?" Edgar said, smiling at her. He stood,
retrieving Marjorie's hand, and bowing. It seemed as if he would
take his leave, and yet a single minute remained.

He looked at her, smiling, and Marjorie felt her heart
beating. "It has been my consummate pleasure, Queen Cleo."

Because Marjorie had risen to accept the duke's hand, she
could feel the pressure and heat of his skin on hers. Etiquette
dictated that he let go, but he still held onto her hand. Curious,
her gaze lifted toward his—a colossal mistake.

Those dark coals focused on her face, and her lips parted.
A sense of recognition swept over her when the duke drew her
closer, lowering his head.

Marjorie tried to move away, but the smell of cloves and
sandalwood lured her closer. At some point she had grasped onto
his coat sleeve, the texture of the velvet feeling luxurious to the
touch. His breath skimmed her cheek, and she licked her lips
with anticipation.

They both heard the sound at the same time. The pounding noise reverberated in the cavernous ballroom. The duke's head lifted, but unlike Marjorie who just stood there immobilized, he stepped back. The sense of loss felt immediate.

The duke did not release the hand, and she watched as he adjusted her wrist, positioning her palm upward. He hesitated, looked at her, and then lowered his head, his lips caressing the crevice of her wrist, pressing two light kisses onto the indentation.

Marjorie gasped, the unpardonable gesture screamed of impropriety. Not letting go, with care, he folded her palm, squeezing gently on her balled fist. "Perhaps we should continue this another time, my queen."

She could only glare at him. Good Lord, she was behaving like a complete ninny.

His smile formed into a frown when he heard the banging again. It was a pounding noise on the ballroom door. Looking thoroughly annoyed, he released her hand, walking toward the doors. Marjorie felt certain someone was about to experience the duke's wrath.

The gilded doors opened before the duke reached them, and a rattled-looking, liveried servant held a note in his direction. The duke snatched it up. After reading it, he left the room, without even saying goodbye.

The footman quickly bowed before Marjorie, then followed him, closing the door.

Marjorie continued to stare at the place where the duke had kissed her wrist, and grimaced.

"Why on earth couldn't he just follow the script?" she whispered.

***

"Edgar, old chap, it's so good to have you home again," said the youthful-looking man standing near the fireplace in the drawing room.

Summoned by Rupert to greet his newly arrived visitors, Edgar reacquainted himself with his surroundings.

The Grangefield drawing room overflowed with odd-looking pieces of furniture. Three burnt-orange colored couches surrounded a short marble-topped coffee table. A ferocious fire hissed beyond a screen-covered grate, and adjacent to each window alcove, stood large potted ferns, positioned like sentries on top of white pedestals. Rupert stood in the center of the room smiling at the same young man who had spoken to him. Another gentleman was also present. He offered Edgar a curt nod, which Edgar reciprocated. Both visitors wore black from head to toe, as befitting men of the clergy.

The voice of the younger man sounded vaguely familiar, but Edgar couldn't place it. Without hesitating, he walked toward him, smiling. "It's not everyday one reunites with their long lost brother."

Edgar stilled. That couldn't be Pierce? How could this gangly youth be the ordained vicar of Grangefield Abbey?

"Pierce!"

With great enthusiasm, the smiling young man accepted Edgar's outstretched hand. They shook with fervor, then joined in a firm embrace.

Memories returned of a high-spirited, fifteen-year-old boy, and Edgar squelched the melancholy, focusing instead on his brother's face. At five-and-twenty, he had grown into a handsome youth, with pitch black eyes and dark hair. From their mother he'd inherited the plump cheeks of a cherub, and that mischievous gleam, which Edgar always associated with pixies running wild in a slowly awakening forest.

"Is this not the grandest of reunions?" Pierce said. "Really old boy, you should have returned home sooner, it's been far too long."

Edgar couldn't help it, his smile turned up a fraction higher. Pierce had grown from a sweet-tempered boy, to a sweet-tempered adult.

Both brothers stared at one another in awe, until they became aware of a disquieting presence behind them.

Turning, Edgar acknowledged the stranger, offering him a curt nod. The man had emerged from a dark alcove: He appeared unimpressed by the Hamilton reunion.

Pierce cleared his throat.

"Sorry; in my excitement I forgot to introduce you, Lyndhurst. Edgar this is Reverend Lyndhurst. He will be assisting me at the vicarage until his post in Shropshire opens up in the new year. I hope you don't mind, I invited him to spend Christmas with us at Grangefield Hall."

"It is a pleasure to make your acquaintance, reverend. You're more than welcome to stay," Edgar said, walking toward Lyndhurst, and extending his hand in greeting.

The man hesitated, then stepped forward to acknowledge the gesture. His hand felt ice cold and skeletal to the touch. After releasing the handshake, the man turned and retreated back to the alcove.

Another lengthy pause ensued. All three brothers waited for Lyndhurst to say something.

"Edgar, I think you may already be acquainted with Mr. Lyndhurst," Pierce said, bridging the silence. "His sister is married to the Earl of Malvern. Wasn't the earl your partner in that shipping venture in India?"

Edgar hesitated. It seemed odd to meet a relation of the earl's so soon after his return to England, particularly when the earl's main seat was in Cornwall, quite a distance from Surrey. They had been firm friends, the Earl and he. When they were not fighting for their country, he and the Earl had spent time engaged in trade. This endeavor had made Edgar a handsome profit, enough to keep his family safe, and supplement his meager soldier's pay.

"That is correct, Pierce. I had the great privilege of soldiering with Malvern in India. Any relation of Malvern's will always be welcome at Grangefield Hall."

The stranger's curt nod acknowledged the enormity of the gesture; however, he still refused to offer any verbal response. The man was definitely being obtuse, Edgar thought.

"I am curious sir, have you taken a vow of silence, or is it usual for you to refrain from conversation?"

Lyndhurst's eyebrows arched, bringing his face into the light, and making visible a distorted left eye. He continued to squint as if he were peering into a dark keyhole.

"Pardon me, Your Grace, I did not mean to offend anyone. Your brother was remiss in notifying you of my strict rules regarding conversation. I seldom speak at social gatherings, unless it becomes necessary."

Edgar noticed the man's mouth had formed a strained smile.

"I have discovered," Lyndhurst continued, "that excessive conversation dulls a man's intellect."

"I see," Edgar managed to blurt out. It sounded as if Lyndhurst had finally decided to put his superior conversation skills into practice.

"I believe a cleric's voice has been designated for a much higher calling. Abiding by these beliefs, Your Grace, excessive banter can be considered trivial, perhaps even damaging to a cleric's ability to concentrate. Thus, I try to use words only when orating; this encourages the flock to spread their wings and listen with eager hearts."

Edgar, stunned, turned to both his brothers, seeking support, but their reactions were equally priceless. Rupert's mustache had compressed under his nose, while Pierce merely looked amused.

Thank heavens Agnes entered the room, wearing the brightest orange dress he had ever seen; a smiling Tiffany in tow. "What's all the excitement? Have we missed something?" she asked.

After what sounded to Edgar like a collective sigh, each brother turned toward her. Rupert moved forward first, offering his wife a peck on the cheek.

What followed next were girlish giggles and cheek kisses between family members. An awestruck Edgar viewed the proceeding with curiosity: His family appeared to be an overly affectionate group of adults.

Mr. Lyndhurst had been forgotten during this happy exchange, except for a last-minute introduction to the ladies, the man retreated into the shadows and sat in isolation on a straight-backed armchair.

"Edgar," Tiffany said. "Lady Tate has given me leave to lead one of your lessons tomorrow. Could we meet before supper?"

"The duke and I have a set daily appointment, Tiffany," Marjorie said, entering the room, shadowed by a stiff-looking Albert. The butler used slow movements as he set down a tray of decanters and glasses. He righted himself, peering over his shoulder with eagle-like dexterity.

"I took the liberty of adding an assortment of stronger beverages to the tea menu, Your Grace."

Edgar approved with a nod, and Albert then beckoned to the three parlor maids waiting outside, who entered with the other trays.

The entire family, with the exception of Edgar, found their favorite seats. Marjorie, Agnes, and Tiffany sat together on the cushioned couch facing the center of the room. Agnes then proceeded to pour the tea.

Pierce vacated his seat near Lyndhurst, dragging a short embroidered stool close to Tiffany. He hunched down beside her; they then proceeded to ignore everyone else in the room, conversing in hushed whispers. On occasion something amusing caused them to snicker and burst out laughing. They were the closest in age amongst the Hamilton brood, and their sibling camaraderie confirmed that they had missed one another's company.

Meanwhile, Rupert tried to engage Lyndhurst in conversation by talking about the severe weather condition, and how this might affect church services on Christmas Eve. The reverend didn't respond, except for the occasional nod. However, when Agnes launched into a discussion about women activists, and the role of women in the church, Lyndhurst's face wore a mottled expression.

Seeing this, Edgar was saved from choking by a ruthless slap to the shoulder blades, delivered by Marjorie, who had come to offer him scones.

"Thank you, madame."

"You're entirely welcome, Your Grace," she said, smiling.

Edgar recovered from the smile. "My sister has informed me that she wishes to lead my lesson tomorrow."

"The lesson tomorrow is dance, which Tiffany excels in. I took the liberty and volunteered her services."

Upon hearing Marjorie's lavish compliments, Tiffany sat up with a straight posture, beaming with delight. Then she sneezed.

"Bless you!" Voices sounded in unison.

"I say, old chap, what's all this about lessons?" Pierce said. "Have you managed to get yourself exiled to the schoolroom? I thought you were too old for that sort of thing."

Tiffany elbowed Pierce in the arm, as if he had ruined a perfect moment.

"I say, Tiff, that hurt," Pierce muttered, offering her a pained expression, while rubbing his ribs.

An odd silence descended over the room, as if a wool blanket had just doused a large flame. Even Agnes, mortified, stopped talking, and sat in stunned silence. All eyes were on Edgar.

"I would refrain from calling me 'old,' brother; particularly if you intend to stay and enjoy a family Christmas." Edgar made an effort to look stern, but he felt his lips curve.

"To answer your question, I have been banished to the schoolroom because Rupert thinks I need a refresher in etiquette, before I am exposed to polite society. Lady Marjorie has agreed to tutor me, she began our lessons today. My objective is to court some unknown woman and make her my duchess. If you had not heard, I must marry, it is a requirement of the inheritance."

"You don't say? No, I had not heard about the lessons," Pierce said, squinting in Rupert's general direction for confirmation.

Turning his attention to Lyndhurst, Edgar continued. "Since I have made you privy to a family discretion, sir, I would appreciate it if you'd not mention this to anyone. As you may have surmised, I find these circumstances rather humiliating. It seems I should admonish my sister for mentioning this in public, but her avid nature prevents me from doing so."

Edgar glared at Tiffany: She immediately pursed her lips, staring at something fascinating on her lap.

As anticipated, Lyndhurst didn't respond, only nodding his head in acknowledgement.

"According to what I've heard whispered in the corridors by the servants," Edgar continued, "Lady Tate is very qualified to deliver this sort of training. She is known to groom grooms," Edgar muttered. "In my humble opinion, I did very well today, wouldn't you agree, Lady Tate?"

Edgar's gaze wandered to Marjorie. Her cheeks had reddened. He wished they were still back in the ballroom and he could complete that kiss he'd started. He remembered the scent of lemons that clung to her hair, and how he'd suppressed the impulse to brush his chin against her ivory cheeks, and kiss every inch of her throat and neck. He'd also wanted to fog up the lenses of her spectacles, and wondered if she needed them to see when they eventually made love.

Marjorie then glanced in his direction, and this prompted him to notice her features. Her lips had parted, looking moist and inviting: The woman indeed had a very kissable mouth.

"Marjorie are you going to answer?" Agnes ventured.

Still she didn't respond.

Edgar continued to stare at her, wondering if she yearned for him as much as he yearned for her.

Agnes redirected. "Marjorie? Edgar was just telling us how he mastered his lesson today."

"Was he, now?" she muttered.

"Yes, dear; do you have a comment?"

Marjorie looked at Rupert, who was now settled on the window seat near Lyndhurst.

"Well, there are several more lessons, and it is too soon to tell if he's mastered anything. The true test will come when we venture to London: The duke will be required to apply those skills when he is in the company of ardent, eligible females."

Edgar bristled. "Agnes, it seems Lady Tate is a harsh taskmaster, unwilling to offer even a hint of praise. Perhaps she is still too dumbfounded by my progress today. What say you?"

Agnes nodded without comment, keeping herself busy offering refills of tea.

The duke now stood nearby. Marjorie tried to ignore him by talking to Agnes, but this strategy became stymied when Agnes decided to step outside the room, calling Tiffany and Pierce to join her. This provided Edgar the opportunity to move into Agnes' vacated spot on the chaise.

Marjorie flinched when Edgar's leg brushed against hers. They were seated so close that their elbows touched. She tried to nudged him away, but this only resulted in her poking his ribs.

"What was that for?" he said, grimacing.

"You are sitting too close, it is considered improper. Move away, or better yet, remove yourself from the chaise."

"Marjorie, I've just started enjoying myself. I fear having tea with my family will be dreadfully dull without some sort of distraction. As I recall, I tried to illustrate how much fun we could have during our recent lesson."

Marjorie gasped. He ignored her discomfort, resting his arm so it draped along the backrest of the chaise.

"Remove your arm this instant," she hissed. "If you don't, I may have to do something drastic."

"How drastic?" he murmured, smiling at his brother, who had glanced in their direction.

Marjorie also smiled at Rupert, gritting her teeth. "I will scream."

"Will you now?"

"It would not be wise to challenge me, Your Grace."

An idle threat, Edgar thought.

Marjorie then trod on his foot.

"Ouch."

"Did you say something Edgar?" Rupert asked.

"Not a thing, Rupert," he said.

Rupert looked dubious, but he returned his attention to Lyndhurst.

Edgar bent to rub his booted foot, inhaling her fragrance. "Lemons," he muttered. "You know, Marjorie, I had no idea interacting with a countrified miss could be so entertaining, albeit painful."

Marjorie shuffled as far away from him as possible, which wasn't far at all. For a second time, she regarded Rupert, as if willing him to notice her. Rupert, however, was lost in conversation and he was doing all the talking.

She might try kicking him in the shins next, Edgar thought, but felt confident that she wouldn't, moving a smidgen closer. He reflected that his behavior bordered on being unpardonable, but they believed him to be uncivilized, so that was how he aimed to behave, at least for now.

"How dare you take such liberties?" she said. "If it weren't for the fact that you have a delightful son, one would think your behavior barbaric."

"I am grateful you find Sabeer endearing."

"Sabeer is a delight. However, at this moment, the boy's temperament and behavior are not in question: *You* need to move away."

"Madame, I must make it known, I have decided to get very well acquainted with you. In fact, I believe we could have a much more animated discussion if we were alone."

"Move away," she hissed. "That will be my last warning, Your Grace. I would prefer you did not embarrass us."

Really what could she do? Knowing this, Edgar opted not to move, which proved a serious miscalculation.

Marjorie waited a scant moment before lifting her arm closest to him. He was not sure what happened, but her teacup somehow dropped onto his lap. The entire contents splashed, then the cup and saucer tumbled onto the carpet.

Reflex forced Edgar to stand up. He stared with shock at the large wet tea stain on the front of his britches, then his temper unleashed in a slew of obscenities.

He now loomed over Marjorie, who had the audacity to glare at him with a startled expression.

Rupert and Lyndhurst emitted a collective "good grief."

Edgar ignored everyone, zeroing in on Marjorie. She stood, now smiling behind a raised kerchief, and choking back what appeared to be mirth. The kerchief properly concealed her reaction, but not from him. Before he or anyone else could comment, she smoothed out the fall of her skirts, and marched from the room, not even offering him an apology.

"I say Edgar, have you gone and upset Marjorie?" Rupert said, in earnest.

Edgar glared at his brother, at the same time dabbing his wet clothes with a serviette. His only thought was, when would he get an opportunity to enact his revenge?

~ ~ ~

Chapter Ten

"Rupert, we're leaving," Marjorie said.

Rupert peered at her over the edge of his newspaper. He'd been sitting on his favorite leather chair by the fireplace when she'd entered the drawing room.

Marjorie marched toward the wall of bookshelves, and then started pacing.

"Well, have a nice time, dear," Rupert said. "And don't forget to wear a heavy coat, the weather looks frigid outside. If Agnes is going with you, make sure she wears her fox shawl; I don't want her catching a cold." He rustled his newspaper. "And, do take a footman, it's very slippery." Then he resumed his reading.

"Good Lord!" Marjorie said, with exasperation. "What I meant to say was, after Iris finishes packing my portmanteau, and I locate Albert, who for some reason can never be found since Sabeer arrived in this house, we will all be on our way home."

She said this glaring at the front page of the *Morning Gazette*, wanting to bore a hole in it so she could see Rupert face to face. "We are all returning to Henley House—today!"

Rupert collapsed the newspaper in his lap. "You're not serious?" He looked as though he was about to have severe heart palpitations, and Marjorie felt a thread of concern for him.

"It's Christmas Eve," he said. "Cook is serving her special Christmas pudding for dessert, and the duke will be receiving his first houseguests.

"Agnes has gone to a great deal of trouble to plan a formal affair. She mentioned that dinner will be twelve courses. Have you also considered that it is snowing outside? A carriage won't be able to travel a mile without getting stuck in a ditch. I suppose that might deter visitors, which in hindsight, may be a good thing. Goodness, how are we going to travel to the village tonight for church services? I better mention something to Henry, he can send a few footmen with shovels to clear the roads." Rupert organized the pages of his newspaper, before setting it down on a small table in front of his chair.

Frustrated, Marjorie flopped onto the chaise. Her nose wrinkled at the sight of the creases on her spruce-green travel cloak. The situation at Grangefield Hall had fast become complicated. Her strange attraction to the duke had somehow managed to cloud her judgement, causing her to behave irrationally.

In addition, Sabeer's presence continued to pose a serious complication. What woman of society would marry a duke with a son who was half-Indian?

"I'm sorry, but I have quite made up my mind," she said, tugging off one of her black leather gloves. "I hope to be well on my way before Agnes comes down for breakfast. I'm positive she will try to convince me to stay."

"Of course she will, but that's beside the point, why are you leaving?" Rupert asked. He had uncrossed his legs, and now strummed his fingers on the leather armrest of his chair.

With difficulty, Marjorie started tugging on the fingers of her other gloved hand. "I find your brother obnoxious; I simply can't work with him."

"I see," Rupert muttered.

Marjorie could have sworn Rupert smiled. But then he picked up his teacup, and the smile had vanished. "Does this have anything to do with yesterday's incident?" he asked, sipping his tea. "Granted, Edgar does have a peculiar way of showing the more playful side of his personality."

"Playful? What are you thinking, Rupert? For all I care he can be as playful as he pleases—but not with me." With triumph, she managed to tug off the second glove. "His arrogance is beyond understanding, and his ability to follow simple instructions nonexistent."

"Edgar is not cooperating with his lessons?"

Ignoring Rupert, she continued her tirade. "Not only does yesterday's incident prove the duke is unmanageable, but what about the boy, Rupert? You never mentioned the duke had a son. Sabeer can't even be presented as his legal heir. I have raised my concerns with the duke, but he doesn't seem to consider this a serious issue. I, on the other hand, do."

Marjorie resumed her pacing. "I feel awful discussing Sabeer as though he were an irritant. Indeed, the boy happens to be the only element of the duke's personality that makes him palatable." She walked toward the hearth, removing a small ivory fan from her reticule, and fanning her face with fury.

"Marjorie, no one except Lyndhurst and I saw what happened yesterday."

"That is also beside the point," Marjorie blurted, fanning faster. "I happen to have experienced the duke's ungentlemanly behavior firsthand. If that man ever enters society, and behaves without a single regard to his social standing, he will be ostracized."

Still sitting, Rupert leaned forward. "I chose you, Marjorie, not because you happen to be a superior matchmaker, but because you have a caring heart. Now, all I ask is that you be patient with him.

"As it relates to the boy," Rupert continued, "as you now know, Edgar married a young woman in India. From all accounts he was devoted to her. I can only imagine that going from a loathsome situation dealing with father, to the unbearable agony of losing a wife must have been torture. In many ways I can understand why he behaves the way he does."

Marjorie realized that she did feel empathetic to the duke's situation. Good Lord, Rupert was right about her, she did have a tender spot.

"I promise," Rupert said, "the first chance I get, I will talk to him."

"You will do no such thing," Marjorie blurted.

"You don't want me to mention our conversation?"

"Absolutely not."

"But I thought ..."

She raised a palm in the air, interrupting him. "You thought wrong. Without a doubt, your brother has behaved rudely, but under no circumstances will I have the duke know how much his behavior bothers me. If he suspects, I will lose all credibility with him."

"Does that mean you have decided to stay?" he said, hopefully.

Marjorie tapped her spectacles till they reached her eyelashes.

"Do you think he's behaving this way on purpose?" She stopped pacing and turned towards him. "Do you suppose he's trying to dissuade me by making me assume he is vulgar and wretched?"

"Perhaps," Rupert muttered.

"If he's trying to sabotage my efforts then I need to be more resilient."

"You're absolutely right!" Rupert said. "I think you're onto something."

Curious, Marjorie looked at him over the rim of her spectacles. Rupert looked sincere, but somehow his tone suggested otherwise.

"You're staying, then?" he said, as if reading her thoughts.

Marjorie didn't answer.

"Marjorie, Edgar needs you; please don't give up on him, or abandon us. I heard from Agnes that you asked Edgar if

167

you could work with the boy. Knowing the circumstances, you can appreciate how much Sabeer needs you as well."

Rupert then sighed a deep sigh. "My dear, you have become very important to this entire family."

"Rupert?"

"Yes, dear," he said.

Marjorie smiled at him. "Have I mentioned you can be very persuasive?"

"Not to my recollection. However, you have mentioned how irritating I can be. Agnes has that same complaint. I believe the last time was on the eve of my wedding. I had prepared my undying love speech, you know the one I planned to deliver to Agnes at the altar. I remember that after the twentieth rendition, you became quite irritated. As I recall your exact words were, 'Oh, do shut up, Rupert!'"

Marjorie laughed. "Yes, well, I suppose now you can add another irritating attribute to the list—persuasion." Her smile faded. "I shall stay, Rupert, and I promise to do my very best to find your brother a wife."

She took a step toward him, garnering his complete attention. "However, under no circumstances will I tolerate being manhandled by him."

"I completely understand," Rupert said.

Marjorie noted that he looked relieved.

"If the duke thinks I'm going to go off and sulk, then he's quite underestimated me."

Rupert bent down to pick up his newspaper, muttering, "I'm sure he has."

Marjorie ignored him. She had already walked to the door, opening it, and walking outside. She turned her attention back to Rupert, frustrated that she could not see his face behind the newspaper.

"Before I am finished with your brother, he will rue the day he ever met Marjorie Alexandria Bowland-Tate."

That said, she kicked back the train of her coat, as if she were a flamenco dancer, and marched out of the room. She slammed the door shut, not bothering to say goodbye to Rupert.

***

At precisely seven o'clock Edgar joined his family and guests in the drawing room.

From information he had received from Jones, who had liberated it from another servant, the Grangefield family always convened the night before Christmas for their traditional holiday repast, and afterwards ventured to the village to attend church services.

This particular evening Edgar didn't feel like celebrating. More precisely, he didn't trust himself to be in the same room as Lady Tate. When he entered the drawing room, a murmur of voices greeted him. He was sure by now the entire family had heard about the spilled tea incident.

"Oh, there you are, Edgar. You look dashing in tails," Agnes said, moving toward him. "It must be a Hamilton trait," she added, blushing as she glanced over at Rupert.

Agnes interlocked her arm with his. "Please indulge me, Your Grace, I would like to introduce you to our guests, Baron and Lady Osterly."

A tall elderly gentleman stood side by side with a short, buxom woman, who appeared much older than Agnes. She was petite, with plump cheeks, and her hair arranged in bright blond ringlets. She carried a large ostrich fan, which she waved in an exaggerated motion across her face.

"The pleasure is ours," Lady Osterly twittered.

Edgar extended his hand in greeting to Baron Osterly. "We are pleased that you could accept our invitation." He then bowed over Lady Osterly's gloved hand, which she had extended so it almost reached his chin.

"Oh, I assure you, Your Grace, I am thrilled to be here," Lady Osterly said. "We've never been invited to Grangefield Hall before, but now that my husband is doing business with the viscount, I'm sure we will be seeing much more of each other." She batted her eyelashes at him before continuing. "You see our original invitation had been for tea, but then the snow started falling, and well, now we are staying overnight; I'm so thrilled!"

Edgar remembered that Rupert intended to sign a land lease with the baron, so he could graze his sheep.

171

"Well, I'm confident your experience here will be unforgettable."

His sarcasm was lost on Lady Osterly. The woman's blond eyelashes fluttered.

Edgar felt grateful when Baron Osterly bridged the silence.

"Without a doubt, this invitation makes up for an otherwise dreary confinement. My wife is forever complaining that country life is not at all glamorous. We just moved here from the North, and cultivating new friendships during the winter has been especially difficult. If you had not heard, Your Grace, I recently inherited the estate on the other side of the village."

"No, I had not heard. Perhaps I should be welcoming you both to Surrey, as well as to Grangefield Hall," Edgar said, offering a smile to each.

A small commotion drew his attention. The object of his lust and mental trepidation had entered the room, causing his smile to vanish. Marjorie had chosen to wear an evening gown with a low neckline, made of ruby red satin—she looked stunning.

He happened to look in Mr. Lyndhurst's direction, and noticed the man leering at Marjorie's bosom: An unpleasant sensation crept over him.

As usual, shadowing Marjorie, Albert entered the room.

"Dinner is served," the Ancient announced. He offered an awkward bow, then exited without being dismissed.

"Splendid!"Agnes said, her lilting voice interrupting Edgar's musing. "Your Grace, as our host, you have been assigned to escort Lady Osterly into supper." She then nodded her head toward Tiffany. "Dearest, you will have the pleasure of being escorted by Baron Osterly." She then noticed Marjorie. "Good, you've finally arrived, and might I add, looking quite festive. Marjorie, you will have the good fortune of being escorted to dinner by both Pierce and Mr. Lyndhurst. Does anyone have any questions?"

"I have one, Agnes," Edgar said, lowering his voice.

"Yes, Your Grace," Agnes replied, releasing his arm, and regarding him.

"Does this list of escorts correspond with the seating assignments for dinner?"

"Why yes, it does," Agnes said with confidence.

"That's what I thought," Edgar acknowledged.

His gaze lingered for a scant moment in Marjorie's direction. Marjorie didn't notice. She had avoided looking at him since she'd entered the room. In fact, she had avoided him all day, Edgar noted with disgust. He knew he would have to apologize to her at some point, the sooner the better. He had behaved badly at tea, and under no circumstances would it be considered proper for a host to manhandle his house guests, even when he did happen to be smitten with one of them.

"Edgar, did you want me to rearrange the seating?" Agnes asked, taking a quick peak in Marjorie's direction.

Edgar noticed. "That won't be necessary, the standing arrangements will suffice. However, in future, Agnes, I would like to be consulted."

Agnes paled.

"I say, that's unkind, Edgar," Rupert said. "Agnes has been arranging the seating for dinner at Grangefield Hall since we were married. She's quite good at arranging things."

Rupert looked red in the face as he twirled the tips of his moustache.

"I apologize for my apparent show of bad manners, madame. My concern lies with the impending arrival of my new duchess. Of course, regarding household matters, I anticipate a smooth transition. However, you must agree, that won't happen unless I'm informed of the goings on at Grangefield Hall."

Agnes flushed, "yes; I understand completely. I had taken the ritual for granted. Thank you for the explanation. In future I will include you in all the household decisions, at least until the new duchess arrives."

"Are you planning to marry, Your Grace?" Lady Osterly asked, fanning herself.

"When the opportunity presents itself, Lady Osterly. It is after all my duty," Edgar replied without emotion. Not leaving

Lady Osterly time to respond further, Edgar said, "Shall we proceed?"

"Oh, yes, by all means, Your Grace." The woman moved an aggressive step forward, grabbing Edgar's elbow.

She giggled: "I say, you're very handsome. I'm quite positive every eligible woman imaginable will be flocking to Surrey once they hear you're on the market."

Edgar didn't respond, turning, and leading the small party through the double doors toward the dining room. Two footmen stood at attention outside, waiting for the couples to pass. Lady Osterly chatted, while Edgar nodded agreement to each of her comments. He then deposited her at her designated seat.

"Where is Sabeer this evening?" Pierce asked, as he seated Marjorie.

Edgar looked over in his brother's direction.

Agnes interjected. "Dinner is later than usual this evening; much too late for a child to stay up and participate, Pierce."

"That is precisely why he won't be joining us, brother," Edgar said. "Besides, he's still recuperating from his illness; I suspect he will need all his energy to open presents tomorrow."

"Who might this person be?" Lady Osterly inquired.

"Sabeer arrived from India with His Grace," Marjorie interrupted.

Edgar frowned at her. She was attempting to avoid mentioning Sabeer in public. Annoyed, he flipped back the tails of his evening coat and seated himself. "I anticipate that you will meet Sabeer tomorrow."

"I look forward to it," Lady Osterly said, peeking over the feathers of her fan, batting her eyelashes at him.

Edgar ignored her, focusing instead on the dining table, which was covered with a pristine white tablecloth. Towards the center of the table, standing in a neat row, were Christmas trees centerpieces, formed with speared pears. Each tree had been decorated with thick garlands of red icing and silver sugar balls.

The seating arrangements had the guests strategically scattered among the Hamilton family members. Having been married to an earl, Marjorie had been seated to Edgar's right, while Mr. Lyndhurst flanked her other side. The man continued to ignore everyone, his attention riveted to Marjorie's cleavage. Edgar suppressed the urge to remove his white dress glove, and offer Lyndhurst a challenge. He tempered his anger when the first course arrived, and Lyndhurst turned his attention to his food. Any thoughts of challenging Lyndhurst to a duel, or asking Marjorie's forgiveness received a reprieve. Edgar sighed, preparing mentally to endure the long night ahead.

***

Marjorie had no choice but to answer questions from both Edgar and Lyndhurst throughout the entire meal. The reverend replied with judicious remarks, ogling her chest for most of the evening.

"I need to talk to you in private, Lady Tate," Edgar whispered.

Marjorie realized that the pain in her stomach had nothing to do with indigestion, even though she had indulged in two helpings of Christmas pudding.

"Would you join me in my study before we leave for the village? This should take but a moment."

Marjorie inclined her head and whispered, "I'm afraid that won't be possible."

Marjorie noticed Edgar swirling his butter knife, and wondered if he contemplated poking out her heart with it.

"I insist, madame," he said through clenched teeth.

Marjorie lifted her napkin and dabbed her mouth.

"Again, I must decline: An evening assignation with you would be an unpardonable breach of etiquette."

Now tight-lipped, Edgar glanced over at Lady Osterly, needing to make sure she was still talking to Pierce. "I need to apologize for my behavior yesterday."

"A meeting will not be necessary, I accept your apology."

"I didn't want to do it here," he said, annoyed. "I wanted to offer my apology in private. My earlier behavior deserves more than just a simple, 'I'm sorry.'"

"I have already said that will suffice."

"You are a headstrong creature, madame."

"Your Grace, I take it that you have finished rendering your apology," Marjorie said, with disgust.

Thankfully, Rupert chose that moment to interrupt, tinkling his crystal wine glass with a silver teaspoon. "Ladies and gentleman." He stood with his wine glass in hand. "I would like to propose a toast." He raised his glass higher.

"To the new Duke of Grangefield. Merry Christmas, Edgar! We are all extremely delighted that you have returned home."

After a round of cheering, Edgar stood. "Thank you, Rupert. I must say, I'm happy to be back in the bosom of my family."

"Here, here!" Pierce said, while motioning across the table to toast with Lady Osterly.

The woman giggled, as she lifted her glass, toasting with the delicacy of a cricket ball hitting a wicket.

***

As custom decreed, the ladies adjourned to the drawing room after dinner, leaving the men to their cigars and brandy. When they rejoined the women, Edgar made a beeline for Marjorie, who stood near the pianoforte inspecting a stack of music sheets.

"You play?"

"I do."

"Will you play tonight?"

"Perhaps tomorrow, Your Grace. I'm rather partial to Christmas carols."

"I shall look forward to it," Edgar said. "Do you think you can forgive my behavior yesterday?"

"Actually, no; that particular incident will be difficult to forget," she whispered, taking a small sip of sherry, at the same time turning over a sheet of music. "In fact, since my arrival, your behavior has been inexcusable. Although you did apologize earlier, I really can't trust the conveyed sincerity."

"I realize I have been difficult to deal with," Edgar said. "In my defense, I consider this inheritance issue a private family

181

matter. I'm afraid the thought of a stranger's interference precipitated my despicable behavior."

Marjorie didn't reply, returning her attention to the music sheets.

"Madame, I have never admitted a wrong to a woman before; I would appreciate it if you would acknowledge the tremendous effort I am making."

"Frankly, Your Grace, I cannot imagine any woman wanting to marry you given the treatment I have experienced."

Although she had kept her tone to a hushed whisper, Edgar noticed that her cheeks had pinked.

"Against my better judgement," she continued, "I have decided to stay and continue your training. Whether you appreciate my decision is unimportant."

Edgar wanted to ask what she meant by that, but she had already walked away, a vision of red defiance. He recalled a similar blow after being punched in the eye during a battle; this time, however, the attack had been a direct shot to his pride.

~ ~ ~

Chapter Eleven

It was well after midnight when those who had attended church services in the village returned to Grangefield Hall by way of a dark desolate road.

A high-pitched whizzing, followed by Mr. Lyndhurst's scream signaled a dangerous presence.

"Everyone to the ground! Gunshots ho!" the duke shouted from his position on horseback.

Marjorie heard the warning. She had opted to travel with Agnes and Tiffany in the Grangefield coach, while the men had chosen to ride their horses. The darkness hindered visibility, but Marjorie watched from the coach window. Being closest to Lyndhurst, Edgar had slid off his horse, and with the honed instincts of a soldier, moved toward the injured man.

The duke caught Lyndhurst, who was about to topple off his horse toward the hard, icy ground. He stooped down, adjusting to the man's dead weight, then lowered Lyndhurst's body onto the snow-covered roadside.

As the wind howled, Rupert and Pierce dismounted their horses, using them as crude shields, crouching down behind them. The brothers looked alert, their pistols drawn, prepared to face any potential threat.

Meanwhile the coach continued to roll forward. Marjorie leaned out the open carriage window, and watched the animals stomping their hooves, still skittish after the gunfire.

She tried to calm herself with slow breathing, but the conditions within the coach were not conducive. Agnes had started moaning Rupert's name loudly, and poor Tiffany, frightened, clutched Marjorie's arm. In contrast to Agnes' hysteria, the girl had become deathly silent.

Marjorie heard Mr. Jones issuing orders in an attempt to calm the horses. The terrified animals pranced a retreating dance, until stomping to a halt. She sighed with relief when the carriage rattled to a stop.

The outriders grabbed the reins of the lead horses. Being their coachman, Jones jumped down from the rooftop, hurling his compact body through the carriage door, which had banged opened when the coach had stopped.

The night then became perfectly still.

"Be calm, Lady Agnes," Jones whispered.

"You, too, Lady Tiffany. If I were you, I'd get down on the floor, who knows where the next gunshots are coming from."

Without hesitation, Agnes clasped Tiffany's skirts, following her to the floor.

Being a soldier like the duke, Jones seemed adept at delivering orders. Taking his advice, Marjorie also slid to the ground.

Jones then whispered, "They shot that Lyndhurst fella and I'm guessing the blighter's in a bad way."

"Oh, dear," Agnes muttered.

"Sorry, milady, I didn't want to upset ye."

"What is to become of us?" Agnes wailed.

Jones focused his attention on Agnes, who had started to gnaw on her upper lip.

"Don't go and panic on me, Lady Agnes," he said. "In our regiment his lordship was known to be the best to 'ave around during a skirmish."

Jones then turned his back on them, assuming a hunched position. He cupped his hands, blowing through his entwined fingers, signaling the hoot of a barn owl. He waited, then blew again, sinking back onto the coach floor, his legs curving under him.

A similar sound echoed back from outside, and within moments the carriage door swung open, and the duke's large dark head appeared.

Agnes shrieked.

"Help me, man," the duke said to Jones. "Grab his arms, I've got his legs."

Unassisted, the duke had dragged Lyndhurst's limp body all the way to the coach. He now bore the man's entire weight between his forearms, chest, and shoulders.

As soon as the ladies rearranged their positions, the duke and Mr. Jones hauled Lyndhurst onto the floor of the carriage.

Marjorie felt grateful that the Grangefield coach could fit so many people, anything smaller and Mr. Lyndhurst would have suffered even more.

"There's plenty of blood, the wound may be serious." Edgar said.

Agnes shrieked. She then clasped her hands onto her extended midsection and succumbed to a dead faint.

"Bloody hell!" Edgar exclaimed. He glared at his sister-in-law's enlarged childbearing frame. She had fallen in her swoon, and was now sprawled on Tiffany's lap.

"Edgar, don't be angry," Tiffany said, "I'll take care of Agnes; you just worry about Mr. Lyndhurst."

Marjorie watched Edgar extend his sister a curt nod of approval.

"Can you manage here, Jones?" the duke asked.

The man grunted his agreement, hauling Lyndhurst back farther into the carriage. The wounded man let out a loud gasp before falling unconscious.

"Are you sound, madame?" the duke asked, still standing outside the vehicle. He had focused his attention on Marjorie, and she felt touched by his concern.

The duke's form was a blur. Somehow during all the commotion she had lost her spectacles.

"I need you to assist Jones; have you handled a pistol before?"

Marjorie offered a distracted "yes," now searching in the dark for her glasses.

"It would appear that you do need those spectacles for more than reading," he said.

Glancing at him, she noticed the glimmer of his teeth.

He extended his arm, handing her something. "No matter," he said, "just point and shoot. Be careful, it's loaded."

Marjorie grasped the handle of a large heavy revolver. During the exchange the duke caressed her fingers, not releasing her hand.

"Don't fire unless you have to," he whispered. Marjorie felt his warm breath linger on her cheek; she shivered. That was all he said before turning and walking away.

"At least I can see when it counts," Marjorie murmured, cocking the pistol and aiming it with as much precision as possible out of the carriage window.

She turned her attention to the other cramped occupants of the carriage.

Agnes, still unconscious, had been lifted onto the bench, and lay in a sprawled position, her head now rested on a pile of fur muffs. Tiffany, wanting to help, had moved to the far corner of the carriage to attend to Mr. Lyndhurst. With instructions from Marjorie, she had torn strips of her cotton petticoat, using them to cover Lyndhurst's wound.

Jones crouched down close to the window near Marjorie. Together they watched for any suspicious movements in the woods.

After several uncomfortable minutes an owl hoot pierced the air.

Jones relaxed his posture, clasping his hands and hooting back. He offered Marjorie a reassuring smile.

"Lady Tate, the duke's just sent the all-clear. The villain must 'av scarpered."

Marjorie noticed he had lowered his firearm and with an uplift of his chin, urged her to follow suit.

Rupert then appeared at Marjorie's end of the carriage, wrenching open the door. Since Marjorie had been holding onto the door handle, she was thrown back.

"Oh, sorry m' dear; are you all right?"

"Rupert, do be careful, I could have blown your head off with my revolver."

Unconcerned, he looked past her into the dark coach. Aided by a dimly lit lantern, which swung from his hand, he peered inside with eagle-like interest.

"What have you done with Agnes?"

"If you would look to the bench, Rupert, you'll see her sprawled there. She fainted after glimpsing Lyndhurst's wound."

Rupert's gaze wandered until it connected with his wife.

"What happened outside?" Marjorie asked, annoyed by his distracted behavior.

"No clues as to who the culprit is; he slipped through when Edgar and the servants were busy combing the woods. I dare say if Edgar had latched onto him, he'd no doubt wish he were dead, or at the very least pleading with the magistrate. How is poor Lyndhurst?"

"The bullet went right through, gov'nor," Jones offered. "Just a trickle of blood, that's all."

"Lady Tiffany mopped up the wound with scraps of her petticoat," Jones continued. "We won't know exactly how serious his condition is until we return to Grangefield Hall. By the sound of all that groaning you'd think he'd been mortally wounded."

"Don't be too hard on the poor chap," Rupert said. "He's probably never been shot before. If it were me I'm sure I'd be making the same amount of noise."

"I doubt that," Tiffany said. "You'd probably have fainted, like your wife here."

Rupert ignored his sister, crawling over Lyndhurst's body to reach Agnes.

"Sweeting, wake up." He bent down to kiss her lips, patting her cheeks. "Agnes, it's all over; dear, you can wake up now."

Marjorie rolled her eyes, suppressing the urge to groan. Wasn't it enough that she was cramped in a carriage with five other people, now she had to endure watching newlyweds being affectionate in public?

Jones also appeared uncomfortable. "I'm off to get an update from his lordship," he said, rising, and pushing the carriage door open.

"I think I'll join you," Marjorie replied, "that will make more room for Rupert." She gently laid down the revolver on the coach bench before following him.

Jones simply jumped down, but that would have been impossible wearing a dress and having no dismount steps. Marjorie opted to move backward, hoisting herself down through the carriage door. She had almost lowered one foot to the ground, when she heard a familiar stern voice.

"Lady Tate, where do you think you are going?" the duke growled in her ear.

Then two hands latched onto the base of her posterior, halting her progress. She shrieked in protest.

The duke moved closer, sandwiching her closer to the carriage. His mouth brushed against her ear, and his voice lowered.

"I don't believe I wish to let you go, Lady Tate."

"Step aside," she said.

He did step aside, but only to stoop down and lift her up like a rocking infant. He then deposited her back onto the coach. "I don't have time to argue with you or play foolish games. I need to dispatch an outrider to fetch the doctor to Grangefield Hall. I suspect even you can't nurse a man with a bullet wound."

Marjorie, now seated on the bench, tempered her anger by righting her skirts.

Now watching her, the duke cleared his throat before lifting a black gloved finger, and pointing it in her direction. "Madame, you will not leave this coach until we have returned to Grangefield Hall, do you understand?" If possible he looked even grimmer than before.

"Perhaps you had forgotten, but there is someone dangerous lurking in these woods. If you continue to behave without caution, I cannot vouch for your safety, or the safety of the others."

He raised his hand in a halting gesture, for indeed Marjorie wanted to object. "Please do not argue with me, not now."

But she could not keep silent. "Your Grace, I do object," she said. "With one breath you ask me to protect the occupants of the coach, may I add with a loaded pistol, and with another breath you treat me like some lackluster twit." She paused to gather her composure. "I am more than capable of understanding the concept of danger, and my behavior tonight clearly demonstrates that I can behave responsibly. Have you considered

194

that it might be you who is not behaving with sufficient due diligence?"

She knew everyone had heard her comments, and shuddered at her own audacity. The duke looked equally bewildered. He seemed rooted to the spot, his expression impassive, his dark eyes glistening with what Marjorie could only describe as astonishment.

He didn't turn and leave, but directed his comments to Rupert, his tone sounding strained.

"Rupert, you will return to Grangefield Hall in the coach." He reached behind Marjorie's head, drawing the curtains closed; she flinched.

"Since Lady Tate has quarrel with my leadership," he said, "you will assume responsibility for the women." Looking at her he added, "Your job is to make sure that they all stay out of my way."

He slammed the coach door shut to punctuate his words. Marjorie watched him through the window. With one practiced lunge he mounted his horse, a large white beast he'd brought back with him from India named Rajah. As soon as his body

anchored to the saddle, the duke flexed the reins, forcing the

stallion to prance forward in a dancing trot.

"Coachman!" he shouted. "Lead the way."

Without objection, the duke's command was obeyed.

~ ~ ~

Chapter Twelve

The cock had not crowed when Marjorie jolted awake, her pulse racing. She couldn't ignore the fact that the duke's presence in her dreams signified something of magnitude— perhaps a warning.

In a flood of awareness, the events of the night before returned. Who on earth would want to shoot a clergyman? And, if the target was not Lyndhurst, Good Lord, who would want to shoot the Duke of Grangefield? As loathsome as Edgar could be, there seemed no reason at all why anyone would want to kill him.

Stumbling in the dark, Marjorie found a dress that didn't require a maid's help to button. With only a handful of servants about at that hour, who would notice if she wore one of her gardening smocks that buttoned in the front?

She left her chambers, making her way to the breakfast room. Here she was greeted by a yawning footman standing at the entrance. "Your name?" she asked.

"Benjamin, milady."

"Merry Christmas, Benjamin. Why are you standing here?"

"His grace hasn't gone to bed yet," Benjamin said, stifling another yawn.

Oh, bother, Marjorie thought, and briefly considered returning to her room to change.

"Have you been here all night?"

"Yes, milady."

"Well, His Grace, wherever he is, won't be needing you anymore, off to bed."

"But I haven't been dismissed by Mr. Henry, milady."

"Benjamin, I shall take full responsibility. Now, go get some rest."

"Thank you, milady."

Benjamin bowed, turning toward the servants quarters. He yawned once more before exiting the hall.

Upon seeing Marjorie enter the room, a parlor maid setting out chafing dishes, shrieked.

"Oh, you did give me a start, miss."

"I apologize," Marjorie said, smiling at her.

The maid curtseyed before departing the scene.

Moments later an anxious Henry arrived, followed by Mrs. Langley, the Grangefield cook. All Marjorie wanted was a cup of tea, but Mrs. Langley had other ideas.

"My apologies, milady, I haven't set out the breakfast dishes. It won't take a minute to fix you up a proper plate."

Without giving Marjorie the opportunity to decline, the stout woman moved toward the kitchen. She returned moments later carrying a large tray of breakfast goodies, all traditional Christmas treats. The assortment included the quintessential fried kippers, accompanied by baked tomatoes and a large portion of scrambled eggs, served over several slices of toast. Henry, smiling, then handed her an additional plate carried in by the parlor maid.

"Your Ladyship, being Christmas Day, Cook added a plate of honeyed pears."

This being more food than Marjorie ate for breakfast in an entire week, she made a supreme effort to look at the tray without wincing.

Pleased with their efforts, the servants departed, leaving Marjorie to contemplate recent events. The traveling party had returned to Grangefield Hall without further incident. Thank goodness the village doctor had come immediately: Marjorie was not sure he would come after the poor reception he had received from the duke after trying to tend to Sabeer. The doctor had examined Lyndhurst's gunshot wound, and diagnosed the injuries as serious but not critical, and the cleric would be confined to bed for an unknown duration.

The question remained, who was the intended target? Marjorie had eavesdropped on a conversation between Rupert and Edgar, discovering that this was the second dangerous incident the duke had encountered since his arrival in England. The first had been a carriage wheel coming loose en route from Portsmouth to London.

The other contentious matter, which caused Marjorie's cheeks to warm, had been the duke's outrageous behavior toward her on the roadside. She had given him no reason to treat her like a dockside madame, and yet he had.

"Good morning, Marjorie."

Good Lord, speak of the devil!

Her hand quivered, causing the teaspoon to rattle in her cup.

"Problems sleeping?" he asked.

She noted that his features registered no emotion, and his outward appearance looked hardly ducal. The haphazard arrangement of his clothes suggested that he had not gone to sleep. He still wore the formal white dress shirt from the night before, now loosely tucked into the waistband of his black britches. His cravat had gone missing, and coarse bristles covered his face, needing the attention of a sharp razor and a very diligent valet.

Regardless of how angry the duke made her feel, she suppressed the impulse to clasp his shirt and drag him closer. Good Lord! Why did she always want to touch him!

Marjorie gathered her composure by staring at the tea leaves at the bottom of her cup; then feeling calmer, she raised her head and met the duke's dark gaze.

"It would appear sleep has eluded us both, Your Grace," she said.

"Edgar, madame; my name is Edgar," he muttered, closing the double doors, ensuring they were alone.

Panicked: That's exactly how Marjorie felt when she again glanced over her shoulder.

"How is Mr. Lyndhurst?" she asked, "and did you have any luck with your inquiries regarding the gunman?"

Before answering, he took an extra moment to take stock of his surroundings.

"Lyndhurst is asleep. The doctor patched him up. Now we must wait until he awakens to estimate how quickly he will recover."

"What about the gunman?"

"Disappeared," Edgar muttered.

He moved toward her, resting his hands on the back of her chair.

Marjorie felt her heartbeat quicken.

She didn't dare look at him, concerned she might reveal some hint of her emotional turmoil. What she felt wasn't fear precisely, but a feeling of anticipation. She realized with disgust, that she enjoyed the feeling of having Edgar close to her.

"You're standing too close," she said. "The distance doesn't adhere to protocol."

"Damn protocol!" he shouted, his hands grasping her shoulders.

Marjorie gasped. She tried to shrug him away, but he didn't let go, tightening his grip. She could hear his shallow breathing. The scent of cloves and sandalwood suffused the air.

The tension felt heady. Both of them chose silence as an alternative to a peremptory display of bad manners.

Although his behavior was entirely inappropriate, Marjorie didn't want him to let go.

"I need to apologize," he whispered, close to her ear, "again."

Confused, Marjorie tried to turn, but what she said next didn't help matters.

"You apologize too often, Your Grace."

"What?" he said, releasing her shoulders.

"I'm sorry, but your apologies never sound sincere."

"Or, is it that you don't, or you won't accept them, madame?" the duke asked.

"It would be easier to accept, Your Grace, if I believed they were delivered with a genuine regard for my person."

Standing and turning, Marjorie attempted to step back, but instead, hit the blunt edge of the dining table. "Look, we both haven't had much sleep in the last twenty-four hours, why not wait until our thoughts clear before we begin delivering apologies?" She noticed the duke's dark expression darken even more.

"However, while I am airing my grievances, I feel compelled to mention that I found your behavior toward me last evening atrocious, and hardly the demeanor attributed to a peer of the realm."

It was then she looked down and noticed his stocking-covered feet. "Good Lord! Where are your boots?"

"With my cravat."

"With your cravat?" She repeated, feeling stupid.

She glared at him. "That is precisely the obtuseness I am talking about, Your Grace. You are a duke, one of the highest orders in the British Empire. Dukes do not wander about in their stockings, or shout at women on dark, deserted highways." Marjorie released a frustrated sigh. "I believe it has become necessary for us to reassess our agreement."

That was when she made a tactical error, she regarded his face. Good Lord! His cheeks looked rather florid. Better not upset him further. But even as she thought this, she knew it would not be possible to keep silent.

"During my stay at Grangefield Hall, your behavior toward me can only be described as boorish, and your lewd advances disturbing. My goal had been to reestablish your position in society by finding you a wife, but at this point my task will be next to impossible. I am no light-skirt, or a woman who can be pawed at." She took in a fortifying breath, and then continued. "You see, there is no connection between us other than what I have just described. Although it is my inclination to leave, I have promised Rupert that I will stay. Bearing this in mind, in the future, please refrain from behaving like a horrid oaf."

Marjorie realized that her voice had raised to a shout. She cringed.

Throughout her monologue the duke had just stood there watching her. Before she could even take a refreshing breath, or revisit her outburst, he stepped forward, and whisked off her spectacles, tossing them onto the table. His arms encircled her waist, hoisting her up as if she weighed no more than a pound of apples.

206

She gasped, but of course, he ignored her, dragging her the short distance forward toward the closed doorway.

When Marjorie had mustered up enough presence of mind to start protesting, he gathered her closer, molding her to his chest. In such close proximity, looking at him caused her vocal cord to stiffen. Good Lord! Had he finally rendered her speechless?

He was staring at her with an odd expression, one she couldn't identify. Not anger, but tension——raw and unchallenged.

Then he adjusted his posture, dragging her further upright. They were nose to nose, and his mouth hovered close to hers.

Bewildered as to what she had done to incite such a reaction, Marjorie squirmed. Of course, she couldn't scream, that would no doubt cause an uproar and have all the Grangefield servants advancing upon them.

If only his mouth just weren't so close.

"You must let me go, You Grace," she hissed.

"I know."

That's all he said before his mouth moved the short distance, and his lips touched hers.

Marjorie froze.

His warm breath and the soft pressure of his lips entranced her. The initial touch felt ruthless, even desperate. Marjorie had not moved, she couldn't. Instead, Edgar gently coaxed her lips open, his tongue invading her mouth. The kiss continued, and for some untoward reason she relaxed. Her only absurd thought was they had to stop——but perhaps not so soon.

Edgar's arms snaked closer about her waist, forcing her body to lean back. His lips invited her closer, his breath mingling with hers. The distinct scent of sandalwood and cloves penetrating her memory.

His lips now kissed her skin, moving to nibble her earlobe. Then he rubbed his bristled cheek against hers in an intimate nuzzling. He hesitated briefly, before trailing kisses along the column of her neck.

Marjorie could have sworn he mumbled something about the sensible design of women's fashions. Then his lips returned to hers, again coaxing her mouth to open.

When she felt a breeze along her collarbone, and his bristle-covered chin grazing her chest, she paused.

"No bodice, madame?" he whispered. "I definitely approve."

Her senses returned like a flame doused by a bucket of water. What had he said? Good Lord! How on earth had he managed to unbutton her gown?

In reaction, her fingers splayed wide on Edgar's stomach, and she shoved him. This turned out to be ineffectual, the duke simply continued kissing her exposed chest.

She didn't mean it to happen, but somehow her fingers slid lower, to the buttoned flap of his britches, grazing the area covering his stiff member. He hissed, his breathing sounding decidedly uneven.

"Madame, if you want to enter my britches, you need only say the word."

Marjorie gasped. The duke peered down at her, probably making sure she hadn't fainted.

"You realize now it will be virtually impossible for me to let you go," he said, lowering his head and gently trailing his lips across her face. His hand lifted the strands of hair, which had fallen across her back. He raised the handful of curls to his nose, murmuring the word "lemons;" the word resounding like a caress.

Marjorie's vocal cords still weren't functioning, perhaps because Edgar now nipped at her lips.

"Come upstairs with me," he whispered.

The cloud of enchantment vanished. Marjorie came to abrupt attention.

"I will not," she stuttered. "What I meant to say was … I …We … must not. I … I … I won't. Good Lord, I don't even like you."

This caused Edgar to smile down at her. He repeated her words. "I don't even like you?' My dear, your body communicates otherwise. It seems you like me rather well. In fact, your hand, if I'm not mistaken, just sang my body's praises."

"Oh, that is absurd," Marjorie said, her hands moving to refasten the buttons of her dress.

"Shall we test my theory again?" he asked, casually twirling a strand of Marjorie's hair about his index finger. He still hadn't released her.

"Somehow," she said, "being close to you makes me dull-witted; it is a wonder I know where I am at this moment."

He smiled again. "My dear, after this morning's events I would never presume to describe you as dull."

Marjorie managed to nudge his arms away. She held her arms outstretched, but that only allowed him to move closer. "No, you don't!"

He tried to distract her by blowing air against her exposed nape. One button still unfastened, she thought.

She looked at his gloating face as he peered at her exposed skin.

She looked down. Good Lord! Two buttons! She batted his hands away, collecting the unbuttoned corners. Her distraction allowed the duke to move forward, and gently push her back against the door.

"Stop. You must stop this absurd behavior at once," she said, with as much reluctant protest as she could infuse into her voice. If truth be told, Edgar's weight felt wonderful, and the way he kneaded her waist seemed added incentive to move closer.

"Look up," he ordered.

"I will not."

Edgar smiled, kissing her cheek.

"Just for a moment," he whispered. "Please!"

His expression appeared reasonable when he nodded upwards. With reluctance, she lifted her head, and spied a large bundle of mistletoe, hanging from a red ribbon on the door jam.

"Thanks to my industrious sister-in-law, we were both just participating in a spot of Christmas cheer. Now, won't you reconsider and come upstairs with me? If it will make you feel better, we can bring the mistletoe. I will even let you unwrap me like a present," he said, smiling.

Marjorie bent her elbows, jabbing Edgar in the ribs.

"Ouch, that hurt!" he muttered, still smiling down at her.

"It was meant to," Marjorie said, trying to regain her composure. "Your interpretation of Christmas cheer is not cheery."

"Well, we don't necessarily need to see eye to eye on this, unless of course we are in bed, madame."

"Good Lord!" Marjorie jabbed him again.

The duke ignored her weak protests.

"Marjorie, it seems I must endeavor to make you like me. You already like what I do to you; apparently, it's just my personality you object to."

"You are without a doubt the most obtuse person I have ever met."

"But you must admit that I am also very entertaining.

"Conceited as well," she added.

"Yes, by all means, let us not forget conceited," Edgar's tone sounded amused. I suppose that is why you're still here, not here in my arms, but here at Grangefield Hall. You have been hired to make me less obtuse, less crude, and hopefully more likable. While you are attempting all of these small miracles, I shall focus on what I do best, our mutual entertainment. Do you think we could add kissing practice to our lessons?"

Her temper flared. She lifted her slipper-covered foot, and stomped on Edgar's stocking-covered toes. He stepped back emitting an oath.

"Oh, bloody hell! Now, that really did hurt."

His shout was loud enough to wake the entire slumbering household. Definitely time to retreat, Marjorie thought.

While the duke was occupied ministering to his foot, she snatched up her spectacles from the table and slipped them on. She then sped toward the double doors, and didn't stop moving until she had reached her bedroom. Once over the threshold, she slammed the door shut, turning the key in the lock. At some point the sun had risen, and streaks of sunshine now filtered

through the heavy, damask curtains.

The room was cold and dark, and the scent of cloves and

sandalwood now lingered in the air. Memories of her unexpected

Christmas present caused her to smile. Indeed, how would she

ever forget this Christmas, or for that matter the unforgettable

kisses given to her by the Eighth Duke of Grangefield.

~ ~ ~

Chapter Thirteen

During Christmas luncheon Marjorie remained uncommunicative. In contrast, Edgar was overzealous. Her annoyance with his behavior kept her fuming, and when the opportunity presented itself, she decided to quit his company, and volunteer to help Agnes plan the afternoon activities.

Agnes's obsession with all things Christmas had propelled her into action. The tallest Christmas tree Marjorie had ever seen in her life now presided in the drawing room. It was fully decorated, each branch dangling with strips of red licorice.

Agnes' chief collaborator, Tiffany, had gathered up all the servants to string popped corn for garlands. As a final touch, the base of the tree bulged with wrapped presents.

Marjorie, en route to the Blue Room to collect Sabeer, heard the boy's loud shouts in Hindi. No doubt he was challenging Albert about something.

Upon arriving, she turned the handle, but the door moved, then stuck. Looking closer, a thin brown arm provided the obstruction. Marjorie pushed a little harder, but from what she could see the arm with tiny bulging muscles, held the door firmly in place.

"You will not be entering, Missy Marge," Sabeer said.

"Why ever not?" Marjorie inquired.

"I have no shirt on."

Marjorie paused to consider this. "Then why not put one on, dear? At my venerable age there is very little that can shock me. Now, be a good fellow and let me in. Is Albert with you?"

"It is Mr. Albert who is causing me this distress, Missy Marge."

"And, why is that?" Marjorie smiled, trying again to budge the door.

"Missy Marge, Mr. Albert is insisting that I cover my person with this most tight clothing. These garments cannot serve any purpose, but to restrict the breathing. I am sure I will soon be expiring, like one of those chickens whose necks are squeezed dead before they are cooked in a curry."

For seven the boy had a sterling vocabulary, Marjorie thought, smiling.

"Mr. Albert, he is also wearing this same collar, but his neck is as thin as most of those chickens. That is why I am thinking, he is always looking the color of cow's milk."

She heard Albert's disgruntled exclamation. Her smile held in place.

She peered through the small crack in the door, and observed a large canopied bed, heaped with rumpled clothing.

It appeared she needed to reason with the boy: Now what strategy would appeal to his ruffled disposition?

"Young man," she began, "this is a very important day in England, I am sure the duke will have plenty to say if you delay the opening of his presents. Perhaps I should also remind you, most of those prettily wrapped packages under the Christmas tree have your name on them."

Marjorie allowed for a healthy pause. "If you are suggesting that a silly shirt with a stiff collar is stopping you from joining the festivities, then we do appear to have a problem, don't we?"

Just in case the boy happened to be watching, her fingertips floated to her temples, and on purpose, she presented a pained expression. "Unfortunately, I must leave and explain this grave situation to the duke. I'm afraid Albert won't be able to stay either; you see, we have our own presents to open."

A silence descended over the corridor. After a full minute Sabeer lowered his arm and the door opened, but only a fraction His brown face peaked through the opening, offering her a clear display of small white teeth and an expression scrunched with indecision.

"Missy Marge, I too am thinking that it would be unwise to delay. You are most correct, Baba will be most displeased." That said, the boy thrust open the door, moving inside the room.

Marjorie, entering, came within inches of bumping headlong into him. He scowled, his attention now focused on Albert, who held his arms outstretched at a forty-five degree angle, dangling what appeared to be a pair of velvet britches. Marjorie peered over her spectacle lenses, squinting at the boy.

Sabeer's shirt, the one that he had been complaining about, appeared at least one size too large. The collar was large about his neck, and the shirt tails fell loose about his thighs; other than that, he was naked all the way down to his toes.

"Good Lord!" Marjorie spluttered, twirling in her slippers until she had turned a complete about face, staring at the door.

"Sabeer, for heavens sake, why aren't you wearing your britches?"

"He refused, madame," Albert said, using an exasperated tone. "He complained that the fabric itched. He planned to attend the festivities as he is presently attired."

Albert cleared his throat. "I tried to convince him that going below stairs without wearing britches would be unwise. After my second attempt, you happened upon the scene."

"I see," Marjorie said.

"Madame, perhaps you could convey to the boy the wisdom of my suggestion."

Marjorie gritted her teeth, preparing to deliver a severe ultimatum.

"Sabeer, you have precisely five minutes to put on your britches and other clothing. If you are not dressed by that time, I will be forced to notify the duke of your behavior." That said, she marched out of the room.

"Albert, I will be waiting outside. When the boy is presentable, which I hope will be soon, make sure he joins me; I do so hate waiting in drafty corridors."

Without looking back, Marjorie retreated, closing the door behind her. She knew this time it would be impossible to hide her smile.

***

Closely observing the dials on her father's watch, precisely seven minutes later Albert opened the door. Marjorie sighed with relief when Sabeer walked into the corridor. Like syrup pouring, the boy moved one shoe-clad foot after the other.

Apparently his new shoes didn't fit either. In fact, nothing in his new wardrobe fit properly. The velvet jacket was too short, barely covering his crisp white shirt. A placate of crumpled ruffles peeked out from the collar of the jacket, which matched the burgundy velvet britches that reached over his kneecaps, covering his all-white stockings. Albert had tied the boy's long hair at his nape with a black velvet ribbon.

All things considered, Marjorie felt satisfied that he looked presentable. She extended her hand, again feeling relief when the boy accepted it without objection. They then proceeded down three flights of stairs, Sabeer holding on with fierce determination.

***

Reaching the main salon, a footman greeted them. He looked at Sabeer, hesitated, then bowed before opening the doors. Apparently word that Sabeer was Edgar's son had already filtered amongst the servants.

The duke noticed them first. Smiling, he moved forward to greet them. He lifted Sabeer into his arms, spinning and hugging him hard, then wishing him a greeting in Hindi. The boy laughed, and hugged him back.

The duke's gaze never wandered far from Marjorie. Her cheeks felt warm, and she knew she blushed. She expelled a sigh when she heard Agnes calling her. Her friend wore a berry-red gown, with strand of emeralds draped from her neck.

She motioned for Edgar to bring the boy over to the Christmas tree. Once there, she handed Sabeer three wrapped packages, and without hesitating, he proceeded to rip open the wrappers.

The first, a velvet pouch, contained jigsaw puzzle pieces. The second was a large box filled with hand carved soldiers wearing sabers. The last package caused Sabeer to frown: It contained several white shirts with stiff, frilly collars, and two pairs of wool britches. Offering a disgusted expression, it took mere moments for him to examine the garments before tossing them aside, and following them to the floor, searching for more presents under the tree.

"Mr. Arnold purchased Sabeer's clothes and gifts in London, and then had them sent here," Rupert said, from behind her.

She turned in his direction and noticed his hands raised in offering.

Marjorie emitted a small squeal of approval when he handed her a red, brocade-covered parcel.

"We don't have too many presents with your name on them, my dear, but this one is very special."

"Oh, thank you, Rupert, I wasn't expecting anything."

"It's a small token, something that reflects how much Agnes and I appreciate you being here. Indeed, there aren't enough words to express my personal gratitude: Merry Christmas, Marjorie!"

He kissed her cheek, then moved to stand next to Agnes.

Marjorie opened her gift in silence, observing the family camaraderie. The duke stood at the far end of the room talking with Tiffany. Even as he tried to focus on a conversation about Greek artifacts, Marjorie felt his gaze wander in her direction,

225

When Tiffany moved away to collect a cup of eggnog from Pierce, Edgar, now smiling, maneuvered toward her.

"Madame?"

She turned to him, a thread of excitement coursing through her.

"Your Grace," she said, fully aware of him. "You appear to have become my shadow today."

"My burden, madame—but a happy one. Perhaps with forewarning you might have ample time to run off and start a conversation with that marble statue over there," he nodded to the corner of the room.

"Don't be absurd," she said, frowning.

"After this morning's events," he continued, "I suppose any sort of conversation between us might pose a challenge."

Marjorie felt her jaw loosen.

"You're gaping, madame."

Marjorie snapped her mouth shut. "Your Grace, I am not a coward."

"Then why are you twiddling your thumbs?"

"I am not," she said, unclenching her hands and clasping them behind her back.

"Then I must have been mistaken," Edgar said, grinning.

"Stop baiting me," she muttered.

"Marjorie, what could you possibly mean?"

"And, don't call me *Marjorie,* I have not given you leave to do so."

Marjorie attempted to walk away, but Edgar gently restrained her arm with his hand. "Don't leave; I wish to talk to you."

"I do not wish to talk to you. This is hardly the time or the place, Your Grace."

"I disagree, madame: No one is close enough to listen, and if someone approaches we can change the subject."

"It is entirely too public," she said.

"I agree, but I can't very well talk to you in private, can I?"

Marjorie had no rejoinder.

Edgar released her arm, grinning as if he had just won a boon.

"Well, what is it you wish to discuss? If you are concerned about your missed lesson, I intend to continue tomorrow; today is a public holiday."

"Actually, I had hoped we would continue what we started this morning."

"Good Lord!"

"Hush now! We don't want to draw unnecessary attention, do we?"

"I don't intend to repeat what happened this morning," Marjorie whispered.

Edgar frowned. "You believe that, do you?" the duke said, sounding amused. "We seem to suit, Marjorie. I don't see why we can't explore the possibilities. Who knows, perhaps I could just marry you, and be done with all of these lessons?"

"Marry me? Don't be absurd!"

"Why is that absurd?" the duke said, looking as if he were contemplating the possibilities.

"Must I remind you, I am only here in a professional capacity. To find you a wife, certainly not to become your wife. I am even getting paid."

"Don't remind me: Good arable land, the price is entirely too high," Edgar muttered.

"It is very fair," Marjorie said, realizing he had changed the subject. She then noticed Agnes watching them; Marjorie smiled at her.

She then rubbed the bridge of her nose, almost dislodging her spectacles.

"So, you *can* see through those things?" the duke said.

"Of course I can, why would I wear them otherwise?"

"I thought you wore them to fuel my sexual curiosity— to tempt me. They do you know—tempt me."

Marjorie spluttered, "I wear them to see: To see you: To see the room."

"Well, make sure you wear them when we are married, I find them far more effective than oysters."

Instead of stomping her foot, which Marjorie wanted to do, she just glared at him.

"I repeat, I am not marrying you." She hated the fact that every time she conversed with him, she ended up talking to his chest.

Edgar seemed to understand her frustrations. He bent down as if inspecting something on Marjorie's shoulder; this gave him the opportunity to allow his mouth to skim her ear.

"I think my plan has merit," he whispered.

She tried to step back, but the movement felt awkward. Her dress caught on the edge of a curio table. She might have toppled it over, but Edgar caught her arm, pulling her forward. She landed against his chest, close enough to smell the sandalwood and cloves that he had added to his bath water.

"There, there, Marjorie, I've caught you," Edgar said, loudly.

"Are you all right, dear?" Agnes inquired, with alarm.

The duke released her, and Marjorie sighed with relief. She felt like grabbing Agnes and giving her a big hug.

230

"Yes, Agnes, I'm fine. The duke rescued me, and all of those glass curios. One more step and the whole lot would have smashed to smithereens."

"That would have been tragic, those belonged to Edgar's Aunt Philipa; they are quite old."

Marjorie recovered enough to change the subject. "How is Mr. Lyndhurst?"

"I understand he was awake this morning, and managed to eat some of Cook's chicken broth," Agnes said. "I think it's a good thing that he keeps conversation to a minimum, the doctor said he needs to conserve his energy."

Marjorie didn't have time to respond; she heard loud female titters. A footman had entered the room, followed by Lady Osterly. The woman's gown was covered from neckline to hem with bright red and green feathers.

"I say, Agnes, did you mention to her this was an informal gathering?" Rupert asked, moving to join them.

"Yes, dear; I believe I told her twice, but she insisted on looking her best for the duke."

Edgar groaned.

"Remind me, Turtledove, why did we invite the Osterlys to dinner?" Rupert said, looking anguished.

"You invited them, darling," Agnes said through clenched teeth. "Remember, Baron Osterly is leasing a section of Grangefield to graze his sheep. Originally, it was an invitation to tea, but then it started snowing, and here they are staying another night."

"Yes, I remember now, we needed the money," Rupert muttered.

Edgar groaned. "Now that I'm back you can rescind that particular contract."

Marjorie wrinkled her nose. "Perhaps, you should wait until you're actually married, Your Grace," she said, smirking at him and at the same time, toggling her spectacles on the bridge of her nose.

The glare he gave her promised retribution.

Lady Osterly floated toward them in a flutter of vivid plumage.

"Your Grace, I've missed your company all day. What has kept you soooo verrry busy?"

Edgar closed his eyes.

Marjorie replied for him. "Oh, that's just the thing, Lady Osterly, His Grace was just remarking how uneventful the day had been without the pleasure of your company; isn't that so, Your Grace?"

Marjorie's smile met Edgar's dark gaze. Even Rupert's muted guffaws were lost amidst the sound of rustling feathers, as Lady Osterly moved a step closer to the duke.

Marjorie presented another bright smile for Edgar's benefit.

Rupert prodded Edgar's arm.

"Yes, Lady Tate, I do recall saying something like that. By the way, where have you hidden your husband, Lady Osterly?"

"My husband, Your Grace?" she said, as if remembering that she had one. "The only thing that entices that man to join the living on Christmas day is the smell of mince pies."

233

"Then it's a good thing we are serving mince pies for tea," Marjorie said, interrupting the duke, who was about to comment.

He closed his mouth, rocking in his boots.

Marjorie continued to smile.

"I say, Edgar, won't you come over here?" Rupert called out, waiting by the doors.

The duke didn't need any further inducements. After making eye contact with his brother, he cleared his throat. "Excuse me, ladies, it appears that I am being summoned."

The two brothers exchanged a few whispered words, then departed from the room.

"Did I say something to upset the duke?" Lady Osterly asked, with an exasperated tone.

"Don't fret, Lady Osterly," Agnes said, her glance veering toward the closed doorway. "I'm sure whatever the secret is, it has nothing to do with us. My marriage has revealed that men can be rather unorthodox creatures. We have all been married, I'm sure you gather my meaning?"

234

"Oh, I do," Lady Osterly twittered, wafting her fan in an exaggerated gesture, causing several plumes from her gown to detach and flutter to the ground.

A reprieve came when the doors of the salon opened, and a footman entered, followed by a maid. The servants wheeled in a rolling cart filled with desserts.

"It must be three o'clock," Agnes said. "I must say, after opening presents I'm feeling quite famished. These days I'm not sure whether my stomach is growling for food, or the baby is demanding some unusual variations in its diet."

All three women laughed.

"Sabeer, have you finished opening your presents?" Marjorie asked, offering him a mince pie. He had somehow entered the bowels of the enormous Christmas tree, and had almost disappeared from view. Because the tree was both broad and tall, he had been well hidden.

Sabeer emerged, smiling, a red bow adorning his neck. He remained on hands and knees imitating a tiger, growling and crawling around the base of the tree.

Marjorie then heard a loud shriek. This soon became a series of shrieks, which evolved into several "Oh my words!" All eyes turned to Lady Osterly, who appeared to be having some sort of fit.

"What is that?" she exclaimed, pointing at the boy.

Marjorie couldn't help but frown. "'That' happens to be Sabeer. I believe the duke mentioned at supper that he had brought someone with him from India."

"That person is a guest?" Lady Osterly spluttered, fanning her face and offering Marjorie a plumped-cheek expression. "You must be mistaken, that boy has to be a servant."

Before anyone could correct her outburst, the woman discovered her sluggish feet, and marched toward the Christmas tree.

"What on earth is the duke doing cavorting with Blackamoors?"

Marjorie, robbed of speech, simply stared at the woman.

"I mean," Lady Osterly managed, "he's not English."

"It is well known, Lady Osterly," Marjorie said, drawing a calming breath, "that not all people in the world are English."

"Don't be obtuse, I know that. But everyone in Surrey is most definitely English."

Marjorie felt her eyes open wide. "I am not privy to information regarding the residents of Surrey, madame. All I know is that boy is here because the duke wishes it."

"You people from the South have rather peculiar notions; I could not possibly linger in the company of a dark person.

"You there! Boy! Leave this room at once!"

Lady Osterly had wagged her fan of plumage at Sabeer, as if wielding a sword.

"I beg your pardon, madame, that boy is going nowhere," Marjorie said, stepping closer to the Christmas tree. "He has more reason to be here than you do."

Lady Osterly gasped, her hands clutching her chest. She stepped back, sitting on a nearby chaise. "Someone fetch me some water, I do believe that I am feeling faint."

237

No one moved to attend to Lady Osterly.

She looked aghast. "This is an outrage! The duke's own family condones this," she said, looking at Agnes and Tiffany. "Don't tell me you two approve of having a heathen living under the same roof as you?"

Marjorie could not ignore the woman's vile comments, but she also knew she needed to focus on Sabeer. He remained perched at the base of the tree, frightened, and staring at Lady Osterly with wide eyes, probably mesmerized by all those red and green feathers. He then started wailing in Hindi.

Good Lord, Marjorie thought, that horrible hag had finally upset him. She could not tell the woman that Sabeer was Edgar's son, the woman was a serious gossip. That sort of news would travel like the wind, and arrive in London before their planned trip at the end of the week: No, that would not serve the duke's cause at all.

Instinct propelled her to move toward the woman. "Since you have upset the boy, I insist you leave, madame."

"I?—I have upset that boy? Surely, you are not thinking properly, Lady Tate. My husband happens to be a baron. We are used to dealing with civilized company, and that creature can hardly be categorized as civilized: He's not even speaking English."

Sabeer wailed louder.

By now Pierce had launched himself up from the chaise and was standing behind Lady Osterly.

"Lady Osterly, you are distraught," Pierce said. "Perhaps I should go and fetch your husband?"

"Reverend, I want that vile person removed from my sight immediately."

Sabeer had receded further into the bowels of the tree, and continued to sob. Marjorie's heart constricted: Good Lord, this was all so awful, and she couldn't do a thing about it.

The vile woman then stood up, moving toward Sabeer, shouting. "You there! Take yourself down to the servants' quarters."

Marjorie felt the first tear roll down her cheek: That poor boy was all she could think. How dare she? How dare that woman presume?

It was then that she saw the duke.

"Your Grace!"

"That will be all, Lady Osterly," he said, as if issuing a command.

The woman stopped her advance. Marjorie offered a silent prayer of thanks. She kneeled down, wanting to coax Sabeer out.

The duke now stood behind the offensive woman. Pierce moved to stand behind him.

"Oh, there you are, Your Grace," Lady Osterly said, offering the duke a sheepish expression.

"I was just remedying a mistake," she continued. "I was just telling this boy to return to the servant's quarters. I suppose being new to *our* ways, I'm sure he just wanted to enjoy Christmas with us," she said, smiling.

Edgar looked red-faced.

"There is no mistake, madame," Edgar said. "This boy remains here. Perhaps it is you who should consider leaving, Lady Osterly? I could arrange for you and your husband to be on your way home within the hour."

Lady Osterly's mouth gaped. "Well, I ... I ... I never! You insult the name of Osterly, sir." It took her but a moment to recover. She fanned her face, then giggled. "You are jesting, Your Grace. That's a relief, for a moment I thought you were serious."

"I have never been more serious in my life," Edgar said.

"He's a Blackamoor," Lady Osterly stuttered.

"That Blackamoor, madame, is my son."

If there were gasps, Marjorie was sure she only heard her own.

Lady Osterly stared at the duke as if he were some hideous creature. She did not speak, even when Pierce escorted her from the room.

The tension didn't lift, not immediately at least.

"Come, lad, it's over. Come to me," the duke said.

241

Sabeer hesitated, continuing to cry. Edgar grabbed Sabeer's arm, pulling him forward.

After clearing the base of the tree, the boy clung to Edgar's neck, his small legs dangling as if he felt faint.

The duke then looked at Marjorie. "I had to say something, that woman insulted Sabeer."

"You did what was necessary, Your Grace."

"The sooner the news is out, the better, madame."

"I just wish we had more time to introduce the boy properly."

"Well, now we will just have to manage," he muttered.

"Come here," Edgar said, his tone gentle.

Marjorie straightened her spectacles. Her hand connected with Edgar's; as if responding to a magician's spell, he pulled her forward so they stood close, he did not let go of her hand.

"Madame, I acknowledge the effort you made here. I realize that for the purposes of my reentry to society, you did not want Sabeer's identity to become public knowledge." He then turned to his family, still holding Marjorie's hand.

"Now, sooner than expected, the world will know I have a son, and that he is half Indian."

H's attention focused on Marjorie. "I want you to know that I will never feel embarrassed by Sabeer's heritage or his lack of acceptance. Although there is no official license that states I married his mother, Sabeer should by rights be my heir. The world of polite society can either accept this fact or be damned."

Marjorie grimaced, even as she thought how wonderful her hand felt in his.

"Marjorie, perhaps the ladies should adjourn," Agnes murmured.

Offering a gentle squeeze, the duke then released her hand.

"It might be best if you followed Lady Agnus' suggestion," he said. "Perhaps you would like to rest before dinner."

But Marjorie would not be dismissed. She looked at Sabeer. She could not see his face, but heard his quiet sobs.

"Why don't I take the boy upstairs? I think we could both cheer each other up."

The duke looked surprised. "Let's see if Sabeer feels the same way."

The boy turned his face toward her. With all the crying his complexion had reddened, but he continued to make small sniffling noises.

She smiled at him, her hands outstretched.

She wanted to sigh with relief when the boy leaned in her direction. She grabbed on to him in a fierce hug, and he buried his face into her shoulder.

Again, the duke looked surprised. "Well, it appears the boy approves, madame: He approves of you. You might want to reconsider our earlier conversation."

Marjorie remembered they had talked about marriage, their marriage to one another. She felt her cheeks warm.

The duke sensed her discomposure. He lifted her chin, trailing a finger down her moist cheek. "Lady Tate, I believe you have the distinction of now being one of the most competent women I know. I dare say, if the opportunity ever arises, I would be proud to serve with you in any regiment."

Marjorie smiled.

Edgar bent down and kissed her cheek. "I'm in your capable hands," he said, smiling.

Marjorie didn't dare respond. Her cheek still tingled where he had kissed her, and she just wanted to stand there forever and stare at him. But at that moment Sabeer decided to hug her tightly, so she turned, retreating with the child in her arms. She then realized how much she adored the boy, and how much she now adored a certain handsome duke, who had somehow triggered a well of affection in her very lonely heart.

~ ~ ~

Chapter Fourteen

"Jones, I will be stepping outside for at least an hour."

"Very good, Your Grace. Will you be needin' the carriage?"

"No. I will walk," Edgar said, glancing at the Christmas wreath hanging from the front door.

"Very well, Your Grace."

Edgar stepped onto the Grangefield driveway. The crisp winter air assailed his senses, causing him to shiver.

The snow had started to melt, glistening white on the surrounding lawns. His boots made crunching noises on the gravel as he walked in the direction of the crofter's cottages.

His thoughts lingered on recent events, specifically the two unplanned incidents since his arrival in England, one of them nearly fatal. To add to these dismal circumstances, he had now exposed his son to the outspoken Lady Osterly. The very mention of the woman's name made Edgar angry.

In recent days, Sabeer had become withdrawn. Indeed, he had not ventured from his room until Albert had informed him of Lord and Lady Osterly's departure.

Marjorie's reaction had been equally subdued, and she had kept out of sight. To his regret, he had not seen her except at mealtimes. He remembered watching as she tried to defend Sabeer, and felt a new admiration for her abilities. To take the position of his protector she had overstepped all bounds of decorum—what a splendid woman!

Notwithstanding her bravery, Edgar realized that his physical attraction to Marjorie loomed ever present. This combination of admiration and lust created a new conflict for him, one he needed to resolve right away.

His thoughts lingered on her lush velvety skin and her long eyelashes. When they occupied the same room, the effect bordered on extreme anticipation. Indeed, he realized that he wanted her all the time, and after the unhappy incident on Christmas Day, his goals had changed where Marjorie was concerned.

He knew he now needed to woo her, melt down her resistance, and make her understand the advantages of marrying him. As much as he felt disinclined to the state of matrimony, it surprised him to realize, a future with Lady Tate as his wife was a palatable idea. Where he had loved Charmine, he desired and respected Marjorie. As a countess, Marjorie also happened to have all the necessary credentials to make him a suitable society wife. Considering their mutual attraction for one another, he felt hopeful that with time their feelings would blossom into love. Yes, the more he thought about it, the more he liked the idea. Now, all he had to do was convince Lady Tate.

His thoughts were interrupted by the sound of voices. More precisely, he heard Sabeer's high-pitched grumbles, some in Hindi. Edgar could not make out the words, but the boy was definitely complaining.

Then he heard another familiar voice, a very patient female voice.

"Missy Marge, my feet are most cold, my hands are most cold, and my nose will be breaking because it has become stiff like coconut bark. I am very much in agony, and I am believing that Jolly Old England is not so jolly."

"Sabeer, do stop grumbling, dear; in time you will get used to the weather here."

"But I have been telling you my legs are not moving; see they are like tree-trunks, soon there will be no more circulation."

The group had moved into view. Edgar watched Sabeer stiffen his torso like a tin soldier. He was covered from head to toe with warm garments, no wonder the boy had difficulty moving.

Marjorie paced alongside him, and the ever-vigilant Albert held up the rear. The old man wore a long black overcoat and tubular top hat. In contrast, Marjorie had chosen a walking coat of vivid Prussian blue, with a matching scarf, her hands neatly tucked into a sable fur muff.

Albert stopped walking. He then made a gurgling noise, attempting to gain Marjorie's attention.

"What is it?" she said.

"We have company, madame."

Sabeer stopped grumbling, looking up.

"Baba!" he exclaimed.

The boy's excitement precipitated a short sprint—

nothing at all stiff about his movements. Within moments he had

reached Edgar's outstretched arms, and hugged him hard.

"What are you doing outside, boy?"

"Baba, Missy Marge is making me wear all of this

scratchy wool, and telling me it would be good to go walking.

My toes will fall from my feet very soon; I now cannot feel my

big toe."

Edgar smiled.

"Does he always complain so incessantly?" Marjorie

asked. A warm mist formed about each of her words, evaporating

into the frosty air.

"I'm afraid so," Edgar replied. "Why is he outside,

madame? Must I remind you that the boy is still recovering from

a severe chill."

"He has been cooped up in his room; he needed some fresh air. Seven-year-olds, particularly boys, are not predisposed to being confined. Perhaps you could remember back to when you were seven."

"It pleases me to hear that you are feeling better after your ordeal," he said, smiling.

Marjorie stared at him. "I don't believe I will ever forget what happened."

"I dare say you won't," Edgar said, lifting his hand to gently brush away a strand of Marjorie's hair, which had floated in front of her eyes.

Albert coughed, reminding them they had an audience.

"I don't think it's a good idea for the boy to be subjected to the cold," he said. "There are still many things in England he is not used to, and one of them is the weather. Albert, please accompany Sabeer to the house; I have a few matters to discuss with Lady Tate."

"Yes, Your Grace," Albert responded without argument.

Marjorie's lips compressed into a thin line, but she remained silent.

Edgar patted the boy on the head, turning him about, and lightly tapping his rear end so he moved forward. "You might want to step lively, Albert; you'll lose him if you don't hurry."

When they were alone, Marjorie objected, "Now I don't have a chaperone: We also need to return to the hall."

"I would like to talk to you, Marjorie, without interruptions. Just conversation, that's all."

He tried to take her gloved hand in his, but she tugged it away, staring at him.

"Just conversation?" she said, unconvinced.

"Just conversation," he responded, "for the moment at least."

This time Edgar grasped her hand, moving them along the path, away from the main house.

"What do you wish to discuss?"

"Christmas Day, the future, our relationship."

"We have no relationship, other than pupil to teacher."

"I think it would be a good idea if we married," Edgar said, without preamble.

Marjorie looked very surprised as she faced him. "I beg your pardon?"

"I said, we should get married. I want you; you want me; I need a wife. You are a suitable candidate. Even my family likes you; and if I thought Rupert had any imagination, I might adopt the notion that he had a hand in all this; selecting you, and then cooking up this ludicrous matchmaking farce to bring us together."

Marjorie stared at him as if he'd gone mad. "It seems you have put a great deal of thought into this decision, Your Grace. As usual, you have failed to take into consideration *my* feelings."

She had stepped away from him, walking down the icy path leading back toward the hall. Edgar couldn't help thinking that he had failed some sort of courtship test.

She was still talking as she walked away, obviously expecting him to follow, which he did.

"First and foremost, your intentions sound far from sincere."

"Marjorie, that's a bald-faced lie and you know it. I am a very sincere person. You might not think so at the moment, but where I lack in sentiment, I make up in sexual curiosity." He smiled.

That halted her, but only briefly. She glared at him, speechless, before resuming her hurried pace. Edgar felt like he was trailing a bloodhound on the scent.

"Second," she continued, "I do not love you." She had shouted this. "By your actions alone, it would appear that you do not love me either."

"Poppycock, madame," Edgar said, using longer strides to catch up with her. He knew he sounded out of breath. "Love is irrelevant," he continued. "Mutual desire is a much better match than love. You desire me; I desire you ... very much, might I add.

"From what I have observed from your character, madame, you have both courage and integrity; I admire those

255

qualities. In my opinion, nothing else is necessary for a successful union."

"I see," Marjorie said, using a crisp tone, her nimble step changing to a march.

Edgar kept up. The path had turned icy, and he became concerned that she might slip. "Slow down, will you? I don't want to have to carry you back if you fall."

Marjorie slowed her pace. A sensible woman, Edgar thought. Obstinate, too, but a sensible woman none the less.

"Are there any more objections?" he asked. "I would like to deal with them all before we return to the Hall and announce our engagement."

She stopped, and he almost bumped into her.

"I don't want to marry anyone," she shouted. "Now, find an argument for that, sir."

"Of course you want to get married; you're a woman, and all women want to get married."

"That is a gross generalization," she fumed. "Perhaps it has escaped your memory, but I have been married before."

"From what I have heard, madame, your late husband was an elderly man, and your marriage was, how should I put it, brief. In addition, I believe he never satisfied you, physically, I mean."

By the way she glared at him, Edgar presumed that he had said the most grossly moronic thing he'd ever said in his life. "Why wouldn't you want to get married?" he asked, wanting to change the subject.

"I don't need a husband," she said. "More precisely, I don't need any permanent fixtures getting in the way of my business activities."

"Permanent fixtures?" he spluttered.

"What good will a husband do me? I already have a sizable fortune and an adequate title; and I can move about society at my leisure. Also, as you already know, I have acquired certain pursuits that a husband, particularly one that is obstinate, unyielding, and boorish, may find objectionable. Hence, I do nott need one, a husband that is."

"Are you suggesting that I am inflexible, madame?"

"I am."

Marjorie halted. "Marriage, Your Grace, for you, is it a need or a desire?"

"What difference does that make?"

Edgar had had enough chitchat. Seeing his advantage, he strode over and lifted her into his arms. The sable muff went flying as he carried her back up the path, away from the Hall.

"Put me down this instant. Why do you always man-handle me?"

She struggled, making his pace difficult, but he managed not to slip.

"Madame, have I mentioned that although you may appear petite, you are not in the least light as a feather."

"That is rude and unkind," she spluttered.

"Merely an observation," he said, puffing. "I suppose this will be practice for when I carry you over the threshold."

"I can walk you know, if you would just ask."

"Yes, but would you actually follow my direction?" Edgar said, through clenched teeth. It was then he spied what

258

he'd been looking for, a gardener's hut hidden by a cluster of trees. He knew from his previous inspection that it was abandoned.

"Why are we going in there?" Marjorie said, having eyed the structure.

"Because that is where I'm going to test my marriage theory."

Edgar entered the building, releasing Marjorie onto her feet. The minute she touched terra firma she turned toward the door, attempting to bolt.

"Oh no, you don't. I have plans for you," he said, yanking her into his arms, and stooping to kiss her. She resisted at first, trying to bite his lips, but he laved and caressed her mouth with more urgency, hoping she would surrender.

"What was that theory?" she asked, breathless.

"That desire is enough for a marriage of convenience, madame," Edgar whispered, kissing her throat.

"Oh …" she replied, as he continued kissing her ear.

"Now, don't move, if you please."

He managed to unbutton her coat, and was disappointed when he found no front closures on her dress. His voice sounded muffled as he moved to kiss her neck. "Clothing worn by English women mystifies me. From experience, Indian saris are far more convenient for this sort of thing."

He carefully unbuttoned her dress, amazed she wasn't resisting. Encouraged, he slid the fabric down to her waist. She gazed about the room, shivering. He was mad to bring her here, but he had to plead his case.

"One moment," he said, shrugging off his gray coat and spreading it across the wood-slat floor, at the same time eyeing the hut.

It had been abandoned some time ago, but thankfully, the windowpanes were still intact, making the single room feel less draughty. He also noted that there was no reserve wood by the hearth. The only useful items appeared to be a few bales of straw, and the remnants of a broken chair. All in all, the room would serve for what he had in mind.

He laid Marjorie down on his coat, and covered her with his body.

"We will be warm soon," he said, hearing his own teeth chatter. "Marjorie, I would like to use this opportunity to convince you about the merits of a physical marriage; our marriage to be precise."

"This escapade of yours will only disprove your theory," she said.

She moved as if to leave, but Edgar had anticipated that she might bolt. He gently fixed his lips onto hers, offering a deeper kiss. "Let's wait and see, shall we?" he whispered.

She hesitated, but then he felt her relax. What had happened to all of her protests, he thought?

"I don't want to get married," she muttered, her eyes closed, as if mustering the strength to stand by her own convictions.

She was still shivering.

"Don't move. Give me a moment to improve our surroundings."

Rising, he removed his morning coat and covered her. His gaze returned to the broken chair in the far corner of the room. Fetching the pieces, he tossed the wooden legs into the hearth, then covered them with some of the straw.

Then he removed a small revolver from his pocket. He noticed Marjorie watching the proceedings with an anxious expression.

"I do understand the concept of till death do us part, Your Grace; there is no need to convince me."

Edgar smiled. "I have plans for you, madame, and none of them include your immediate demise. There will, however, be a loud bang in your future. I recommend that you cover your ears."

Edgar emptied the gunpowder from one of the bullet casings, sprinkling the granules over the piled straw. He cocked the pistol, and fired it into the hearth. After a loud bang, sparks flew, and in no time a fire blazed.

"You are quite resourceful, Your Grace," Marjorie offered.

"A military career lends itself to such things," Edgar replied, crouching before the flames, and prodding the burning wood with one of the chair legs.

"One day I would be interested to hear about your adventures," Marjorie said.

Edgar realized she was still huddled in his jacket, her teeth chattering. "Stories can wait, I have something more collaborative in mind."

"Oh, and what would that be?" Marjorie said, smiling.

He removed his shirt and cravat, and set them aside. Then he lowered himself next to Marjorie, draping his arm about her shoulders. It was now time to explain his feelings, and for the first time in his life, he didn't know where to begin.

***

Marjorie asked herself again, why she was sitting on the floor of a deserted hut, in the middle of winter, with the Duke of Grangefield? Good Lord, had she turned into sort of wanton?

A part of her realized that her body and mind wanted Edgar Hamilton, and not just wanted, needed. She had endured years of a loveless marriage, where intimacy had become a matter of routine. Now she had the opportunity to experience true passion, while satisfying her considerable curiosity at the same time.

They were sitting in a locked embrace, watching the flames in the hearth. The duke stroked her cheeks with his fingers. He had already removed the pins and ribbons from her hair, spreading out her tresses, while placing gentle kisses on her ears and neck.

Marjorie felt foolish wanting to touch him. But not knowing how to proceed she didn't move. Her husband, the earl, had always made love to her fully clothed, and after the deed was done he would adjourn to his rooms.

Being enamoured with the duke seemed enough justification to be alone with him like this. Whatever happened, would happen just once, and most important, she would not sacrifice her independence in the bargain.

"Marry me," Edgar whispered.

"I cannot."

"Cannot, or won't?" he mumbled, biting down lightly on her earlobe.

"Both. I happen to value my carefree lifestyle more than I do marriage."

The duke continued his assault on her ear. He lowered her dress and shift to her hips, exposing her nakedness to his gaze.

Marjorie allowed it, there was no denying how much she wanted this to happen between them.

He continued to watch her, her breasts already aroused. His mouth covered one of her nipples, and he groaned while laving them with his tongue. Encouraged by her moans, his hands wandered to the small of her back. She scaled his shoulders with her fingernails, reveling in the feel of his warm, naked skin against hers.

When he trailed kisses down the length of her belly, Marjorie mumbled, "I don't need a husband." It was true, she didn't need a husband, but she did need passion. If their relationship would always be like this, she knew she would want this man forever, and becoming his mistress could yield several advantages.

Edgar had been right, her late husband had been too old for her. He had been the first man she had lain with, and after his death she had not taken any lovers. Now, being with Edgar like this, she knew she would not want to make love to anyone else.

"You're quite sure you don't need a husband?" the duke said, nipping at the skin on her belly.

"I'm too busy," she muttered, her breathing sounding irregular. "I sell crops, you know?"

"Yes, I know. You're a most accomplished woman of agriculture," Edgar said, as he moved his hand beneath her skirts, massaging her legs.

"Marriage would be inconvenient," she said.

"But you're being selfish, you know," Edgar whispered, kissing her breastbone. "I happen to need a wife."

"Yes, I suppose there is that to consider," she said, yelping when Edgar bit down on her nipple.

"I'm sorry, I feel very urgent at the moment."

Marjorie shivered, not from the cold this time.

Edgar kissed her mouth.

"We still have entirely too many clothes on, madame,"
he mumbled.

Marjorie nodded.

"Marjorie"

"Yes."

"Lift up."

She moved her hips, and Edgar tugged away her coat.
Her dress and chemise followed. He dragged them down her
legs, then loosened her stockings. She watched him hesitate, as
he eyed the complicated laces on her walking shoes. "You will
have to keep those on, I don't have the patience to untie all those
knots."

She was too engrossed with touching his chest to
respond.

When he stopped to examine his progress, Marjorie
looked at herself. Except for her pantalettes, stockings and shoes,
for all intents and purposes she was naked.

"Everything about you is delicious, madame. Your breasts alone remind me of ripened berries that would make my mouth water." He bent down to bite and suck at one of her pebbled nipples.

Marjorie moaned, moving her fingers through his hair, while gently holding his head in place.

"Patience," he muttered.

His hand slid down, tugging down her undergarments. His mouth continued to lave her skin, while his fingers probed the soft hairs on her mound, his fingers dipping into the crevice, separating the skin and smoothing the dark hair. Then his head moved downward.

Marjorie sucked in air when his lips made contact.

His tongue moved with precision, probing the soft warm passageway. Marjorie stilled her hands, wavering as to what to touch next.

The duke seemed to respond to her changes, and he knew when her hips lifted, and her stomach muscles clenched.

"Oh, good bloody Lord!" She cried out.

It seemed an eternity before she recovered.

He smiled. "I believe it's my turn now."

He unfastened the buttons of his britches, releasing his engorged member.

He stopped to look at her, a serious expression looming.

"I will take precautions," he said.

Marjorie nodded. Apparently he did not want to force her into marriage, and a baby would ensure that.

He didn't wait any longer, raising himself above her until they were lying chest to chest.

Using one sure movement he entered her body. Her squeak of protest came first, but then her body adjusted to accommodate him. He moved deeper still, stopping briefly to adjust the position of her legs. He continued to stroke her skin, kissing her shoulders, at the same time thrusting his hips. He entered her again, to the hilt this time, stopping to kiss her neck and breasts. Marjorie felt the tension building between them, and the flow of energy increased with each precise movement. A heady scent of sandalwood, cloves and lemons filled the air.

"Now!" he whispered in her ear. "Come with me now."

She felt sure a pained expression creased her face. Her eyes felt as if they danced in her head, and her lips tingled. This time when her release came she screamed out his name, and Edgar buried himself deep within her, before pulling away. His release was immediate, his seed smearing on her exposed belly.

"Oh my!" she said.

"Oh my, indeed," Edgar panted. He fell to the side, shifting her so they spooned.

"Marry me, Marjorie. This is all the proof we need. If you say yes, next time we won't have to worry about precautions."

Marjorie didn't respond. She stirred, turning to regard his face.

"I will ask you again: Do you love me, Edgar?"

The duke stroked her back, his face contemplative, as if he were considering her question.

"Of course, I have feelings for you, Marjorie. At this moment they are very strong feelings."

"But, do you? Do you love me?" she said, almost afraid to hear his answer.

"Marjorie, to my recollection, the strongest feelings I have ever owned have been for my late wife. But I should make known that my feelings for you cannot be described. If you must have an absolute answer now, it would be I don't know how I feel."

"Then I cannot marry you," Marjorie said, her glance moving to the dusty floor slats.

"Considering my current legal circumstances, marriage would be a practical decision, madame." He sounded exasperated. "If it is the words you want to hear, I will gladly say them."

"No! I want you to mean them," Marjorie said, attempting to rise.

She moved away from him. She noticed him gaze at his shaft, lying limp between his thighs. He grunted.

Grateful to still have her shoes on, Marjorie reached for the pile of their clothing. She poked about until she found her shift, which she used to clean off his seed from her belly,

discarding it onto the blazing hearth.

"I will not marry again without love," she said, knowing

she needed to explain properly. Her voice sounded muffled, the

fabric of her dress covering her head.

"My late husband and I had nothing in common. Ours

had been a marriage by arrangement. If I ever considered tying

the proverbial 'knot' again, the circumstances would have to be

different: I do not want or need anything 'practical.'"

She hunched her shoulders, scooping her arms into the

shoulder holes of her dress. Unable to hold the two ends together

and continue dressing, she gave up, leaving the garment gaping

open, searching for her pantalettes.

"Is this what you are looking for?" he said, lifting a scrap

of white material by one finger.

He lay before her on his coat, his other arm supporting

his head. He was smiling. He hadn't even bothered to fasten his

britches.

Marjorie could see that his member had once again become rigid. She ignored the impulse to undress and rejoin him.

"You will have to come and retrieve it from me," he said, still smiling, and waving the pantalettes like a flag.

Marjorie hesitated only a moment, before walking toward him. She leaned over, her finger latching onto the cloth. She clung on, but unexpectedly the duke yanked her forward. She screeched, falling forward with a thud across his chest, allowing his arms to encircle her, and his mouth to descend on hers.

She struggled to extricate herself, but she had to be honest, she wasn't trying too hard. The duke could make her senseless with just kisses, and soon her lips parted, yielding to him.

"I can't say I love you in earnest, that would not be honorable," Edgar whispered in her ear.

"Then I can't marry you. I won't marry you, or anyone else for that matter," she said. "I shall find you a suitable wife, someone who is compatible; I will keep my end of the bargain."

She scrambled away, her pantalettes clasped in her hands. Putting them on, she searched for her coat.

A silence loomed between them as the duke stood and began dressing. Marjorie watched him buttoning his trousers, and then his jacket. He lifted his gray coat from the floor, shaking it out, and shoving his arms into it. He seemed distracted as he crouched down to smother the flames in the hearth.

Outside the hut he turned, holding her in place by the collar of her coat. "I have one last question, madame."

Marjorie knew that it wasn't the cold chill that forced her chin to rise. She wanted to look deep into his soul, and listen to him say the words she longed to hear.

"Do you love me?" he asked.

Startled, Marjorie stepped away from him, and his hands fell away.

She knew her face had formed a grim expression.

"No, Your Grace, I do not love you."

She turned away, feeling tears sting her eyes. She would not allow him to see her like this, to see how sorry she felt. It was wrong to want something from him that she could not give in return. He muttered something else, what, Marjorie was not sure. The word sounded like "liar," but she didn't dare look back. She could feel his presence, walking behind her like a great dark shadow. With only the echoes of crunching ice and gravel resonating across the fields, she couldn't believe her ears when the Duke of Grangefield started to whistle.

~ ~ ~

Chapter Fifteen

A shrill scream followed a short silence. Then there was a loud commotion outside the conservatory door. Sabeer could be heard wailing in Hindi, which brought Edgar to attention.

He stood up from the brown chaise, and moved toward the door.

"What in the blazes is going on?" Rupert mumbled, poking his nose over the top of his newspaper.

"We will soon find out," Edgar muttered.

Marjorie and Agnes had stopped their conversation, both standing up. "Is that Sabeer crying?" Agnes said.

There was no chance for anyone to answer because Sabeer chose that moment to run into the room. He stopped to look about before his gaze fastened on Marjorie. He ran straight toward her, and without warning embraced her skirts, crying and wailing the whole time.

Edgar watched as she gathered the boy into her arms and sat down, moving him onto her lap. The boy sobbed and moaned, all of it in Hindi.

Marjorie adapted to the situation without hesitation. She again wrapped her arms around the boy, who was dressed in his nightshirt. He was holding on so tightly that her spectacles inched toward the tip of her nose, but she ignored them.

"There, there, what has happened, dear? Why are you so upset?" she cooed, patting his back, looking toward Edgar with a bewildered expression.

Edgar had to admit he felt awed by her composure. It had been hours since they'd returned from the gardener's hut and he still felt on edge. In addition, Sabeer never had bad dreams, and knowing this made him feel even more anxious; something of magnitude had frightened him.

Sabeer still had not said anything coherent. He continued to sob, hugging Marjorie's neck as though she were a lifeline. Edgar surprised himself by not feeling any resentment: One thing was obvious, the boy had good taste; he liked Marjorie.

Nevertheless, he didn't want Marjorie to shoulder this problem alone. With determined strides he approached his son.

"Sabeer," he whispered.

The boy ignored him, crying louder, the sound of his sobs absorbed by Marjorie's shoulder: Edgar had never seen him so disturbed.

He moved the last step, stooping down, attempting to scoop up the boy. But Sabeer would have none of it, clinging onto Marjorie.

"Sabeer," she said, "you are holding on too tight, dear."

Sabeer lessened his hold, but still didn't let go.

Eventually his wailing subsided, replaced by hiccups.

Edgar realized this was the first time the boy had relied on anyone other than him for comfort. He was not precisely sure how he felt about that.

"Come, boy, why not give Lady Tate a chance to breathe?"

Sabeer objected in Hindi, but Edgar successfully lifted him into his arms, moving him towards the brown chaise. "Was it a dream?" he said, sitting down and setting the boy on his lap.

Sabeer did speak, but in Hindi.

"English; everyone wants to hear what happened."

Sabeer then noticed he had an audience. This somehow made him feel better, and he started again, excited.

"The man ... One eye. His robes long, Baba. His knife also long and most sharp-looking. The man's eye was gray like a goose. The knife, he pointed to my nose, then to my heart." Sabeer stopped to take a breath.

"Oh, my," Agnes muttered.

Rupert had his mouth gaping. "Do you suppose that was a concise paragraph?" he said to his wife.

Sabeer continued his jabbering, and Edgar was having a difficult time stringing together the events.

"Slower," Edgar said. "We all want to understand what happened to you."

"He had a big knife," Sabeer started.

"Who had a big knife, dear?" Marjorie asked.

"The man."

"Where was this man, dear?" Marjorie asked.

"Standing by my bed, Missy Marge."

"What was he doing in your room with a knife?"

The boy stared at her as if she had lost her front teeth.

"Sabeer, that is not a difficult question," Edgar said. "Lady Tate is trying to establish the facts. We all want to help you interpret your dream."

"No dream, Baba. The man was big, this big." Sabeer stretched up his arm, pointing a finger to the ceiling. "He was wearing robes like in the sultan's army."

"Robes, aha! Now that explains everything."

The adults all turned in Rupert's direction.

Realizing he had misspoken, Rupert returned to reading his newspaper.

"Continue, Sabeer."

"Baba, I dreamed about the beach at Calangute. The sun hot, the water very blue. Mr. Jones, he stood close by, holding a big jug filled with ice water; he was serving me ..."

"I get the picture, Sabeer. Get on with it."

Sabeer looked put out for a moment, but Edgar felt relieved that he had stopped crying.

"I am hearing a noise, but not from the beach. I am thinking this noise is of a decidedly disturbing nature. Then with my eyes open, there above my head is a knife, the size of Major Pottersab's steel sword."

"Major Potter, was our commander in Delhi," Edgar offered in explanation. "Sabeer didn't like him."

"He was a very angry-looking man, Baba," Sabeer added in his defense. "Major Pottersab would hold his sword to my nose."

"Get back to the man in your room with the big knife, dear," Marjorie said.

Edgar noted that she had not once looked at him since they had returned from the gardener's hut. Even now she avoided eye contact, her gaze focused on Sabeer.

"The man is holding the knife to my nose," Sabeer continued, "he had only one eye showing; I am thinking his eye was glass, like the blind man who sits on the temple steps."

"One glass eye. You don't say," Rupert muttered, from behind his newspaper. "I never had dreams about glass-eyed men. Fascinating!"

Sabeer wrinkled his nose in Rupert's direction. "Baba, he was big. Big like Mr. Henry, but he was speaking like Mr. Albert, through his nose."

"Like Mr. Albert?" Agnes asked.

"He means English, Agnes; as in the Queen's English," Marjorie said.

Agnes nodded her understanding.

"He would say your name, Baba. He would say it again and again."

"What exactly did he say, Sabeer?" Edgar asked.

"The time has come, Hamilton.' Baba, he would say this looking at the sword pointed to my head."

"I say, this boy has very colorful dreams," Rupert added from behind his newspaper. "Once I dreamt about a pirate. He robbed people from the village and carried a saber."

"Baba, my eyes were open," Sabeer protested.

"It is well-know that some people dream with their eyes open, Sabeer," Agnes said, kindly.

"I was most awake, Missy Marge."

"Yes, we believe you, dear. Why not tell us the rest? What happened next?"

"He cut me here, see."

Sabeer held his neck out for Edgar to see. There was indeed a barely decipherable scratch under the boy's chin. He could have scratched himself in his sleep, Edgar thought.

"Sabeer, Grangefield Hall is a very difficult place to enter unseen; let alone venture above stairs."

"I do not lie, Baba."

"I never said that you were lying," Edgar said.

The boy started crying again.

"Why don't we install a cot for you in my room, just for tonight?" Edgar said. "And, when Marjorie and I leave for London tomorrow, for added protection, I will arrange for Albert to sleep in your room."

"Mr. Albert, he is snoring through his mouth."

"Well, he's the only option at the moment. Other than leaving you with Mr. Jones."

"That's probably why he had the nightmare," Rupert said. "When did you tell him you were leaving?"

Sabeer frowned.

"This afternoon, after I told you," Edgar said to his brother. "Lady Tate decided we should take advantage of the New Year's Eve festivities so I could meet eligible ladies. I thought it best to inform Sabeer."

There was a knock at the door and Albert entered.

"I was told to come to the conservatory, Your Grace."

Edgar smiled. "Were you really told?"

"Actually, I heard that something frightened the boy."

"He had a bad dream," Marjorie said.

"My eyes were open," Sabeer protested.

"Albert, will you take the boy back upstairs, please?" she added. "Just for tonight, a cot should be placed for him in His Grace's room."

Albert extended his hand to Sabeer.

The boy looked at it, wrinkled his nose, but accepted it. Before letting go, Edgar hugged him.

"Stay with him until I retire, Albert."

"Yes, Your Grace."

"Albert, tomorrow I will be leaving for London, so I can continue the duke's training," Marjorie said. "You will be remaining at Grangefield Hall."

Albert looked startled for a scant moment, before regaining his composure. He nodded, then moved toward the door with Sabeer in tow.

"Albert."

Albert stopped. "Yes, Your Grace."

"It is only temporary—you staying here. I will need someone to keep an eye on Sabeer: Someone I trust. You see, I will be taking Jones with me to London."

Edgar was sure he had never seen it before: Albert actually smiled at Sabeer. Then hand in hand, the old man and the boy left the room.

"Well, what do you suppose all that was about?" Agnes said to Marjorie once the door closed.

"Probably just a bad dream," Marjorie responded.

"I wouldn't be too sure," Rupert said. "I'm positive father's ghost still wanders the hallways at night."

"Don't be ridiculous, dear," Agnes said, glowering at her husband.

"Well, what else could it be? No stranger could have gained access to the hall."

Edgar noticed Marjorie looking at him for the first time. She felt it, too, something was definitely wrong. A great deal had happened since he had arrived, and some of it unpleasant. First, the carriage wheel coming loose when he had traveled to

London; and then Lyndhurst shot for no reason. Perhaps these were unrelated incidents and he was making far too much of the situation. He could also not dismiss the fact that Sabeer had a vivid imagination.

Regardless, worrying about some faceless, nameless villain didn't serve his purpose. His concentration had to be focused on convincing Marjorie of their impending marriage. Even now, instead of feeling satiated after making love to her, he wanted her again.

He was no longer an impulsive young boy. As a soldier he had learned how to be patient, particularly when it came to what really mattered; which at that moment was, doing everything in his power to protect his future and his family.

~ ~ ~

Chapter Sixteen
Grosvenor House, London

"I told the footman I wanted to surprise you," Edgar said, entering Marjorie's study.

She had been preoccupied penning a list of women she wanted to introduce Edgar to at Lady Howard's Grand Tea Social that afternoon.

"You have succeeded, Your Grace," Marjorie muttered, trying to sound disinterested.

"I have not seen you in three days, madame. I had some misguided notion that you might have missed me."

"Yet another misconception on your part. Did I not mention that I would be busy arranging your social calendar?"

"Forgive me if I don't believe you," he mumbled.

Marjorie pinned him with a stare. Her late father, Lord Bowland, had taught her five different stares. Marjorie used stare number five, posing her mouth into a compressed stiff line, her eyes steering daggers at Edgar's chest.

289

"'Stare, but never look 'em in the eye,'" that's what her father had told her.

However, any attempt to prove her point was lost on the duke when he walked toward her, and raised his hand, caressing her cheek.

Marjorie swatted his fingers away.

"I can't help myself," Edgar said, staring at the fireplace.

"Try! For the love of heaven, try!" Marjorie muttered, moving away from him toward the door, at the same time pulling on her leather gloves with impatient tugs, and then buttoning the closures at the wrists.

"Is Tiffany waiting in the carriage?" Marjorie asked, looking out of the open doors into the small hallway.

"She and Rupert are meeting us at Howard House," Edgar mumbled.

Marjorie pinned him with another stare, number two.

"No need to be concerned," he said. "It's only a short coach ride to Leicester Square, and there's not much I can do to you in that amount of time; more's the pity."

Marjorie's eyes formed slits, stare number three. The duke had to be up to something. Now upset, she exited the study without waiting for him. One of her footmen appeared, immediately opening the front door. Without waiting, Marjorie stepped out into the frosty day, sensing that he walked behind her.

They descended the short flight of stairs in silence, her hand extending toward Mr. Jones.

"Good day," she said.

"Lady Tate," Jones replied, his expression intent, his cheeks pink from the cold. He assisted Marjorie onto the first rung of steps leading into the coach. Valet, nursemaid for Sabeer, guard, and now London carriage driver—indeed the man had many talents. He had become, for all intents and purposes, Edgar's right-hand man.

"Jones, if I should bang on the roof, I expect you to stop the carriage and come to my assistance," she said.

Edgar laughed, and Jones looked at the duke quizzically.

"I mean it, Your Grace; I'm not stepping into this vehicle until he promises."

His smirk disappeared. "Oh, good grief, madame, the most I will do is hold your hand."

"You won't even do that. Make him promise."

"Jones, tell her what she wants to hear or we will never leave Grosvenor Square."

"I promise, Lady Tate."

"Satisfied?" Edgar said, with disgust.

Marjorie offered him a look of disdain as she boarded the coach, and Edgar shrugged at Jones, before following her. As they settled onto the cushioned benches facing one another, the coach started moving.

Lady Howard's invitation marked the first formal engagement on Edgar's social calendar, but Marjorie didn't feel at all comfortable about attending with him. Making love to the duke had been a mistake. Not a mistake in the sense that she hadn't wanted it to happen, but now she realized she cared for him, and a part of her even wanted to accept his proposal.

To make matters worse, the incident with Sabeer's nightmare, confirmed to Marjorie that she cared for the boy as well. The promise of having a family and being a mother were tempting, and if marrying Edgar meant she could have those things and physical pleasure as well, then perhaps being in love wasn't so important after all.

If only Agnes had traveled to London with them. Her friend might have helped her sort out her feelings, but she was too close to delivering her baby, and had remained behind at Grangefield Hall. Albert and Sabeer had also been left behind. After the incident with Lady Osterly, Edgar had announced that the boy would not be leaving Surrey unless hell froze over. Marjorie understood why Albert had been left behind, but not having him with her felt particularly difficult. She could always count on Albert for his unabridged loyalty; his resistance to change; and finally, his ability to be stubborn at the least opportune moments. Good Lord, how would she manage in London without him?

"Stop brooding," Edgar said, interrupting her thoughts. "Albert will return to your side, eventually."

Marjorie's head snapped up. "I'm not brooding."

"Well, what do you call it then?" Edgar asked.

"I don't call it anything."

"You miss him, don't you?"

"Yes, but that's neither here nor there."

His smile widened.

She glared at him. "How did you know?"

"My dear, it would seem you have taught me yet another invaluable lesson—how to read your mind."

"Don't be absurd," she said, turning her head to stare out the window.

"As much as you want to deny it, we are destined to be together."

"You do have the most peculiar notions, Your Grace."

He didn't laugh. "That's why you've deliberately stayed away."

"I don't know what you're talking about," Marjorie said.

"You have deep, unrequited feelings toward me," Edgar said, with a smirk, which forced the wicked dimple in his chin to appear.

"I refuse to discuss my feelings with you," Marjorie said. After that she refused to say another word for the remainder of the coach ride.

When they arrived at Howard House she got out, paying very little attention to Jones, but overhearing his conversation with the duke.

"I didn't tell her I can't hear any banging when the coach is moving at a clip," he said, sounding concerned.

"Not to worry, Jones, I managed to suppress my vulgar urges. I'm sure Lady Tate would thank you herself, but at the moment she is too upset with me."

Jones nodded, and then remounted to his position on top of the coach. He drove the vehicle toward the outside curb, and parked with the other coaches.

"He's most put out. You must have said something to offend him," Edgar said, smiling.

Marjorie huffed: "Stop talking nonsense!"

Entering the large foyer of Howard House, they were greeted by the butler, who took their coats.

Laying a hand on Edgar's forearm, she allowed him to conduct her up the wide embankment of stairs leading to the main salon. The modest-sized gathering occupied the formal sitting room of Howard House.

Lady Howard had gone to great lengths to create a festive air. There were two glistening crystal chandeliers adorning the ceiling, each completely lit, a huge extravagance for a mid-afternoon soiree.

All about, servants wearing the mauve-colored Howard livery, served tea and cakes. Several couches and a chaise lounge had been arranged in the very front of the room, and toward the rear, card tables had been set out, and a small groups had gathered to watch the games.

Marjorie noted that Lady Howard had arrived to personally greet them. "Lady Tate, it's so good to see you again. I believe the last time was at the Cavendish Gala. I am so pleased you could attend today."

Following protocol, Marjorie gave a low curtsy, tipping her head. She had chosen to wear one of her new gowns, a confection of sky blue wool, the neckline trimmed with a cream-colored lace. The same cream-colored ribbons adorned her hair.

"Thank you for extending the invitation, Lady Howard."

"Who is your handsome escort, dear?"

"I believe you are well-acquainted with the Hamilton family. I have the great pleasure of introducing you to the Duke of Grangefield."

Lady Howard's cheeks pinked, she looked as if she would succumb to a faint. Instead, she flipped open her ivory fan, wafting it using a vigorous motion.

"How good of you to attend my little tea, Your Grace."

"Thank You, Lady Howard," Edgar said, bowing.

Marjorie had to acknowledge that he looked very ducal in his gray worsted-wool tailcoat, white cravat, and pinstripe britches.

"Since you're new to the London scene, Your Grace, I would be honored to introduce you to my guests. It isn't everyday I play hostess to a handsome duke," Lady Howard twittered, her eyes gleaming with admiration behind her fluttering fan. "You don't mind do you, Lady Tate?"

"Not in the least, Lady Howard. This would be a small coup considering the duke must reacquaint himself with society. Indeed, I do believe Viscount Hamilton and Lady Tiffany are also here; why don't I go search them out, while you introduce the duke to your guests?"

Lady Howard ignored Marjorie, hooking her arm in Edgar's, and whisking him away.

Marjorie watched Edgar glare his annoyance over his shoulder. She smiled at him, but the look he gave her promised retribution.

***

"I say, good job, Marjorie," Rupert said, appearing at her side. He waved to Edgar, as they watched him disappear into the crowd.

"With any luck we won't see him for the rest of the afternoon."

"I suppose we won't," Marjorie mumbled, without exuberance.

"Thanks to you, he now knows how to behave in a social setting," Rupert said, watching her face.

"Yes, I suppose he does," she muttered.

"He also knows his family obligations," Rupert said.

Marjorie turned, noticing her friend's anxious expression.

"Yes, he does, Rupert," Marjorie said. She really hadn't meant to snap.

"Good. Then I shall go and find Tiffany. I'm sure one of her suitors probably needs rescuing." He disappeared without giving her a chance to apologize.

Why were her emotions in turmoil? Good Lord, she already missed the duke, and knowing that Lady Howard was introducing him to marriage candidates made her angry: This realization came as a surprise.

Perhaps she should marry him; if not her, then it would be some other woman, and that would really make her feel miserable.

Edgar Hamilton could be insufferable, obstinate, and crude, but his core personality, from what she had observed, remained loyal and kind.

So why was something telling her this wasn't enough? No, if she did marry again, it had to be for love.

"Woolgathering, m' dear?" Edgar asked.

Surprised, she turned toward the familiar voice.

"Perhaps. Are you having a good time, Your Grace?" she asked.

"Not especially," Edgar whispered in her ear.

"Oh. Why not?" Marjorie ventured, splaying her sandalwood fan in front of her face, fanning the scent into the air.

"Well, the main reason is I have not been alone with you in several days. If left to my own devices for so long, anything could happen," he said, smiling so that the wicked cleft in his chin became more pronounced.

Marjorie snapped her fan shut, then tapped him on the forearm. "Stop that. You need to concentrate on your objective."

"But I am, my dear," he said, looking at her.

"I am not your objective," Marjorie hissed. "Oh, bother!" she said, fumbling in her reticule. "This should keep your thoughts occupied on something more productive.

Here is a list of eligible marriage candidates." She unfolded a small scrap of paper, at the same time adjusting her spectacles.

"I wish you wouldn't do that," Edgar said.

She ignored him. "What about Mary Hereford?"

"Already met her," Edgar said. "Not suitable at all."

"Why ever not, she's a viscount's daughter?"

"Because she kept referring to me as Elgard. She said it twice, Marjorie."

She noticed his attention had wandered to someone or something behind them, which caused her to frown. She also noticed he was smiling.

"The next young woman on my list is Lady Isabella White. She should be here with her father, the Earl of Denbigh."

"I've met her too. She doesn't wear spectacles," the duke said. "I've decided to add spectacles to my list of requirements for a future bride."

Marjorie had had quite enough. "Your Grace, I take exception to your ..."

"Your Grace," a soft female voice interrupted.

Edgar and Marjorie both turned.

"I had no intention of being so forward," the woman continued, "but I hope you will allow this small lapse in protocol."

The woman had straw-colored blond hair, and stood almost as tall as Edgar. She wore a dove-gray gown, with a black chiffon scarf draped across one shoulder, fastened at the waist with an ornate emerald brooch. Around her neck dangled a delicate chain, holding a gold wedding ring.

The woman's demeanor could only be described as ethereal. Her features were complemented by blond eyelashes and rosy cheeks. Even her smile reminded Marjorie of an angel.

Edgar appeared equally enthralled. He watched the woman with a look of appreciation, one that made Marjorie want to kick him in the shins.

"The Countess of Malvern, Your Grace." The woman said, curtseying. "I believe you were well-acquainted with my late husband."

As if reawakened from a spell, Edgar came to attention. He stepped forward without hesitating, and bowed, accepting the Countess's uplifted hand and kissing it.

"My dear, it is an absolute pleasure to make your acquaintance," Edgar said, his face glowing.

Marjorie then had to endure watching the couple stare at one another. Finally, she coughed into her fan to gain their attention.

"Oh, pardon me," Edgar said. "Permit me to introduce Lady Tate, the Countess of Penmore."

"How do you do?" Marjorie murmured.

The Countess offered her an incomplete curtsey, her full attention remaining on Edgar.

Marjorie had to admit they made a striking couple; the thought caused a knot to form in her stomach.

"The Earl and I were business partners in India," Edgar stated.

"Yes," the countess said. "I have been briefed about his business interests by my solicitors. They also mentioned your name. I would like to take this opportunity to personally thank you for your generosity, Your Grace."

"I wish I could have done more, Countess, but my hands were tied by legalities. Malvern insisted on leaving the ships and routes to me. He also left me a considerable portion of the operating capital."

"I have no cause to complain, Your Grace. What do I know about running a shipping empire? Frankly, I'm relieved that my late husband left me a generous stipend and very few legal issues to deal with."

"Uh ... Perhaps I will go for a walk," Marjorie said, "that way you two can catch up."

"Stay," Edgar said.

But Marjorie had already turned to leave. Edgar clasped her upper arm.

"Madame, I want you to stay," he said, using a commanding tone.

"Well, if you insist," Marjorie said, through clenched teeth.

The Countess frowned, now all of her attention focused on Marjorie, who sensed the woman was now annoyed.

"Lottie? Lady Howard wants to show us her new oil painting."

All three of them turned toward the sound of the male voice.

The man had a similar height to the duke.

"Oh, hello, Nigel. Your Grace, permit me to introduce a family friend and my escort, Lord Crosswell."

"Nigel, may I introduce you to the Duke of Grangefield."

Lord Crosswell appeared surprised to be meeting the duke. His features held an odd expression. Indeed, he looked angry, his moustache quivered, and his eyes, Marjorie felt sure, bulged as if he'd been caught off guard. He also wore a gray eye patch, which made him look even more menacing.

"Grangefield?" he stuttered.

Edgar, Marjorie, and the Countess of Malvern, all stared at him.

"Forgive me if I don't dwell on pleasantries: I doubt we could be friends, Grangefield," Crosswell said.

Marjorie and the Countess gasped in unison. The duke's mouth pinched.

Lord Crosswell leaned forward. "I'm sure you remember my sister, Virginia Crosswell."

"I do remember," Edgar replied. "My condolences."

Marjorie sensed that Edgar's body had stilled, his features looked pained, perhaps even remorseful.

306

Crosswell didn't respond. Instead, he tugged at the Countess' arm. "Come, Lottie."

Before the Countess could raise a word of protest, she was swept away.

"Good Lord," Marjorie said, fanning her face at a rapid clip. "What on earth was all that about?"

"His sister killed herself after she was left at the altar," Edgar said.

"How dreadful," Marjorie said. "But what does that have to do with you?"

"I am the one who left her at the altar."

"Oh, my word! I do recall Rupert mentioning the story to me."

"I suppose Crosswell has a strong reason to dislike me; what do you think?"

Marjorie understood how much Edgar had suffered because of his fragile past. "I think I would have to hear all the details before I gave my opinion."

Edgar smiled at her. "Have I mentioned what a splendid woman you are?"

"Not in public," Marjorie said, knowing her cheeks felt warm. "I would like to hear the story, if you care to tell me."

"Ah, yes, the story. Well, the late duke, my father, decided to arrange a marriage for me when I was seventeen. This was because I happened to be the son that never conformed.

"Of course, I wasn't ready to marry anyone. And, to make matters worse, my father informed me about my marriage the night before the wedding."

"The night before?" Marjorie said, stupefied.

"Bold and full of bluster, as he often was, the duke came to my suite that evening, and told me that it was marriage, 'or else.'"

"Or else, what?"

"I don't remember there being an 'or else.'"

"I say, that's dreadfully unfair," she muttered.

"I would agree, madame. That is why I packed my things and left that same night.

I managed to board a ship at Portsmouth, and one year later, when more troops were needed after the uprisings in India, I joined the British Army. At the Battle of Delhi, where Malvern was killed, ironically, I saved two men, and as a result, was promoted to captain of the guard."

"Then you're a hero."

"Madame, there are no heroes on the battlefield."

A short pause ensued. Marjorie then looked at him.

"So that is why your father added a stipulation to his will?" Marjorie said.

"Correct. Sadly, Rupert informed me by letter that Virginia Crosswell, my intended bride, had taken her life; she was only sixteen."

"Oh, how awful," Marjorie said, adjusting her spectacles, and peering at him with a look of intense interest.

Edgar continued. "Apparently, she had a frail disposition, and the embarrassment had been too much to bear."

"You know what's curious, Edgar."

"Yes, dear."

"Lord Crosswell didn't seem surprised to meet you. He was surprised to be introduced, but he didn't seem shocked. As if he knew you were in England."

"Marjorie, news does travel. No doubt Lady Osterly already informed every busybody she knows."

Marjorie shuddered. "What a horrible woman."

"I agree." Edgar said, looping Marjorie's hand through his forearm, then patting it in place. They moved toward a doorway hidden behind several large potted ficus plants.

"Where are we going?"

Edgar smiled, offering her a full display of his dimples. "Just wait and see, madame. I have planned a little surprise for you."

~ ~ ~

Chapter Seventeen

Marjorie frowned.

"When did you get a chance to go scouting?" she asked.

"When Lady Howard finally released my hand, I slipped away. Please don't do that," Edgar said.

"Do what?" Marjorie said, with all innocence.

"Blink. You know how those spectacles of yours drive me bonkers: I can barely speak when you wear them."

Marjorie's eyelashes fluttered. "Your Grace, without a doubt, you are the most unstable person I have ever met."

"That sounded like a compliment, Lady Tate," he said, smiling.

Without waiting for her response, Edgar led her through a doorway. They passed into a narrow corridor, before arriving at a small room built entirely of bricks and glass panels. It was a hot and humid room with a musty odor. Most surprising of all, it was filled with pink orchids.

"Oh! How lovely!"

"I thought you might like this." Edgar sounded smug.

"I've never seen so many flowers in one place. Well, not unless you count Kew Gardens."

"You will have to take me there sometime, I've not had the pleasure."

Marjorie glanced at him. Her spectacle lenses had fogged, and his image was blurred.

"I'm sure you will want to tour London accompanied by your new duchess. By the way, how did your wife-hunting exploits go this afternoon?"

"I'm not looking for a wife anymore, Marjorie."

"Of course, you are; that is why we came to London."

"I made my decision today."

"I beg your pardon?" Marjorie said, realizing her tone sounded more relieved than distressed.

"I said, I came to my decision about marriage this morning."

"Without mentioning anything to me or Rupert?"

"Marjorie, I merely agreed to this matchmaking farce to placate my family. I never had any intention of 'wife-hunting,' as you so eloquently put it." He pulled her forward so they were at arm's length, and then held her in place as if she might bolt. "I've decided you're the only woman I want to marry."

"Don't be ridiculous. I already told you I won't marry you. You really must face realities; the idea here is to find a woman who is willing to marry *you*."

"But you are willing, Marjorie; all I have to do is convince you."

She tried to wrench away, but was unsuccessful. "Let go," she muttered, knowing full well her protest sounded weak.

"You don't sound convincing."

"I do," she said.

The duke tugged her the short distance forward, his lips descending over hers. He coaxed her lips open, his tongue joining with hers.

After several deep kisses, Marjorie realized to her chagrin that she participated. The duke, also sensing this, continued to trail kisses across her cheeks.

"I have missed you, madame," he said, breathless, his lips now nipping her earlobe. His hands had moved behind her back, attempting to unfasten the buttons of her gown.

"Stop! What are you doing?" Marjorie squeaked, trying to shake his hands away.

He stopped, standing quite still, reluctant to look at her face. "Why must I stop?" he said, between labored breaths. Marjorie noticed the pulse throbbing at the base of his neck.

"I can give you a dozen reasons. Let me see. Oh, yes; we happen to be in a hot house that is quite dirty; I am wearing one of my new gowns; we are in a very public place; I don't wish my gown to get crushed; you don't love me. How many more reasons do you need?"

Edgar laughed. "You don't want me to wrinkle your gown?"

"It is a very pretty gown."

"Well, you have me there. I agree, on you that gown is very pretty. Now, consider the situation further: If Lady Howard were wearing that same frock, I'm sure I wouldn't want to tear it off her body, as much as I want to tear it off yours."

Marjorie smiled.

Encouraged, Edgar bent down and kissed her neck.

Marjorie objected again, but not so vehemently, until she felt her feet lift off the floor. "Why do you insist on carrying me everywhere?" she said, her words sounding muffled by his coat.

"I like carrying you," he said, moving behind a tall screen. "Here we will be concealed from view, and I can have my way with you without fear of discovery."

Marjorie's mouth gaped.

The duke had lowered her so her feet touched the floor, bracing her back against a large panel of bricks and glass. If she turned her head a fraction, she could see the street below through the window. It wasn't easy identifying shapes because the glass had been painted white.

His hands left her waist, moving to open the buttons of his shirt. "Put your hands on me, Marjorie; I need to feel you touch my skin."

Feeling dazed, she obeyed, and Edgar continued to kiss her face.

Her touch seemed to ignite his passion. He had raised her skirts, stroking the skin under her garters. His fingers trailing upward, soon finding her mound.

Marjorie moaned when his fingers caressed the moist opening. She heard herself whimper as Edgar increased the strokes, his fingers slowing their assault to massage the sensitive skin.

Her hands moved to cover his exposed nipples, molding them with her palms, as she continued to stroke his chest. Her fingers then traveled lower, gently pressing his ribs, and grazing the flat planes of his abdomen. Realizing she wanted to be closer, she pressed her face against his chest, smelling the sandalwood and cloves.

"I want you so much, Marjorie," he murmured, his breathing labored.

"But someone might see us."

Her argument sounded unconvincing. His fingers had not left her, and the tension in her body had increased.

"I promise, there will be no noticeable creases to your dress." His voice sounded strained, his hands moving to her waist as he lifted her.

She heard herself say, "Don't stop."

This time it would be because it felt right, Marjorie told herself. She would tell him why later, and he would accept, and then they would marry. "Hurry," she said.

"Always in a hurry, madame," he muttered, turning her slowly so her hands padded the rough wall, her face toward the brick. Then he moved closer. "Try not to collapse your arms," he whispered. His nose and lips now nuzzled the back of her neck, as he raised the skirts of her dress and her chemise, lowering her pantalettes.

Marjorie felt one of his hands fumble near his britches, then she felt the thick warm skin of his shaft press against her buttocks.

"Why like this?" she said, her whisper sounding desperate.

"Trust me," he muttered, then entered her with one thrust.

She was thankful that her scream of pleasure was muffled by the wall, although still quite audible.

"Are you all right?" he asked, his cheek touching her ear.

She managed a nod. Her limbs felt languid as her body became accustomed to the wonderful invasion, then Edgar's shaft penetrated deeper, the pressure building. His hands had moved to cover her breasts, massaging each mound through the fabric of her dress.

The protection of his frame supported her body against the wall, while he kissed her neck.

"You feel like heaven," he murmured in her ear.

Marjorie gasped when he adjusted position, withdrawing, and reentering her.

She started to feel warm, and her breathing sounded ragged. She grew more anxious as the sweet pressure of desire continued to build.

Edgar now kissed her mouth, and within the next heartbeat, came her unannounced climax. Edgar's release followed a fraction of a moment later. Afterwards, he let go of her shoulders, laying his hands flat on the cool glass on each side of her face.

They remained facing the wall. Edgar's breathing had steadied, but he continued to press her body against the wall, his hands moving to massage her breasts.

"We really must consider doing this in a bed next time. One that has a soft mattress," he said.

They laughed together, and he turned her so she faced him, kissing her mouth.

"Now, madame, give me one good reason why I would want to marry anyone else."

She didn't reply. She couldn't.

***

"Perhaps we should marry, Edgar."

"What?" Edgar said, incredulous.

They had left Howard House in the ducal carriage, and were sitting side by side holding hands.

There were no words to describe what had just transpired between them. Edgar had come to realize that not even with Chamine had the physical attraction been this overwhelming, so binding between two people.

"I will marry you," she repeated.

As if his prayers had been answered, he looked at her, his eyes narrowing. She was a curious little thing, he thought.

"A wise decision, madame, but what may I ask caused this reversal in my fortune?"

"I am making a practical decision."

Edgar remained silent, watching her. She stared out the window, though there was no view to speak of.

"You need a wife," she continued, "we seem to suit, and this would benefit Sabeer."

"Sabeer?" Edgar asked, surprised.

"Well, of course, Sabeer, he is your son."

"I am well aware of that. What has Sabeer got to do with us getting married?"

Marjorie looked at him as if he had egg on his face. "Sabeer and I have a fondness for one another. He responds to me."

"He responds to me, too, what is your point?"

"Sabeer needs a female influence," Marjorie said.

"Possibly. Are you telling me you want to marry me because you want to become Sabeer's mother?"

"Well, he is a factor, Your Grace. I care for you deeply, of course."

"Of course," Edgar said, without enthusiasm.

"I thought you would be pleased with my decision," she said, turning toward him.

"I thought I would be as well," he muttered.

"But you're not."

"Madame, I had thought that a marriage should be about how well we suited. Perhaps even about how well this would reshape the inheritance issue. I had not been prepared to hear a declaration regarding the maternal bond formed between you and my son."

"There's no need to raise your voice, Your Grace."

"Edgar, madame; must I remind you, my name is Edgar."

"I thought you would be pleased," Marjorie said, in a quiet voice.

"I am pleased, but now I am also curious. If Sabeer were not a factor would you still want to marry me?"

Marjorie looked at him. "I'm ... "

"Not sure," Edgar finished. "Well, that certainly gives me some perspective."

"Of course, I care for you, but I want love as well, and if not from you, the boy is more than willing to fill that void."

"I see."

"I don't see why this is so difficult for you to understand," Marjorie continued. "It has been established that I don't need to marry anyone; I don't need your fortune; and I don't need your title. Sabeer likes me—I like you both."

"Again, I suppose I should feel fortunate," Edgar muttered.

"Good Lord! Why are you being so difficult? I like *you*, Your Grace. If I did not like you then this conversation would not be taking place."

It was then the coach halted, and Edgar noticed they had reached Grosvenor House. "Bloody hell!" he muttered.

Marjorie ignored him.

Jones had already opened the door to the carriage, lowering the steps, and Marjorie descended.

"We need to discuss this further, madame."

"Do we, Your Grace?"

"You make a valid point: Of course, Sabeer's feelings must be considered."

Jones looked at Edgar curiously.

It was a slight distraction, enough for Marjorie to walk toward her door.

"Perhaps you are the one who should consider the situation further," she said.

"Marjorie," Edgar said, but it was too late. She had already entered the house, and the footman had closed the door behind her.

~ ~ ~

Chapter Eighteen

"She says in her letter that she's leaving."

"What are you mumbling on about, Rupert?" Edgar asked, looking up. He had been sitting behind his desk in his study, reviewing the invitations he had received in the afternoon post.

"I received a letter from Marjorie. She says she will be leaving London after the New Year's Eve ball. She says that there is nothing more for her to do since Lady Howard offered to coordinate your London activities. Marjorie wants to get back to her life. Did you know she deals in trade?"

"Yes, blast it, Rupert, I know," Edgar said. "I also know she is ambitious, talented, and she doesn't want to get married unless love is involved, she's been through one arranged marriage already."

"Well, I'm not privy to whether she wants to get married or not," Rupert said, stroking his moustache.

"I am," Edgar said, standing and walking toward the spirits cabinet. "Brandy?"

"No, thank you; a bit too early for me. I say, that ball is tonight, has your costume arrived?"

"It has, and don't bother asking me what it is."

"Why all the secrecy? If you're going as an army soldier then just say so."

"I'm not," Edgar said, "and the reason I don't want you to know is because I don't want Marjorie to find out about it."

"You mortally wound me, brother. Are you suggesting I might say something?"

"I am."

"Oh, I say, that's so unfair," Rupert said, plopping down on a leather armchair.

Edgar ignored his pout. "Did she explain why she is leaving?"

"I told you, old boy, she says her job's done here. She can't work with you. She won't even accept payment now. She considers you to be her most uncooperative student."

"Oh?" Edgar said, trying to sound disinterested. His brother, he had discovered, could be quite perceptive at times.

"That's what the letter says." Rupert paused to twirl his moustache tips, making him look quite dastardly.

"She mentioned something about you not looking for a wife anymore. I want to tell her that's rubbish, and of course, you're still looking."

"I hate to shatter your illusions, but she's right, I'm not looking for a wife anymore."

"What?" Rupert said, flabbergasted. "But we agreed."

"No, I agreed to go along with your plans to be trained, I never agreed to getting married. I have made other provisions to circumvent the conditions of father's will: I will not be cajoled into marrying anyone."

"What have you done?"

"I have authorized my solicitor, Mr. Arnold, to petition the Queen for an adjudication proceeding. Since the inheritance reverts back to the crown after the waiting period, the queen has the authority to rescind her interest and return the Hamilton

fortune to the rightful heir."

Edgar stopped pacing. "I have already heard from the

palace. Her Majesty has agreed to support my motion."

"Oh, I say, well done, Edgar."

The duke looked at his brother's relieved expression, and

felt relieved himself. He'd wanted to tell Rupert when the decree

had arrived, but Marjorie had proved to be a distraction. Now

she had decided to return to her estates. Three days of separation

had been long enough, the thought of being parted from her

indefinitely sounded unbearable.

"How dare she decide to leave without completing my

training? A bargain is a bargain; this won't do at all," he muttered

to a small potted plant.

Taking the wrong meaning, Rupert answered for him.

"Of course it will do. This news is stupendous, Edgar; I did dread

seeing you married to the wrong woman." He walked to the

spirits cabinet. "Changed m' mind. We need to toast our good

fortune." He perused the various decanters.

"Want a topper?" He lifted up the brandy decanter.

Edgar nodded.

"Why so glum-looking?" Rupert said. "If I were you I'd be hopping with joy. Instead, you're frowning at that plant as if you were contemplating slicing off its roots."

Edgar's chin raised at his brother's wry humor.

"What's bothering you?" Rupert asked.

"Marjorie."

"Oh, it's 'Marjorie,' is it? Did she approve this little lapse in protocol?"

"Shut up, Rupert."

"That bad, is it?"

"She is without a doubt the most obstinate woman I have ever encountered," Edgar muttered.

"Then it sounds like you've met your match," Rupert said, laughing.

Edgar didn't join him.

"I take it there are feelings involved here?" Rupert said, pouring two brandies, then walking toward Edgar with one of the glasses.

Edgar grunted his thanks without answering.

"Well, it seems to me that something drastic needs to happen, and it has to happen before she leaves London tomorrow," Rupert said.

Edgar again didn't respond. Instead, he lifted his glass, taking a moment to smell the bouquet before gulping down the contents. His body shuddered as the alcohol warmed his gullet. He pondered the word "drastic," then nodded.

"Do you need any assistance with that plan of yours?"

He noticed Rupert had returned to the spirits table. His brother smiled at him, lifting the decanter in Edgar's direction as if toasting.

"I will let you know," Edgar said, lifting his empty glass in a salute. Then he realized he too was smiling, and released a sigh of relief. Finally, like a good soldier, he had formulated a plan; and he knew without a doubt, the battle could now be won.

***

The carriage jostled, coming to a stop outside the Montjoy Mansion. The drive to south London had taken well over an hour and Marjorie felt cold to the bone. A brisk wind whistled through the air, and although most of the snow had melted, the streets were covered with a gray sludge, making driving conditions miserable.

Her costume for this event had been chosen on a whim. In Marjorie's opinion the garment revealed entirely too much, making it impracticable for an evening jaunt around London in the heart of winter. But her choice had been motivated by anguish because she would not be seeing the duke for some time, and she wanted to look especially nice. The idea of leaving him made her want to cry, and during the last twenty-four hours she had done her fair share of weeping. The next time she would see him he would probably be married, the event as inevitable as a rain shower on English soil.

Marjorie looked toward the rear. There were many carriages waiting behind hers.

"Over to the left, gov'nor," one of the Montjoy footmen called out, guiding her coachman to the curb. The coach moved a short distance and then stopped, joining a formation of carriages along the gravel pathway leading to the entrance of the mansion.

The carriage door opened, and she shivered when a blast of cold air sailed through the flimsy materials of her cloak and gown. Removing the red tartan blanket covering her legs, Marjorie extended her hand to the waiting footman, who wore a white wig and a formal, midnight blue jacket.

"Lady Tate," he said.

"Thank you," Marjorie acknowledged, as he helped her descend.

"I'd wrap up good an' warm, milady, there's a line to get in."

"Footman?"

"Yes, milady."

"Has the Grangefield party arrived?"

"They have, milady. About twenty minutes ago."

He then escorted her toward the main entrance.

Entering the well-lit foyer, she sighed with gratitude when she felt a blast of warm air. It appeared their hosts had spared no expense, the entryway had been well-screened to limit the drafty condition of their ancestral home.

Marjorie removed her cloak, passing it to a maid, and then adjusted her gloves. They fit all the way to her elbows. She knew full well they distracted from the theme of her costume, but protocol dictated that she wear them.

She heard the rich strains of a Viennese waltz as she entered the main ballroom. A sea of colors and costumes greeted her. She spied two woodland nymphs, as well as the goddess Diana.

The woodland nymphs giggled, and a monk passing by, waved to her with his bible.

Marjorie smiled. She knew all of them, but they hadn't recognized her. A thick band of kohl outlined her eyes, and a black, shoulder-length wig covered her head. It felt decadent not wearing a corset, but this allowed her gown to hang straight down over her hips, tied at the waist with a gold cord. She languished in the feel of the white silk. The sheath style had no sleeves, and her left arm was fully exposed. On her right arm she had worn a coiled, gold bracelet, spiraling from wrist to elbow, and decorated with a cobra's head. To finish the look she had chosen an amulet choker, formed in a half moon design, which covered the full expanse of her chest.

Marjorie looked beyond the cavernous dance floor with its throng of waltzing partners. Rupert had agreed that a member of the Hamilton family would be waiting for her. Indeed, the ballroom appeared endless. She realized that looking for a friend in such a large crowd would be a monstrous task. In the distance, an even larger throng had gathered around the edge of the dance floor.

Thank heaven she spied Tiffany. The gal stood out in most crowds. Her bored expression suggested that she needed rescuing from her conversation partner, who sported the costume of a court jester. Marjorie immediately recognized Lord

Albey, and understood why her young friend appeared so bored.
Tiffany yawned twice behind her fan, as Lord Albey described
something using large hand gestures, which caused the bells on
his costume to jingle.

Tiffany's attention wandered from Albey on several
occasions. When she spied Marjorie, she smiled.

"Oh, I'm so relieved you are here," Tiffany said,
straightening the arrow quills in the scabbard of her Goddess
Diana costume. Lord Albey frowned, and Tiffany blanched at her
rudeness.

"What I meant to say was, Rupert has been looking for
you. He's out there," she said, pointing to the dance floor. "Lady
Montjoy nabbed him as soon as the quadrille started."

Tiffany looked down. "I say, what a clever costume. I'm
positive Edgar will be thrilled. Did you know that you both
complement one another? But then again I'm sure you haven't
seen him yet, he looks quite magnificent."

Not wanting to appear rude, Marjorie turned her
attention to greet Lord Albey. "Good Evening, My Lord."

"Good evening, Lady Tate."

"Lord Albey, do you mind if I separate you from Lady Tiffany for a few moments? I would like to locate the retiring room, and would enjoy some company."

Lord Albey looked disappointed, but he bowed, which caused the bells on his hat to jangle.

"Not at all, madame. If you will excuse me, ladies." He took one last, longing look at Tiffany, then walked away, his costume making more jingling noises.

"What a loud ensemble," Marjorie said, squelching the impulse to cover her ears.

"He says it's authentic," Tiffany mumbled.

"It appears the young lord is quite besotted with you."

"Yes, I know," Tiffany said, sounding unenthusiastic. "They all are. Unfortunately, it's my dowry they're all besotted with.

Marjorie, did you know that Lord Albey is destitute? His father lost his entire fortune in a card game last year, and afterward shot himself."

"No!"

Tiffany lowered her voice. "Lord Albey is trying to recoup his fortune by marrying an heiress."

"How appalling!" Marjorie said.

"Did you really want to visit the retiring room?" Tiffany asked.

"Of course not. How else was I supposed to distract Lord Albey?" That was when Marjorie noticed him watching them. "Perhaps we should walk over there, just in case he suspects. By the way, where is the duke?"

"He's behind you, near that large fern, talking to the Countess Malvern."

Marjorie squelched the impulse to turn in his direction.

"They've been talking and laughing for the last twenty minutes. The countess seems to have caught his attention."

Now curiosity forced her to turn.

Indeed, the duke and countess stood huddled together, whispering and laughing. She could only see the top of Edgar's head. Even at Howard House, Marjorie had thought they made a striking couple, a vision of light and dark, mingling in perfect accord.

"Should I wave him over?" Tiffany asked, "I'm sure he will notice me above the crowd; we're the same height you know."

"Don't do that," Marjorie said; "Let's not interrupt them. Perhaps the duke is practicing some of the skills I taught him."

Marjorie looked up, noticing Tiffany's frown.

"Are you really planning to leave London tomorrow?" Tiffany asked.

"Yes, I have quite made up my mind," Marjorie replied, distracted. She had somehow focused on the back of Edgar's head, as if willing him to turn and notice her.

"I will miss you."

"I shall miss you, too, dear. I have had a lovely holiday, but it's time that I returned home. I'm sure Lady Howard will be an excellent sponsor, and judging by her eagerness yesterday, she will be quite open to introducing your brother to a bevy of eligible women."

They heard the jingling noises at the same time. Lord Albey walked toward the far end of the ballroom. Marjorie noticed Edgar's attention drawn to Albey as well, but then he turned, this time in her direction, and their eyes made contact. Marjorie saw him make a quick bow before the countess, then move toward them.

"Good Lord, he's coming this way," Marjorie mumbled.

"You can let go of my arm; it's not Julius Caesar, just Edgar," Tiffany said, smiling.

Feeling foolish, Marjorie did let go of Tiffany, almost tripping over her skirts trying to regain her balance. Good Lord, he did look magnificent!

Edgar had chosen the garb of a Roman centurion, perhaps even Mark Anthony, she thought with amusement. His smile appeared focused on hers. The wicked dimple in his chin looking prominent on his newly shaven face.

This particular centurion wore sandals on his bare feet, and his long muscular legs were naked to the thigh. He had donned a white skirt with a burgundy and gold trim, that met at his upper thigh. Another much shorter skirt topped the first, this one made of vertical metal panels. A shiny metal breastplate covered his chest, and he wore a laurel leaf crown on his head.

"My queen," Edgar said, bowing over her hand.

"Your Grace."

"I say, Edgar, that's a tad informal, someone might hear," Tiffany crooned. She had raised her lace fan, and was fluttering it over her face to hide her smile.

"I whispered," Edgar said, smiling.

"Yes, well, that's still no excuse for a lapse in protocol," Tiffany replied.

"He did whisper, Tiffany," Marjorie said. "Regardless, none of this will matter in the morning, I will be on my way home," she said, even as she noticed Edgar frown.

"I just heard about your plans."

"I felt obliged to mention my decision to Rupert first." Marjorie fanned her face with her ostrich fan. The fan had a painted blue eye in the center, which she imagined blinked at her with disapproval.

"I do, however, apologize for not informing you as well."

"You can apologize properly on the dance floor. Shall we?" Edgar had extended his hand to her. "They're about to play a waltz."

"I realize that," she said, now annoyed with him.

"You've passed your mourning, almost a month now, dancing together won't cause a scandal."

"What about Tiffany?" Marjorie said, glancing at her friend's flushed expression. "She's a debutante; we can't leave her alone."

Edgar ogled his sister. "I suppose not," he muttered.

"Don't be absurd, I'll be perfectly all right," Tiffany offered.

"Wait a moment," Edgar said, turning swiftly, which caused the metal panels of his skirt to clink.

Marjorie sighed, longing for a private place where she could go and collect herself. The moment she had glanced at the duke she had started to feel warm. The way she felt, marrying him would have been a sensible conclusion, and Marjorie was always sensible, even if it seemed foolish wanting a man who didn't love her.

To her annoyance, Edgar reappeared with the Countess Malvern in tow, costumed as a harem girl.

"Lottie has agreed to keep you company, Tiffany."

"Lottie?" Marjorie and Tiffany both squeaked in unison.

Edgar frowned at them. "For heaven's sake, I meant the Countess Malvern."

Marjorie's features felt pinched. Her spectacles trembled on the bridge of her nose.

"I told you not to do that with your spectacles," Edgar whispered in her ear.

Marjorie blanched at the sexual implications. Her hand quivered as she accepted his, and once joined, they moved with the elegance of Egyptian monarchy toward the dance floor.

After performing the customary bow, Edgar laced his arm around her waist, moving them both into the square step movement of the waltz.

Even though her legs were not as long as Edgar's, Marjorie kept up with him. Her head lifted, her arms poised in the required position. With Tiffany's help he had practiced enough at Grangefield Hall, and all the slips, trips, and fumbles had been mastered. They glided together in perfect accord, their features impassive, their movements as smooth as a soft breeze.

Marjorie felt like laughing out loud at the sheer perfection of their union. But this would be the last time he would hold her, the last time their eyes made love, and their heartbeats thrummed like the strains of a celestial harp. Good Lord, why did she have to go and fall in love with him?

Marjorie looked up at his face. As if sensing her anguish, the duke drew closer. They observed the arm length standards required for a waltz, but just barely. Their hands were interwoven, and she could smell his scent of sandalwood and cloves. He said something to her, but she could not understand him above the taps of slippers and boots, and the dulcet strains of the large orchestra. He, too, seemed to sense her confusion.

She attempted to question his whispered words with a tilt of her head, even as their feet moved in time, and her gown brushed against his naked legs.

His look of complete possession made Marjorie shiver. Their gazes were locked, and he repeated the words again, mouthing each one with care. His lips parted one more time, they arched with purpose and perfect alignment, and finally Marjorie understood: He had said, "I love you."

His head lowered to meet hers, as if he wanted to kiss her right there on the dance floor, in front of everybody. Marjorie stopped moving. The ballroom began to darken; the footmen were extinguishing the candles in the wall sconces.

She realized Edgar had guided them toward a concealed portico, where they were well out of sight from prying eyes. In partial darkness his lips met hers.

The moments ticked by, and the kiss lingered on. Beyond them across the dance floor more candles, flickered, like a blanket of bright stars, and the orchestra violins played a soft serenade.

In her jubilant haze, still being kissed by Edgar, and being entwined in his arms, Marjorie heard a strong baritone singing "God Save the Queen."

Edgar kissed her again, with more urgency this time.

"Happy New Year, Marjorie," he said, breathlessly.

"Happy New Year, Edgar," she replied, knowing her own breathing sounded uneven.

Edgar embraced her again, then kissed her forehead. With reluctance, he released her, and a moment later he was whisked away by a boisterous crowd of merrymakers.

His expression marked his displeasure at being parted from her, but Marjorie still felt surprised by his declaration.

Good Lord, had he really said he loved her? She couldn't believe it.

She felt a thrill, followed by outright disbelief. Marjorie wanted to cry with happiness, but the sensible part of her needed convincing, before she could completely give her heart away.

That anxious feeling would not leave her, even as she maneuvered through the large crowd. There was now no denying the swirl of emotions she felt. As much as she needed to calm herself, she acknowledged this was the wrong time and place to try, particularly when she became swept away by a swarm of boisterous and jubilant revelers.

~ ~ ~

Chapter Nineteen

Marjorie found herself at the other end of the ballroom.
After the Auld Lang Syne had played, the servants proceeded to
re-light the wall lamps.

She noticed Rupert and Lady Montjoy had cornered
Edgar. They were exchanging their mutual felicitations. Edgar
seemed pleased, almost enigmatic, and far too confident.
Marjorie kissed several familiar cheeks, and a few not so familiar
ones covered with heavy makeup.

Tiffany rescued her from the crowd. But then Lord
Albey appeared, claiming a dance, which left Marjorie standing
alone. Enjoying the solitude, she stood in a small alcove
concealed by several Greek statues.

"He's a monster," she heard a male voice stammer. "It's
rumored the military discharged him, without even a
handshake," the man continued.

Marjorie slid closer to the wall. She hated
eavesdropping, but the voice sounded vaguely familiar.

"Is that true, or are you making it up? You've been known to tell a tale or two, Crosswell, and this one borders on being libelous. I certainly wouldn't want to be you if the Duke of Grangefield gets wind of what you've been saying about him: He's rumored to be very adept with pistols."

"It's true," Crosswell said. "The man was stripped of his rank and booted out of the military on his rear end."

Marjorie stifled a gasp. Lord Crosswell was stirring up mischief with Lord Buccleuch.

"Didn't you hear? He even brought one of those dark people with him from India," Crosswell said.

Marjorie realized that if Edgar got wind of this, Crosswell would no doubt be meeting his Maker at dawn.

"A young boy," Crosswell crooned.

"You don't say," Buccleuch replied.

"As dark as sin, and quite stupid by all accounts."

"Why in the devil did he bring him to England? We don't need foreigners here, particularly Blackamoors," Buccleuch postulated.

"Well, I've heard it said that a life in the military changes a man's carnal pleasures. It's rumored that when left to their own devices, soldiers can become a tad unconventional when it comes to pleasures of the flesh: Do you catch my meaning?"

Marjorie held back another gasp.

"You don't say," Buccleuch said, sounding shocked.

Marjorie envisioned his monocle sliding from his eye, and his mouth hanging open.

"I've also heard that there have been strange goings on at Grangefield hall. Naked people in deserted huts, locked doors, muffled voices."

Marjorie clasped a hand over her mouth. She wanted to walk out from her hiding place and punch Crosswell in the nose. How did he know about the goings-on at Grangefield Hall? Unless, of course he'd been spying on them.

"And, where did you hear that?" Marjorie recognized the additional male voice and her mouth fell open.

"Grangefield!" Buccleuch spluttered.

"Crosswell," Edgar acknowledged. "If I were you I'd concentrate on lowering my voice in public. Did I hear you mention something about Grangefield Hall?"

Marjorie couldn't see Edgar's face, but she recognized his deliberate tone. She also heard a nervous tapping, probably Crosswell, she imagined his boot was tapping on the marble tile.

Crosswell's voice now quivered when he spoke. "I was just telling Buccleuch here that I heard you brought a boy with you from India."

"I did. May I ask how that concerns you?"

"I wasn't spreading tales," Crosswell said.

"That's good to know. If you were, then there may be consequences."

Marjorie imagined Edgar red-faced, with his hand poised at the hilt of his dagger, prepared to cut out Crosswell's heart.

"There's been a lot of strange goings-on at Grangefield Hall since you arrived," Crosswell muttered. "That's what I've heard."

"Who have you heard this from?" Edgar sneered.

"It's just hearsay," Crosswell said.

"You told me it came from a reliable source," Buccleuch muttered.

"I misspoke."

"Since you may not be familiar with military code, Crosswell," Edgar said, "it seems only fair that I familiarize you with it. If any serviceman hears either his name, or the names of his family besmirched in public, it is his duty to right the matter, to the death if necessary."

"I say, are you threatening me?"

Marjorie heard boots shuffling, imagining Crosswell stepping as far away from Edgar as possible.

She should intervene, she thought, the quicker the better, before things got out of hand. Straightening her shoulders, she stepped out of the alcove. "Oh, good. I have found you at last, Your Grace."

Standing in between the three men, she faced the duke.

Edgar frowned at her.

"Happy New Year, Lord Crosswell, and also to you, Lord Buccleuch," Marjorie said, curtseying. "You will excuse me, but I must whisk the duke away. It is quite late, and his brother and sister are waiting to depart in the foyer. I believe the Grangefield carriage has been summoned."

With more bravado than she felt, she extended her arm, waiting for the duke to proffer his. He did so, albeit with reluctance.

The metal slats of his Roman skirt clanked as he bowed, but when he turned his head, his angry gaze lingered on Crosswell. "I meant what I said: Those who have tested my temper have not lived long enough to describe it."

Without explanation, Edgar squeezed Marjorie's upper arm, ignoring her yelp. He then escorted her out of the crowded ballroom, toward the foyer.

***

Marjorie noticed the frost covering the Montjoy lawn. It was well after two in the morning and the guests were starting to depart. Nestled in her cloak, Marjorie waited on the terrace.

"Footman?"

"Yes, milady."

"Would you fetch the Penmore carriage?"

The footman looked confused.

"I'm the Countess of Penmore."

"Yes, milady, I know."

"Well, if you know, why are my coach and driver not here?"

"I'm not sure, milady."

"I beg your pardon."

"Your driver left half an hour after you arrived."

"He left?" Marjorie said.

"Yes, milady."

"But I told him specifically to wait for me."

"I think he was told to leave, milady." The footman looked stricken. "By that gent over there," he said, pointing. "He told your bloke that he could go 'ome."

Now shivering, Marjorie looked toward the throngs of people huddled at various points on the stairwell, all of them

waiting for their carriage names to be called out. Edgar stood on
the very top step with his back turned away.

"You mean that man wearing the long burgundy cape
with the fur collar?" Marjorie pointed toward the duke.

"Yes, milady. Earlier, I overheard him mention to your
driver that he'd be taking you home in his carriage."

Her face pinched with anger. She glowered at the duke's
back, while he continued saying his goodbyes to the Countess
Malvern. The woman's arm had latched onto his in a proprietary
manner.

Marjorie's ears had not yet recovered from the tongue-
lashing the duke had given her about her interference with
Crosswell. Well, thank goodness she hadn't agreed to marry him,
he had to be the most ungrateful man she had ever met. Her goal
had been to avoid him after the ball, now he had gone and
interfered with her plans to get home.

She inhaled a fortifying breath, before marching up the
stairs, just in time to watch the Countess Malvern move a step
closer to the duke. Marjorie seethed, not knowing why she

disliked the woman. The countess seemed nice enough, and she always looked like an angel, which didn't help matters. Without a doubt, she would make a perfect duchess. However, that wasn't her concern at the moment. Edgar was to blame for her predicament, and now he had to account for himself.

"What have you done with my coach and driver?" she snapped at his back.

Several people within hearing, turned toward them. Edgar, unfazed by this lapse in protocol, looked over his shoulder at her as if he were examining a fly that needed swatting. He didn't answer, perhaps because he was still angry with her. Instead, he bid the countess goodbye, and then waited for the woman to leave.

"Don't you dare look at me as if I were an ogre," Marjorie hissed. "I saved you from a potentially damaging situation; you should be thanking me." She folded her arms wanting to appear determined. "Now, tell me what have you done with my coach and driver?"

Edgar again didn't respond. He studied her face as if she were a valuable piece of porcelain.

Rupert, standing close by interrupted their protracted silence. His cloak had concealed his Henry VIII costume, however, he still wore the matching crown.

"Marjorie, we are taking you home. It is not safe for you to be traveling alone through the city. One driver and a footman are hardly enough protection at this time of the morning." He then adjusted his crown. "This is all my fault; I was supposed to tell you about the change in plans. By the way, Happy New Year! I didn't get a chance to greet you earlier."

Marjorie felt like unleashing her anger on someone, but she knew it would be wasted on Rupert. Instead, she snorted, her lips compressing into a stiff line.

"Ah … Good! That's settled then," Rupert said. "I thought you'd be so angry you might want to shoot me with one of Tiffany's arrows. By the way, where is Tiffany?"

Marjorie groaned, nodding below to where Tiffany stood on the steps, saying her goodbyes to Lord Albey.

Too late, she realized that the duke had stepped toward her, and interwoven his arm with hers. "I believe the coaches have arrived," he said, without preamble.

"Coaches?" Marjorie said, surprised.

"Yes," Edgar said. "Two coaches create a better show of force."

She didn't believe him.

Then Rupert left, muttering something about fetching Tiffany. Something felt amiss, but Marjorie didn't know what.

Once assembled, the small group moved toward the vehicles. Edgar lifted Marjorie up to the first step, he seemed to be in some sort of hurry. Before Marjorie could protest the seating arrangements, the door of the carriage closed.

"But I need a chaperone!"

"You have me," Edgar said, smiling.

She frowned.

"Anyway, at this time of night no one will notice."

She gazed out of the window. Of course, it was pitch dark, and there was no view to speak of. When her teeth chattered, Edgar had the perfect excuse to move next to her from the opposite seat. He positioned her in the crook of his arm, ignoring her protests. Soon she gave up the struggle to sit straight, simple exhaustion forcing her head to fall on his shoulder.

"I'm sure you will feel warm in no time," he whispered.

She half-dozed, nestling closer to him. At one point she imagined his hand moving to stroke her back; she sighed, relaxing against the padded cushions. Sleep felt wonderful, it also helped her forget, at least for a moment, about being alone in the dead of night, with the man she loved.

***

Edgar nudged her arm. "Marjorie dear, wake up. We will be resting here before we continue our journey."

She yawned, licking her lips.

"Home at last. I can't wait to soak my feet, they feel quite stiff." She had forgotten how angry she had been prior to her nap, and Edgar didn't think it was wise to remind her.

She peered out of the window, squinting.

"Where are we?" she asked.

Edgar adjusted her tilted spectacles.

"We have stopped at an inn on the East Road."

"Why?" Marjorie responded. She stared at him, waiting for the rest of his explanation.

But Edgar didn't offer any more information, he just moved to open the door.

Her arm shot out, grabbing a fist full of his fur collar. "Why have we stopped here?"

"I already explained; we will rest here before we continue our journey."

"But I don't understand?" She sounded confused. "Why aren't we heading home—home toward Grosvenor Square?"

"I am taking you home, madame, home to Penmore. Rupert and I thought it would be easier and safer to simply head out tonight, particularly since you planned to leave London tomorrow. This way I can serve as your escort, and at the same time, enjoy more of your delightful company."

He really wasn't lying, Edgar thought, he just wasn't telling her the whole truth. The whole truth would serve no purpose, but to make her angrier.

"But I don't need your escort," she said. "And, what about my luggage; and my servants?"

"I took the liberty of making all the arrangements. Your servants and luggage have already left London. This is far more expeditious, don't you agree?"

"No, I don't agree," Marjorie shouted. "I am not staying here. More precisely, I am not staying here with *you*."

"Well, if I must arrange a separate room, I will. However, I do think it would be best if we occupied one room," he said, smiling at her horrified expression.

"I repeat, I won't stay *anywhere with you*. Now, I would like to go home—to my home in London."

"Be patient, madame," he said, opening the door of the carriage, where Jones stood waiting.

"Did you explain everything to the innkeeper?"

"Yes, Your Grace."

"Everything?"

"Everything," Jones replied, using one of his curt soldierly responses.

Edgar felt relieved she hadn't asked more questions. No doubt, telling her about the short detour they were taking to Grangefield Hall, and arranging for Pierce to marry them at the vicarage, would only complicate matters. As far as Edgar was concerned, the less Marjorie knew about his plans the better.

Realizing that she was the only woman he wanted to marry had been a revelation. Now he hoped convincing her would not be too difficult. The timing had to be just so, or all his plans would go awry. He extended his hand:

"Come along, m' dear."

"I'm not getting out of this coach."

"Of course you are," he said with confidence.

"I'm not." She scooted toward the other door, but Edgar anticipated her move, nudging Jones into action.

The burly driver rushed around, opening the opposite door, and extending a hand to assist Marjorie down.

"I suppose you are traveling to Penmore with us, Jones?"

Edgar noted that Jones said nothing, looking down at the dirt-covered pathway.

"Don't abuse my valet, my dear." He extended his hand to her. "Come along; nothing will be gained if you keep making a fuss."

"When the situation goes beyond the bounds of acceptable behavior, you don't want me to make a fuss? Really, Edgar, you can be quite obtuse at times."

Edgar didn't respond. "Must I remind you, you're the one who wanted to leave London in the first place."

Marjorie huffed, giving him a "I hate you" look, before reluctantly taking his hand. "As soon as I am permitted to warm myself in front of a nice fire, I will have a full explanation."

"I thought I just gave you one," Edgar replied, using his best no nonsense tone.

Marjorie descended, and Edgar led her toward the inn and the waiting innkeeper. The balding man stood at the door, wringing his hands with glee. A lamp hung on a nail close by, illuminating his bald head.

"Bartholomew Potts, Your Grace, at your service."

He had spoken to Marjorie as though she were a duchess.

He then bowed over his extended belly. "I'm right honored to have you both spend the night at mi'inn. We have all the creature comforts you'll be needing."

Edgar didn't bother to correct his misuse of her title. Instead, he dragged her along using the crook of her arm.

"I say, slow down, you're walking too fast," Marjorie complained.

"Which room, innkeeper?" Edgar asked, ignoring her.

"It's Bartholomew Potts, Your Grace."

"Which room, Mr. Potts?" Edgar repeated.

"First door, up the stairs," he said, offering a startled expression. "It's been ready for hours. I'll just go fetch the hot water for washing," he mumbled, before disappearing inside the inn.

"Tell him the hot water can wait until morning, Jones," Edgar said, looking over his shoulder.

He then led Marjorie through the poorly lit entryway and up a short flight of creaking stairs. When they reached the first door, he opened it as if he were expecting an ambush.

Marjorie strode passed him into the room, removing her long gloves, finger by finger with angry tugs.

Edgar watched with amusement as she inspected the room. Her eyes stopped at the oversized bed, covered with a laundered white sheet. Another sheet and three folded blankets had been piled on top of a nearby chair, and a blazing fire crackled in the hearth.

Edgar felt too tired, and he didn't have the energy to explain anything to anyone. Planning this little undertaking had taken most of the day. All he wanted to do was go to bed, and if she would allow it, hold her in his arms.

Too bad her expression looked determined. She had already tossed the sheet and blankets onto the bed, sitting down on the chair, her fists clenched on top of her lap.

"You're time is up, Your Grace. I want some answers, and I want them now."

Edgar sighed. The battle was afoot, and with regret, he realized his adversary was refreshed, and ready for the fight.

~ ~ ~

Chapter Twenty

"Well?"

"Well what?" Edgar replied, unfolding the sheet and each of the blankets, and spreading them out on the bed.

"You know very well what. I would like some answers, if you please." She had tipped back her spectacles with such force that Edgar imagined her finger had poked through the glass lens.

"I told you, I'm escorting you to Penmore."

"Stop spouting nonsense," Marjorie spluttered. "You and I both know that I don't need an escort to Penmore. Now, why have you brought me here?"

If she wanted to interrogate him, Edgar thought, he might as well be comfortable. He moved to the door, unbuckling his sword belt: It dropped to the floor. Next, he removed his cape; the metal breastplate followed; and then the armored skirt of metal slats. Finding no place to put them, they clattered in front of the door in a heap, looking like a pile of weaponry discarded by a fleeing army.

He stretched, then walked toward Marjorie. All he had on was the short white shift, his erection all too evident.

He smiled when he saw her shiver.

"Are you cold, madame?"

"No!"

"Hot, perhaps?"

"No," she said, clearing her throat. "I'm waiting, Your Grace."

He sat on the bed, removing the laurel leaf crown and placing it on the floor. "Actually, we are headed for Penmore; however, we will be making a short detour to pick up Sabeer at Grangefield Hall. Then we will proceed to the village, where Pierce will marry us at the vicarage."

"I see."

She sounded calm, even rational, he thought.

"We will be married tomorrow."

"Don't be absurd," Marjorie said, standing up too quickly. She lost her balance, falling back onto the chair.

"You said you would marry me, and I procured the license," Edgar said.

"I suggested we marry. As I recall, you found some objection with my reasoning; we did not agree to anything. Now, if we have concluded this discussion, I would like to go home. As I understand it, you can cross out the name on that marriage license and replace it with the name of someone more willing."

Irrational, Edgar thought. He felt almost sorry that he had to mislead her, but now he had no choice. Standing, he walked toward the hearth. One by one he doused the three lone candles using the pads of his fingers.

"What are you doing?" Marjorie asked, sounding nervous.

He didn't answer until he returned to the bed, pulling back the top sheet and blankets.

"I'm preparing to go to bed," Edgar replied.

"You can't do that."

"Of course I can, I'm tired."

He sat down on the edge of the bed, tugging off the chemise and drawing it over his head, this left him naked. For modesty's sake, he slid his legs under the sheet and blankets, covering his body to the waist. Only a lone candle illuminated. Stretching out, his fingers snuffed the flame, immersing the room in pitch darkness. Any remaining light came from the fire in the grate.

"Good Lord! Why on earth did you do that? Now I won't be able to get to the door," she muttered.

"The door is locked. If I were you I wouldn't try."

"Have you gone mad, Your Grace? I must go home at once, by tomorrow my reputation will be in tatters." She took an anxious breath. "If that happens, even the Queen won't receive me. I demand that you arise this instant and return me to London."

Edgar smiled, now he definitely had time enough to declare his new found feelings to her. "We will be married tomorrow; your reputation will no doubt be improved by our union; you will not need to make an appointment to see the

370

Queen. It is well-known marrying a duke bestows certain

privileges, like barging into the palace unannounced."

Marjorie snorted. "I will not be barging into the palace,

and I certainly won't be marrying a duke tomorrow."

Edgar had to concede she did sound very upset, perhaps

he should take pity on her. He fanned the bed sheet. "First, I

don't know how to say this without upsetting you, but we are not

returning to London until I have rested.

"Second, I don't want to force you to do anything against

your will. That said, I promise that after we have both had a good

night's rest, we will discuss the situation to our mutual

satisfaction. If you decide that you still do not want to marry me,

I will return you home. Together, we can find a suitable excuse

to explain your absence, without any consequences. Now, please

come to bed."

The crackling of the flames in the hearth were the only

sounds he heard. Edgar felt reasonably assured that Marjorie

understood the terms of her exile, and would not attempt

anything stupid, like climbing out of the window, which thankfully she had not thought of.

Edgar heard a loud clink, then something dropped to the floor. That had to be the gold amulet she wore around her neck: What a relief she had decided to be sensible.

He then heard her feet pad the two steps toward the bed. In the dark he could make out that she touched her face, and then secured a small bundle under the bed.

Her spectacles. Damn! He had wanted to remove those himself.

Then she flounced on the bed, bending down to remove her sandals. He imagined she still wore her cape, and probably everything else. Her feet lifted, and adjusted under the sheet, and then she took several seconds to arrange each article of clothing before lying prostrate, like an entombed mummy.

Edgar sighed, raising onto one arm so he could see her face in the firelight.

"At least take off your cloak," he whispered.

"No."

"You will feel more comfortable," he offered.

"No."

"Are you still angry?"

She didn't reply. Edgar smiled. "Silence is an encouraging sign."

She snorted.

"Let me at least unpin your hair; I know you need help with that wig."

She didn't respond. Taking that as a sign of her willingness, he hoisted himself up to a seated position. Thankfully there was enough light from the fireplace to get the job done.

Within moments he had dislodged the hairpins and removed the short wig. He fanned out her dark curls, spreading them across the pillow. The scent of lemons permeated the air.

She sighed.

"Better?"

No response. Edgar smiled, again repositioning his body so he laid next to her, on his side.

"Marjorie?"

More silence.

"I want you to know that I'm not proposing we marry because of the terms of the will."

He slipped his arm across the top of her pillow until his hand could caress her cloak-covered shoulder.

She tried to shrug him off, but Edgar persisted.

"I admit, you caught me off guard when you mentioned your affection for Sabeer; and I needed some time to understand the situation better. I now realize how important it is that the two of you like one another, and I feel doubly fortunate that Sabeer has become fond of you."

No answer.

"Only Rupert knows this, but shortly after arriving in England, I took the liberty of writing to the Queen via my solicitor. If you will recall my marriage to Chamine was performed in a Hindu ceremony, and there was no official license or proper witness. According to English law, marriages must be performed in a church to be considered legal.

"In my correspondence, I made a formal request to Her Majesty. If the inheritance should revert to the crown, which it will if I don't marry before the specified time indicated in my father's will, the fortune should be returned to me. The Queen agreed, and now I no longer have to marry anyone."

He paused. "What I am trying to say, and making a complete hash of it is, I care for you, Marjorie. The feelings I have for you are different from those I had for Chamine, but I can honestly say they are very heartfelt.

"In conclusion, Lady Tate, I have discovered that I am quite in love with you."

Edgar supposed a simple kiss would have amply conveyed her sentiments, but instead, Marjorie's chilled feet landed on his bare legs. He would have yowled, but instead, he pulled her closer to him.

He raised himself up until he could see her eyelashes flutter. His lips brushed her mouth, then trailed kisses across her cheek, returning to her lips. Her mouth opened, and he deepened the kiss.

"I do love you," he repeated.

"I believe you," she said, trailing her fingers across his cheek. Her breathing sounded ragged as she clasped his bare arms. "I fear I will always need you, my lord." It sounded as if this statement had been difficult to disclose.

Edgar understood her restraint, placing another light kiss on her lips. "As usual, you have too many clothes on, madame," he whispered, untying her cape.

Within moments the garment lay spooled on the ground next to the bed. The sheer silk fabric of her costume stretched across her puckered nipples, allowing Edgar's hands to find them. He massaged, and she moaned her approval. Her thighs spread, and he wedged his hand between them, caressing her.

"No bloomers?" he said.

She shook her head.

Reaching with his other hand, he loosened the ties of dress. It didn't take long for her gown and shift to join her cape, and then she was naked.

Edgar lifted her arms above her head, moving on top of her. His legs clasped about her thighs.

She squeaked a small protest when Edgar redistributed his weight.

"Did you select that delicious costume for my benefit, madame?" he said, smiling at her.

"Yes." The tentative response sounded more like a moan.

"Are you ready to admit that you care for me, too?"

Silence.

Edgar couldn't wait, covering her mouth with his. He knew that the kiss felt rough, but he also knew he needed to convey his deep longing for her.

His arousal felt erect and ready. She would be his wife in a matter of hours, and after that she would be his forever.

Edgar noted that her breathing sounded uneven as he massaged her skin, at the same time kissing her mouth. Then lifting her hips, he entered her without hesitation. He savored each pant, each moan, each cry, as his thighs smothered her hips.

The scream of pleasure was hers.

"Say the words, Marjorie," Edgar whispered in her ear. "Tell me you will marry me; I need to know how you feel."

Marjorie embraced him tightly. He sensed her release would happen soon.

"Say it."

She didn't respond.

He thrust again. She moaned. He pushed deeper, securing his body into hers. Their release came quickly, his seed pouring into her.

When his body relaxed, Edgar returned to his side of the bed, Marjorie clinging to his side.

"At least you want me," he muttered.

"I do. God help me, I do," Marjorie whispered in his ear, kissing his cheek.

"Will you marry me tomorrow?"

She kissed the base of his neck, while caressing the hairs on his chest. She had draped her naked body across his. "I w..."

Before she could finish her sentence, a loud banging sound came from below stairs. A dog started barking, and Edgar raised himself up, his body alert and honed for combat.

Marjorie moved away from him, scrambling beneath the bed for her spectacles.

"Don't move," Edgar said, searching for his discarded toga in the dark. His fingers latched onto it, and in two movements he slipped it over his head, then stood beside the bed.

"You can't see."

Edgar snorted. "Of course I can see."

"You can't, it's too dark."

"As usual, madame, your powers of deduction never fail to amaze me," Edgar said.

"You will hurt yourself," Marjorie said.

"I will not ... uuff!"

"I told you."

Edgar said nothing, rummaging through the pile of armor and clothing.

After putting on his sandals and cape, he made judicious movements, until he reached the door. He could hear the sound of male voices in heated conversation. First, he recognized the innkeeper's voice, the man was repeating the same phrase:

"He's not here, I tell you."

He sounded as if he were shouting to a large riotous crowd.

Moving toward the hearth, Edgar lit two candles with the smoldering embers. He secured one in a candle holder, raising the other toward Marjorie.

"Is that enough light for you to get dressed?"

"I think so," she said, standing up. He was rewarded with a magnificent display of her naked back, buttocks, and the rigid outline of her spine.

"We will finish this later," he said, hearing a slight hitch in his voice. "I promise."

Marjorie looked over her shoulder, smiling at him. She then shrugged into her shift and the white silk gown.

The voices were getting louder.

"I know he's bloody well here, you can't tell me
otherwise," a man's voice insisted.

Edgar recognized the voice.

"That's Rupert."

"No! He will discover us together," Marjorie
stammered.

"He knows we are together," Edgar said.

"He *knows* we are together? Together *like this*?" she said,
draping her cape about her shoulders.

"He helped me make the arrangements."

"He helped you?"

"Marjorie, I'm sorry I had to deceive you, but you were
being difficult, and I had to do something drastic. However, now
we must find out why Rupert is here, his sudden arrival is not
part of the plan: I fear it must be something important, or he
wouldn't have come. "

"Rupert knew?"

"Yes, Rupert knew," he mumbled, trying to ignore her
frown as he opened the door.

Rupert had been about to knock, his two fists poised as if they were about to batter down the door.

"What has happened?" Edgar asked, looking at the urgent expression on his brother's face. Edgar heard something behind Rupert, and watched as a troop of people marched up the narrow staircase.

"I tried to stop 'em, Your Grace," the innkeeper said, shouting from behind the pack, "but that toffee-nosed gent insisted that he knows you. Says he's your brother: Kept saying it, he did. Plus, that old geezer, the one with all them wrinkles—he scared me half to death. Don't smile much, does he?"

It was then Edgar noticed Albert. In sentry formation, behind him stood Mr. Jones, knotting the ties of his britches.

"Albert, why aren't you at Grangefield Hall?"

"What has happened?" Marjorie said, from behind Edgar's shoulder. "Did I hear you say Albert is here?"

Edgar groaned.

She repositioned her spectacles. "Good Lord! Albert do come in and sit down, you look exhausted."

382

"Didn't I tell you to stay inside?" Edgar said, using a raised voice.

"You did," Marjorie said.

"So why didn't you listen?"

"To you?" she said, "don't be absurd."

Edgar raised his hands in a defeated gesture, looking to Rupert for an explanation.

"What has happened?" he asked his brother.

If it were at all possible, Rupert looked even more morose. The fingers of one of his hands fidgeted with his moustache.

"Speak up, man! What has happened?" Edgar bellowed.

"It ... It's Sabeer."

Edgar cheeks felt warm. His hands grabbed the lapels of Rupert's heavy topcoat, dragging him forward with enough force that both men stood toe to toe. "What about Sabeer?" Edgar shouted.

"I'm sorry to be the one to inform you, Edgar," Rupert said, fear etched on his face. "I ... I ... Oh, God," he spluttered. "Sabeer has gone missing."

"What?" Edgar said, astonished. "What do you mean, missing?"

Rupert licked his lips. "He's been kidnapped. A note was left in his room."

He paused. "But they don't want to keep the boy, Edgar. They want to give him up, that's what the note said."

The duke glanced over his shoulder at Marjorie; her complexion had paled. At some point she had hooked her arm in his, whether it was for restraint or comfort, he was not sure.

Rupert continued. "As I said, they want to give the boy up, but only if they can exchange him."

"And, what do they want to exchange him for?" Edgar asked.

Rupert glanced down at his shoes, hesitating. Then he looked up, his expression serious.

"Edgar, the note said Sabeer is just the bait—they really want you instead."

~ ~ ~

Chapter Twenty-One

Edgar glared at Marjorie. "For the last time, I said you're not going."

"Don't be absurd, Your Grace. Of course, I'm going."

"Madame, I have given you leave to call me by my first name, after all, we are going to be married."

"You are?" Rupert asked, his eyes blinking with astonishment.

"Yes, damn it, we are," Edgar replied.

"I have not agreed."

"Whether you agree or not is beside the point. In light of recent events, because I can't marry you as planned, and I can't return you to London, your reputation will soon be in tatters."

"Regardless, as I said," Marjorie stated, adjusting her spectacles, "I have not agreed."

Edgar was furious. "We will argue about this later; at the moment I have other things on my mind. Rupert, where do we go from here?"

"What?"

Edgar shouted. "Where in the hell do they have Sabeer?"

Rupert uncovered his ears. "The East End. Sounds very melodramatic, but apparently he is being held in a deserted warehouse."

"Jones, get the carriage ready."

"Yes, Your Grace."

Jones bolted down the risers, taking two steps at a time. Edgar turned toward Rupert. "We must alert the authorities in London; whoever took Sabeer must be caught and charged with kidnapping. Albert, how long has the boy been gone?"

Marjorie noticed Albert had difficulty standing, his eyes also looked bloodshot.

"I noticed his absence at approximately four o'clock last evening, Your Grace. After finding the note, I had the grounds searched thoroughly. Not finding Master Sabeer, I headed straight for London."

Satisfied, Edgar turned to his brother. "Rupert, take Albert and Marjorie back to my London house. After that, round up the police and bring them to the docks; I will travel there now to search for Sabeer."

"You're going alone?" Marjorie asked, stupefied.

"I have no choice," he said. "Anyway, I won't be alone, Jones will be with me."

Marjorie inched a cautious step forward. "The dangers appear unclear, therefore Albert and I must go with you."

Edgar scoffed. "That is out of the question. I want you safe in London. Also, if you had not noticed, your faithful retainer can barely stand on his own two legs, he's exhausted."

"Albert can take a nap during the coach ride to London, isn't that right, Albert?"

"Yes, madame," Albert muttered.

"That's settled," Marjorie said. "We will see you in the coach. Come along, Albert."

She located her reticule, and then adjusted her spectacles, before heading toward the staircase.

One of Edgar's sandal-covered feet stomped down hard on the edge of her cloak. The material bunched, clasping at Marjorie's throat.

"I repeat, you are not going anywhere."

"I'm choking, Your Grace."

Edgar lifted his foot, and she lurched attempting to steady herself. The cloak unclasped, cascading to the floor.

"Madame, if I have to go and locate a rope to tie you to the bedposts, I will. The only place you are going is back to London."

"I am free to do as I please, whether you agree or not, Albert and I are going with you. The boy means a great deal to me, and I have quite made up my mind."

Edgar bent down to retrieve her fallen cloak.

"This is not the time or place for you to behave like a shrew. Do what you bloody well like," he growled, moving past her, heading downstairs.

***

Astonished, Marjorie stared at his receding form; why had he relented so easily?

"Do you suppose this means I can go?" she asked Rupert.

"It appears so," Rupert said.

"Do you think he means it?"

Rupert didn't get a chance to respond, hearing Edgar bellow for them to get a move on.

"Madame, time is of the essence," the duke shouted. "We need to be on our way if we plan to head for London."

Suspicious, Marjorie looked down the staircase. She watched the duke unfurl her cape, shaking it to remove any dust. Taking her cue, she descended the stairs, followed by Rupert and Albert. Edgar held out the garment like a large banner.

"Put this on, I don't want you catching a cold."

Marjorie moved toward the cloak, and into his embrace, relishing his concern for her comfort. She lifted her arms to button the clasp. The next thing she knew Edgar's arms had encircled hers in a vice-like grip, and a handkerchief had been stuffed into her mouth. He then dragged her backward, while she kicked in protest. Gagging, Marjorie noticed the innkeeper

holding open the door to a small closet. Edgar pushed her inside,

and the innkeeper shut and bolted the door.

Marjorie spat out the handkerchief, shouting an

unladylike expletive she'd heard one of the servants saying. She

proffered a satisfied grunt as she kicked the closet door, then she

yowled with pain, staring at her open-toed sandals. Bad decision,

she thought.

She heard Edgar giving instructions. "Stay with her,

Albert. If you so much as touches that door, and I live to hear

about it, you will face the consequences, which could include a

demotion to lower footman."

Albert must have nodded, because Marjorie didn't hear a

response. Good Lord! Lower footman status, that must have

upset him, she thought.

"This is for her safety," the duke added. "If she tags

along, she will either get in the way or get injured. You do

understand, don't you?"

Albert probably wore his grim expression, Marjorie thought.

"Don't worry, man, she adores you," the duke continued, "eventually she might even forgive you."

All the while they ignored her screams and threats. Of course, she had not stopped shouting, except to tend to her stubbed toe, which Marjorie felt sure would become quite bruised.

"Enough dilly-dallying, let's be on our way, Rupert." That was the last she heard of Edgar before her world became devoid of the Eighth Duke of Grangefield.

***

Marjorie, with her throat quite raw from shouting, had settled down on the floor of what appeared to be a wine closet, absent the wine bottles. Her obstacles included two large beer kegs and several glass jars covered with muslin clothes. Mead, she thought after bending closer to smell the jar covers.

She had nothing to sit on, so she crouched on the floor. She had used her time alone to assess her feelings for Edgar

Hamilton. She had already forgiven the duke for his abominable behavior. Logically, she agreed, the mission would be dangerous. Beyond that, Marjorie felt angry. She had never considered herself incapable of anything in her life, and she simply could not start thinking that way now. Damn him to hell, no man had the right to debase her abilities.

"Albert! Are you out there?"

Marjorie heard the shuffling of feet, then the clearing of a male voice.

"Albert, I promise not to tell the duke if you open the door."

No answer.

"Albert!"

A chair scraped against the wood floor.

"Albert, he needs our help. Just because he was a soldier doesn't mean he's invincible. It would be another matter if Rupert had gone with him, but Rupert is heading in a different direction, which leaves the duke alone; except for Mr. Jones, of course, who I suppose is quite capable, but still just a single person."

No response.

She had to find a way to get out of this dismal little room.

"Albert, go fetch the innkeeper."

She sensed his hesitation.

"Albert, if you don't go get the innkeeper, I will make a solemn promise of my own, I will demote you to the rank of silver-polisher; I can do it, you know."

The next sounds were scrapings, followed by two distinct sets of male footsteps and heavy panting, followed by scratching at the closet door. Marjorie concluded that the scratching sounds were being made by large dog paws. The panting could either have been the innkeeper or his dog, Marjorie was unsure.

"Stop that, Rollo! You don't want to be frightening Her Ladyship," the innkeeper muttered.

Marjorie heard the dog give a big sigh before lumbering down beside the door.

"Milady, how may I assist you?" the innkeeper said.

"You can unbolt this door, if you please."

"Now, I can't be doing that, Your Grace."

Marjorie ignored his reference to her being the duke's wife.

"Why ever not? The duke has left, and so has his brother. There is no reason why I should remain locked up in here."

"Well, His Grace insisted. He told me you weren't to see the light of day until tomorrow."

"Did he pay you?"

"Ten shillings now, and a full gold piece tomorrow," the innkeeper said with enthusiasm.

Marjorie saw her opportunity for freedom. "You realize that the duke has embarked on a rather perilous mission. Did you consider that he may not return to pay you that gold piece?"

A deafening silence followed. The innkeeper evaluated his situation—sensible man.

Marjorie decided to exercise her advantage. "The duke could get shot, he could fall and lose his memory. Indeed, a great deal could happen between now and tomorrow."

She held an ear to the door, waiting for his answer.

"You had me going for a minute, Your Grace. Being that your husband was a captain in the army, I'm sure he knows what he's about, and having you in the closet is part of his plan."

It seemed the innkeeper would not be convinced.

"Well, if you are certain you want to take the risk?"

"When it's time for your breakfast, I'll let you out," he said.

No, that wouldn't do at all, Marjorie thought.

"I say, innkeeper. Mr. Potts, is it?"

"Yes, Your Grace."

"I'm more than certain Albert, standing beside you, can vouch for me. I'm a woman of considerable financial means."

"He's nodding, milady. He seems like a gent that can be trusted. He's been sitting out 'ere like a dog guarding a blooming bone. Not even Rollo could hav' done a better job."

"Well, Albert has always taken his responsibilities very seriously."

"Yes, Your Grace."

"As I was saying, Mr. Potts, if you open the door, I will double the amount the duke has offered you, and I will add a good supply of potatoes—fresh potatoes; enough for a full year."

"You got crops?"

"Indeed I do, Mr. Potts," Marjorie said, smiling, "I have all sorts of crops."

"Got carrots?"

"Yes, I grow carrots."

"How about turnips?"

Marjorie's breath hitched. "I say, Mr. Potts, potatoes and carrots are my absolute limit."

"Well, need I be reminding you, milady, you're the one who's locked in the closet."

"Yes, I suppose you're right," Marjorie said, disgusted. "What else do you want?"

"My missus likes her greens, she does."

"Well, I suppose I could add some peas when they are in season."

"Then you've got yourself a bargain, Your Grace."

Marjorie heard the bolt being struck, even as she mumbled to herself that the price had been entirely too high. Her vision soon adjusted as dim light filled the closet.

"Shall we shake on that, milady?" Mr. Potts said.

"Oh, I suppose so," Marjorie said, extending her hand to his sweaty palm, at the same time stepping toward freedom.

Albert stood behind him.

"Don't worry, you didn't touch the door," Marjorie said, responding to his anxious expression.

"I had every confidence in your abilities, madame."

Marjorie smiled.

"All right, Mr. Potts, what will it cost me to borrow both you and your gig for a quick jaunt to London?"

"No gig, Your Grace. All I have is a market cart with a pony. I also know a couple of quick back roads to London."

"Then it will have to be the market cart and pony," Marjorie said, realizing that this would slow down their journey to London.

The innkeeper still looked undecided.

"I should mention," Marjorie said, "Albert doesn't know how to drive any sort of conveyance. For some reason he has never bothered to learn because he thinks it's beneath him, which of course it is. Unfortunately, I don't have a lower footman at my disposal. That being the case, I will need a driver, and you appear to be available. I presume you know where the docks are?"

Mr. Potts didn't reply.

Marjorie felt her nose wrinkle. She adjusted her spectacles. "How does a pitcher of flaxseed oil sound?"

"You got oil as well?" he said, with awe.

"I do indeed," Marjorie said, not thrilled at all with this bargaining experience.

The innkeeper's expression now carried a huge smile. He jerked the corners of his black vest over his protruding stomach, which Marjorie noticed had not been properly buttoned.

"My missus will be right pleased, Your Grace."

"I'm sure she will," Marjorie replied, dryly. "In fact, Mr. Potts, I'm sure she'll be doubly pleased that you drive a very impressive bargain."

~ ~ ~

Marjorie huddled in her cloak, grateful it was heavy enough to ward off the early morning chill. The main road heading toward the heart of London brimmed with early morning activity.

"I'm positive the duke will not be pleased to see us," she said.

"I would concur, madame," Albert replied, with a morose tone.

"I'm also positive His Grace will have a fit."

"Again, I concur, madame."

At that moment Marjorie had more to worry about than Albert's curt responses. With Mr. Potts driving the market cart, they had entered the city over an hour ago. The docks were in a less traveled area, and it was well-known that cutthroats and thieves frequented the streets leading eastward.

Mr. Potts produced a concealed pitchfork from under the hay, which he moved close to his side. Marjorie noticed that

Albert had inched closer to her, his hand resting on the edge of her cloak. She supposed he wanted to catch her if she fell down, or perhaps even ward off some hoodlum, who might decide to molest her. To help, she arranged her cloak so the garment completely covered her head, as well as the white silk of her gown, making her look like a monk en route to Canterbury Cathedral.

"Mr. Potts mentioned that we have almost reached the docks," Marjorie said.

"Yes, madame?"

"Do you think I should contrive a plan?" Marjorie ventured.

"I don't think so, madame."

Marjorie looked at him, surprised. "Why ever not?"

"I don't think it would be wise for me to say; my position being in jeopardy, and so on, and so forth."

Marjorie straightened her back. "Your position was never in jeopardy, and you well know it."

"I would still rather not say, madame."

"I insist."

Albert regarded her. The wrinkles on his forehead had bunched, which usually indicated that he was displeased about something. He moved his hand from the edge of her cloak, adjusting his bowler hat, then plucked off a strand of straw that had dared to land on the sleeve of his gray coat.

"Your plans, madame, at times have a tendency to go aground."

"Go aground?" Marjorie repeated.

"Madame, it might be best to locate His Grace before making any 'plans' of your own."

That said, they both ignored one another for the remainder of the journey, although Albert's hand did reattach to her cloak.

"It's just around the bend, milady," Mr. Potts shouted.

The cart turned the last corner, and they entered an alley leading toward a cluster of warehouses.

"It's the second building on the right," Potts said. "That's the address I heard that Rupert-fella give Mr. Jones."

Jasper, their pony, started snorting, then his trot becoming more skittish.

"It's all right, lad, we'll be stopping in a minute, then I'll give you some of that sweet hay from the back," Potts said.

Marjorie noted that Jasper understood the word hay, rearing his head appreciatively. But he now brayed louder, and Mr. Potts continued to have trouble controlling the reins.

"God help 'em, milady!" Mr. Potts shouted, "Look up there!"

Marjorie smelled something peculiar. Looking up, she saw the thick smoke.

"Good Lord! The warehouse is on fire!"

Her hood fell down as she looked about for signs of life. She realized in that section of the city no one would respond to a fire; in addition, there would be no one to ask for help.

"Can you see the duke, Mr. Potts, or for that matter, Mr. Jones?"

"No, milady, there's too much smoke."

"Oh, dear, I do hope we're not too late."

Albert produced a handkerchief, and immediately covered his mouth. "Madame, the smoke is quite thick, and the fire appears well out of control."

Marjorie coughed, covering her mouth with her hand.

"Jasper's frightened, I can't go any closer," Mr. Potts said. "I'll let you off here, then see to the cart."

"Yes, by all means, Mr. Potts," Marjorie said, noticing the icy pavement, and carefully jumping off the cart.

Albert also disembarked, and Mr. Potts then steered the cart away.

"Albert, I must find His Grace." She knew she sounded unsure, and her heartbeat now raced: She had never felt so anxious.

"That would not be wise, madame," Albert said.

With all the thick smoke surrounding them Marjorie was glad that he stood close by and had grabbed a hold of her cloak.

"But the duke could be hurt, or even dead."

The last word she had been said as an afterthought, but that didn't stop her eyes from tearing.

She moved a step toward the burning warehouse.

"I hope the duke has located the boy by now," she said.

Then a large rough hand appeared, jerking her to the ground.

"Albert, get to the ground," Edgar shouted.

"Oh, Your Grace, there you are," Marjorie said, relieved. "I'm so glad to see you."

She offered him a huge smile. There was less smoke closer to the ground, and she could see his face. She wanted to smooth away all those angry lines on his face.

"I'm so glad you're all right," she said. Then her gloved fingers lifted and stroked Edgar's cheek.

The wicked dimple, which appeared in Edgar's chin whenever he grinned, had recessed to form a large cleft. He wasn't pleased to see her; Marjorie frowned.

"Oh, do stop looking at me like that, Your Grace."

From their crouched position he started to shake her shoulders. Marjorie's hair spilled out of its knot, and quickly became covered with flying ash.

"I can assure you that I am quite awake, Your Grace, no need for you to make sure."

"Marjorie," the duke said, with deathly calm. He had stopped shaking her.

"Yes, Edgar."

He paused. "Marjorie, why are you here?" he asked.

"I have come to help you find Sabeer."

"Do you think I am incapable of a simple rescue?"

"No, of course not."

"Then why did you disobey my instructions?"

"I didn't agree to them in the first place."

He stared at her, his expression unreadable.

"Marjorie, I delayed rescuing Sabeer because Jones spotted you and Albert on the back of that cart. With the added danger of the fire, I could not risk having you in harm's way.

Now time is running out, and your arrival has complicated

matters. "

"But, you love me."

"We have established that fact," he said with a patient

tone. "But now I must go search for Sabeer."

Marjorie's eyes started to tear. Edgar pulled her closer,

kissing her forehead.

"Marjorie, nothing is going to happen to me. However,

you must stay here with Albert. I have to go inside that building,"

he pointed, "the information provided by the kidnapper said

Sabeer is in there." He adjusted her spectacles. Marjorie clung to

his arm, as he tried to set her away from him.

"I'm coming with you," she said, then noticed his angry

expression. "Well, at least as far as the entrance."

"All right," Edgar said, "but you will stay outside; do you

understand?"

She nodded, looking up at his face, still sniffing, and

drying her tears with the edge of her cloak.

Edgar wanted to hone his point. "These buildings are old and not well-maintained. From this vantage point the fire appears minimal, but it is difficult to tell how quickly it will spread. If it gets worse, the roof might collapse." He held her at arm's distance. "Promise me you will stay here, Marjorie."

"I promise," she replied, her voice hushed.

Edgar then hurried off; he didn't look back.

***

Marjorie gnawed on her knuckles, watching Edgar disappear into the smoky haze, and then enter the burning warehouse.

Looking for Albert, she discovered that he had been standing beside her all along.

"Albert, the duke has instructed me to stand over there."

"Very good, madame."

"Mr. Potts has not returned," she said, needing to occupy her thoughts with idle chatter.

Albert didn't respond. Marjorie felt sure his face was scrunched with concern, which always made his wrinkles appear more pronounced.

"Madame," he said, "I would not worry about the duke. I'm sure His Grace and Mr. Jones can manage. They are former soldiers and they know how to deal with villains."

"But today His Grace is not fighting a battle, he is fighting some unknown menace, and there may be more than one."

Marjorie had almost forgotten that they were alone and in a very crime-ridden part of London. She also knew that although Albert had not moved far from her side, with all the smoke about, now she could not see him.

What she had not mentioned to Edgar was she had never been good at keeping promises, particularly ones that did not make sense. She lowered her hands to her sides, her decision made. Without mentioning her plan to Albert, she moved toward the blazing building.

***

When Edgar entered the building, a thick smoke filled the corridor. To avoid becoming asphyxiated, he had crouched down, covering his mouth with the edge of his cloak, crawling forward. Looking up, it appeared that the roof was ready to collapse: Finding Sabeer was now was a priority.

The fire had spread to the walls of the east quadrant, the direction he was heading. His saving grace had to have been the weather, which remained a combination of frigid cold and soft breeze, helping to temper the flames. Then he spotted the shattered glass belonging to a once flaming hurricane lamp, laying a few inches away.

He stilled. The sound came again. He heard a faint coughing, accompanied by mournful weeping. Edgar immediately recognized the Hindu prayer. The prayer repeated in between coughs.

"Sabeer?" Edgar shouted.

No response.

The coughing sound stopped, which caused him to wonder if he'd imagined it. He crawled toward the sound, and that was when he met his first obstacle, a tall wall of crates.

He came alert hearing a loud creaking, followed by the sound of several hinges opening. Instinct caused him to move to the right, just in time to avoid a falling ceiling rafter. With a huge roar, it came crashing down in a flurry of flames and sparks.

He recovered, and that was when he saw it, the fallen crates had created a wide opening. At the end he spied Sabeer, lying prone on the ground, quite still, his arms and legs bound together: The boy appeared unconscious.

"Thank you!" he whispered, feeling a mixture of agony and relief.

Moving as expeditiously as possible, he shoved at crate after crate, until he had created a clear path leading to the boy. His hands were bloody and splintered, but he ignored the pain, too obsessed with his mission.

A shuffling noise behind him forced him to find cover. The smoke had thickened, but his senses remained sharp. He crouched lower, assuming an attack pose, and waited.

Removing a small pistol from the concealed pocket in the lining of his cloak, his fingers itched to pull the trigger. Based on the nearing noises, he knew he would get his chance soon enough. He could now hear the footsteps and the swishing of fabric; the combatant apparently wanted to make this easy for him. Indeed, he would have shot without compulsion, but then he noticed an unusual glinting of gold, and then a familiar cloaked figure emerged from the smoke.

"Bloody hell!" Edgar blustered, recognizing the apparition.

"Oh, thank heaven," Marjorie said. "Have you found Sabeer?"

Edgar still crouching down, was rendered speechless.

"Oh, dear, you have hurt your hands," she said, plucking them up, and then lifting them higher for closer inspection.

Edgar felt his mouth lolling. He stifled his shock when he caught sight of another flaming rafter about to fall to the left of where Marjorie stood. He dragged her forward just in time, and held her tightly in his arms. The descent had been soundless, yet deadly, the flames now lapping at the hem of her cape.

"Madame," was all he could say, before three more beams fell from the ceiling, missing them by a hair's breadth.

"Stay by my side," he growled.

"Oh, yes, I intend to."

He heard fear in her voice, and her hand had grabbed his cloak.

"We're going through there," he said, pointing toward the gap between the crates, while reaching to clasp her hand.

They moved forward, dodging the small flames, and soon reached Sabeer.

Edgar had never seen the boy look so lifeless. Someone had stripped him down to his drawers, his hands and feet were tied with coarse rope.

Marjorie stooped down to untie the ropes.

"He can't be dead," she wailed.

"No, he's still breathing. It's a miracle considering all the smoke he's inhaled. We need to get him out of here," Edgar said.

Lifting Sabeer into his arms, he waited for Marjorie's hand to latch onto the back of his cloak. She seemed to know his silent commands and complied.

They moved back through the tunnel of fallen debris, avoiding the flames skirting the floorboards. The blaze quickly consumed the crates and was well out of control. Edgar feared the warehouse would come down around them.

"We'll have to move toward the back," he shouted, above the boom of the roaring flames and crashing timbers.

"Try to keep up."

Marjorie nodded.

"So you came through the front, did you?" a voice said.

Edgar and Marjorie were surprised to see Lord Crosswell in their path. He stood facing them, an apparition in the swirling smoke and orange flames. He carried a revolver, and pointed it at Edgar's chest.

Thank goodness Marjorie hadn't screamed, but with some force she had grabbed onto his cloak, sending him staggering. Edgar managed, just barely, to steady himself, readjusting his weight, while keeping his arms latched about Sabeer.

"Grangefield, I see you accepted my invitation," Crosswell said, offering up a maniacal laugh.

"You're responsible for all of this?" Marjorie said.

"I'm afraid I am, Lady Tate. Actually, I'm hoping the fire will be blamed for your deaths," Crosswell replied. "You see, that's an important part of my plan. The only piece I was not sure about was when the duke would arrive, but then he did," Crosswell said, again laughing like a madman.

"You set this fire?" Marjorie stuttered, incredulous.

"I waited until I spotted his carriage, then I broke the lamp. With all this dry wood it took no time at all." Crosswell's focus shifted to Edgar. "You're awfully quiet, Grangefield, what are you up to?" he nudged the revolver in Edgar's direction.

"Allow Lady Tate to take the boy and leave," Edgar said. "You want a clean shot when the time comes, don't you?"

"Perhaps," Crosswell said, disinterested. He pulled out a second revolver from his coat pocket. "See, I came prepared. Now, kindly lower the boy to the floor." He wielded one of the guns, indicating to Edgar he should do just that.

Edgar had no choice. He lowered Sabeer, but that was when he spotted Jones. The man had hidden behind a tall stack of smoldering crates, aiming his rifle in Crosswell's direction. Marjorie stood diagonally in his line of fire: Edgar knew at that angle he wouldn't have a clear shot.

"You've been a thorn in my side for ten years, Grangefield," Crosswell said. "I've wanted to see you dead; I've never wanted anything so badly in my life."

"It appears that you're about to get your wish," Edgar said, "but why not let the boy and woman go? They have nothing to do with this," Edgar said.

"Do you think I'm stupid enough to leave witnesses? You were responsible for my sister's death, Grangefield, how could

419

you expect mercy? Of course, I realize you didn't put the noose around Virginia's neck, and you didn't pull the chair from under her feet, but you may as well have," Crosswell said with vehement rage. "Once a coward, as they say. A coward who ran away, instead of being there for my sister."

Marjorie gasped, but Crosswell ignored her. "The pathetic part of this story is that poor gal waited in the chapel for five hours. She even waited another ten days, knowing you had already left England."

"But Edgar didn't kill her," Marjorie said, "she had a choice."

Crosswell laughed. "Really, madame, how many choices are there for a jilted woman in our social setting?"

Edgar didn't hear her attempt to refute what Crosswell had said. Marjorie knew too well the social implications.

"After she'd killed herself," Crosswell continued, "you might as well have signed a death warrant for the rest of my family. Father died three months after the scandal broke. Mama then had to sell our home and belongings to pay off his gambling debts. She lived only a few years after that," Crosswell said, cocking the trigger of his pistol. "Are you satisfied, Grangefield?"

Marjorie gasped, and Crosswell laughed his madman's laugh, the hideous sound echoing through the burning chamber.

Edgar then heard Marjorie cough loudly, she had noticed Jones. She was about to say something to him, but Edgar stepped sideways treading on her toe.

She yelped, staggering backward.

"You did that on purpose," she spluttered. "I was just trying to … "

"I know what you were trying to do," he hissed. "Be so kind as to not vocalize your thoughts."

"What are you two conspiring? Not planning on escaping, I hope," Crosswell said with a sneer.

Unseen, Edgar managed to slip his right hand into the concealed pocket of his cloak, getting hold of the pistol. Without creating suspicion, Marjorie tried to step as far to the side as possible, most likely to give Jones the space he needed for a clear shot; but it still wasn't enough.

"Do you both mind kneeling down?" Crosswell said, moving the revolver in a threatening manner.

Edgar saw his advantage, and nodded to Marjorie in agreement. They both knelt down.

"I do apologize, Lady Tate, your time is up. It's too bad really, you were never part of the plan, and I have nothing to gain by killing you; but alas, here you are the unfortunate witness." He positioned the pistol toward her chest. "I want to make Grangefield suffer, so I believe I will shoot you first."

"I'm sure you will receive your just rewards soon enough." Marjorie said, with confidence.

"Whatever do you mean?" Crosswell asked, observing her.

"I mean ... "

Edgar gave her a sharp nudge in the arm, she yelped.

She glared at him, but said nothing.

Crosswell laughed at their antics. His pistol hand lowered and was now idle by his side. Then the cocking sound of a rifle alerted him, and he looked about.

Edgar chose that moment to lift his revolver. In one smooth motion he aimed the weapon at Crosswell's shoulder, knowing that he only had one chance.

Then he pulled the trigger.

~ ~ ~

Chapter Twenty-Three

Crosswell screamed, his pistol clattering to the ground. He staggered before collapsing to his knees onto the hot floorboards.

Jones emerged from his hiding spot, training his shotgun directly at Crosswell's face. He managed to kick away the two fallen pistols.

"Up," he growled.

"Good timing, Mr. Jones," Marjorie said, offering him a broad smile.

"Thank you, milady," Jones replied, without taking his eyes from Crosswell.

"Your brother has arrived, Your Grace," Jones said.

"He also has excellent timing," Edgar said, without emotion, at the same time bending down to cover Sabeer with his cloak.

Rupert entered the warehouse, rushing toward Edgar, followed by two uniformed members of the Metropolitan Police.

425

"Scotland Yard could only spare two men," he huffed.

"Good work," Edgar replied, relieved to see reinforcements.

"They can escort Lord Crosswell to Newgate. The charges are kidnapping and attempted murder."

Edgar glanced at the burning warehouse ceiling. "Outside! Let's get outside," he shouted.

Rupert glanced around him. "A sound idea, brother," he said, moving toward the exit.

Crosswell had already been chained and was being led outside by the police. Jones stepped forward to pick up Sabeer.

"Be careful with him, Jones, I'm not sure the extent of his injuries."

Jones nodded.

"What about Marjorie?" Rupert shouted from the doorway.

Edgar had almost reached the exit, turning to check on her progress.

She was still standing where he had left her, but something didn't look right; she appeared to be tugging at the skirt of her gown. Good Lord, her dress was caught on something.

"Edgar, look up there!" Rupert shouted.

He did. A ceiling rafter was about to come lose, and it was right above Marjorie's head.

Reacting, Edgar sprinted in Marjorie's direction. Reaching her, he pulled her into his arms.

"My dress, it's caught," she shouted, above the din of hissing wood and crackling flames.

Edgar's instincts told him they had to move, and in a hurry.

"Edgar, get out of there!" Rupert shouted.

His brother's warning came too late. The ceiling creaked one last time. The burning wood made a loud heaving noise, just before he heard Marjorie scream his name.

Then everything went pitch black.

***

"He is a thoughtless man."

"Yes, madame," Albert said, bouncing on the cushioned bench of the moving Grangefield coach.

Marjorie held Edgar's head in place on her lap, clamping down extra tight when the coach hit a bump in the road. The burning rafter had fallen, and Edgar had been hurt.

Whilst in the process of transferring Sabeer into one of the coaches, Jones had heard Marjorie's scream, and dashed back inside the warehouse. He'd acted without delay, carrying Edgar's unconscious body outside.

Soon afterward, two coaches moved at an ungodly pace, making their way toward the duke's London residence.

"I tell you the duke is inconsiderate, stubborn, ill-tempered, and unyielding," Marjorie said, stroking Edgar's forehead, and brushing away his hair from a large bleeding gash.

"He should not have returned to save me. I could have managed without his assistance."

"Yes, madame."

"Albert," Marjorie said, "if all you can say is 'yes, madame,' I suggest you not say anything at all."

"Yes, madame," he intoned.

Marjorie rolled her eyes. "Men!" she muttered.

She trailed her fingers across Edgar's face, caressing the stubble on his chin.

"How could he? I did not need saving. Men always presume women need saving."

Albert didn't reply. His elderly frame became jostled every time the carriage hit one of the many nasty bumps in the road.

"Jones, do drive slower," Marjorie shouted, angrily.

"'Ere, you just told me to go faster: I wish you'd make up your mind, Lady Tate," Jones shouted, with irritation.

"You're right, Jones; by all means, go as fast as you please."

Marjorie heard Jones grunt, but the coach continued to move at the same clipped pace.

Within the half hour they arrived at Grangefield House. The coach that transported Sabeer had arrived first, and the boy had already been removed to one of the bedchambers.

Three footmen waited by the steps. As soon as Jones set the break, they carried Edgar's unconscious body into the house.

An hour later the doctor arrived. He tended to Sabeer first. The boy had awakened from his unconscious state, only to start crying, before again falling asleep from exhaustion.

The doctor's diagnosis of Edgar included a large bump on the head, and several cuts and minor burns to his hands, which had been bandaged.

The doctor could not say when or if the duke would awake, which caused Marjorie to become both restless and anxious. Good Lord, if Edgar didn't recover she would never forgive herself.

"Rupert, we should get a second medical opinion," Marjorie said. The duke's bedchamber was very spacious, and Edgar had been laid out on his very large bed. Other than his bandaged hands, an even wider bandage had been wrapped around his forehead, covering the nasty cut above his left eye.

Rupert didn't reply; he was seated on a chaise close to the bed, watching Edgar like a vigilant parent.

Wanting to shatter the heavy silence, Marjorie said, "I've never known him to be so inanimate."

"The doctor mentioned we should talk to him," Rupert said, "he might be able to hear us." He then stood, moving toward her. He looked at her, his expression serious.

"He will be all right, Marjorie."

"He is a most obstinate man, Rupert. I'm sure he's doing this just to make me feel guilty about not keeping my promise: Perhaps he blames me."

"I wouldn't start presuming things," Rupert said, walking toward the door.

"I should go check on Sabeer," he said. "When the boy realized Edgar wasn't there, and he wouldn't be coming, he became hysterical. He eventually cried himself to sleep. I left him with Albert; I hope you don't mind."

431

"No, of course not," Marjorie said. "Albert dotes on the boy. It is unfortunate that between Lady Osterly and this kidnapping business, Sabeer has suffered a great deal."

Rupert didn't reply, and without her noticing, he quietly left the room.

Needing to stay busy, Marjorie tied back the curtains at the bedpost, exposing Edgar's face to the dimming light from the window.

The duke's face had not seen a razor in two days; even unconscious he looked intimidating. His naked shoulders and arms were covered with a crisp white sheet.

Marjorie noticed his long black eyelashes grazed the tops of his cheeks. His mouth had fallen open, and his breathing was even. She skimmed her fingers over the bandage on his forehead, sweeping away his dark curls.

"You are the most exasperating man," she whispered.

As usual, she felt the need to touch him, tugging at the hairs on his naked chest. If he'd been awake, no doubt he would have yowled; but he didn't make a sound, only his nose twitched.

432

"You must wake up, Edgar—I mean now! It is most inconsiderate of you to sleep the whole day away."

Holding his hand, she turned to look out the window; there was very little view with the darkening sky. "Your Grace, you are needed here because a great deal must be done."

She squeezed his hand. "You see, Crosswell has been remanded to the lower courts and is awaiting trial. As the prime witness, your presence will be required. I suspect the authorities will charge him with kidnapping.

"Rupert also mentioned that Crosswell confessed to shooting at you on Christmas Eve. Since he shot Mr. Lyndhurst instead, he will also be charged with assault."

Marjorie lifted Edgar's hand, cradling it to her cheek. She had seated herself on the bed at an angle to his prone body, now stroking his knuckles.

"Sabeer is most disturbed because you have been asleep for so long."

Marjorie thought she saw Edgar's eyelids flutter, but dismissed this as a cloud on her spectacles.

"Indeed, the boy has been beside himself. It's not everyday one is kidnapped and left to perish in a burning building. Really, Edgar, you must wake up!"

Marjorie pinched his hand not too gently, but he did not stir.

"Last but not least, our marriage plans: How can we discuss the terms if you are spending hours at a time in bed? There must be terms, you know. I just can't give up my business interests without a productive discussion beforehand. Not that I would, give them up, of course."

His skin had warmed, a good sign. She even imagined his thumb caressing her palm; silly, she was just being wishful.

"On the subject of marriage," Marjorie continued, I will admit, I experience immense pleasure in your company. What I am trying to say is: Oh, really, this is most difficult. Well, you see … I have fallen in love with you. There, I have said it out loud for all the world to hear!"

She glanced at Edgar's chest, watching it rise and fall.

"So, since I do love you, it is quite inappropriate for you to spend this very important moment unconscious." She squeezed his hand with a tad too much pressure, and thought for a moment he flinched. Then she bent down to his ear and yelled:

"Wake up, Your Grace. I just told you that I am in love with you; be so kind as to appreciate the effort I am making."

She watched, surprised, as his eyelids fluttered open. He smiled at her, his arms snaking about her waist like a vice. He ignored her "Good Lord," dragging her forward until she lay nestled across his chest, one of her legs dangling over the side of the bed. They were now face to face.

"I heard you, madame," Edgar's hoarse voice groused in her ear. He licked his lips. "In fact, I heard you all three times," he croaked.

Marjorie struggled in his embrace, not knowing whether to feel relief or outrage.

"Your Grace, I am delighted you are awake," Marjorie said, straightening her spectacles.

"Have I not told you not to do that with your spectacles, madame?"

She smiled at him.

Edgar continued. "I might have missed your declaration of love if you had not pinched, prodded, and plucked me into awareness."

Marjorie's cheeks warmed.

He released her a fraction, lifting her arms about his shoulders; this allowed her to rest her head on his bare chest.

"I do love you," she said, tilting her head up and kissing his chin.

"Yes, I believe you do," Edgar replied, pulling her closer.

"The only question remains is, will you marry me?"

Marjorie sighed. "Well, I suppose so. England has not been safe since you arrived. In between roadside shootings and kidnappings, there's no telling what will happen next. It appears that someone must keep a close eye on you, and that happy burden has fallen upon me." She then kissed his cheek.

Edgar smiled, his eyelids fluttering closed.

"How is my son?"

"Physically very improved. He was very lucky not to get hurt in that warehouse. I'm positive he will feel much better once he hears that you are awake."

Edgar winced when he tried to turn his head.

"Is the pain awful?" Marjorie whispered, snuggling into his arms. "The doctor left some laudanum if you need it."

Edgar stroked her back. "It doesn't hurt if I stay very still and imagine you naked."

Marjorie laughed, nudging him in the ribs.

He winced.

"Oh, I'm so sorry."

"How sorry?" Edgar asked, his hand lowering to lift her skirts. Marjorie looked over her shoulder, while shooing his hands away.

"Really, Marjorie, it's just my head and hands that hurt, the rest of me is functioning quite well."

She attempted to sound appalled: "Edgar, someone might come in."

He offered her a tender kiss.

Her lips moved with his in a slow gentle dance, causing Edgar to groan.

"Madame, I died a thousand deaths watching that warehouse roof collapse almost on your head. In the future you will not frighten me like that again."

"Mmm," Marjorie replied, her tongue caressing his lower lip.

He grunted with approval, kissing her cheek and stroking her back. "In all things," he muttered, "you will follow my direction to the letter."

Surprised, Marjorie looked at him. "Don't be absurd," she said. She noticed his frown. "Since we are on the subject of independence. As a courtesy, I am informing you that after we are married, I will be continuing my business interests. Is that understood, Your Grace?"

Edgar's face held an odd expression. "Madame, I realize there will be occasions when we don't see eye-to-eye. However, I will endeavor not to interfere with your odd pursuits; in exchange for my generosity ... "

Her mouth opened to voice an objection, but he kissed her with a firm smack on the lips, pulling away quickly, then lifting one of his fingers and placing it on her lips.

"As I was saying, in exchange for my generosity, I expect some degree of authority."

Marjorie stared at him with a willful smile. "Well, I suppose even I can manage 'some degree of authority.' What about Sabeer?" Marjorie asked in concern.

"Sabeer accepts my authority." Edgar said.

"No. What I meant, Edgar, is will he mind me being his mother?"

"I can't believe you are worried about what the boy thinks," he replied. "If you had not noticed, he happens to adore you. I am confident Sabeer will embrace this idea without objection."

His lips moved to hers. "Speaking of embraces, care to seal our bargain with another kiss?"

They were interrupted by the sound of a man clearing his throat. With reluctance, they turned, still entwined, in the direction of the door.

"So good of you to join us, Edgar," Rupert said. "How are you feeling, old man?"

"Other than a severe headache, you still look and sound like one of my annoying brothers."

Rupert smiled. "I can see Marjorie is keeping you entertained. I suppose there's no chance of you dropping off for another long nap?"

"None at all. Actually, this might be a good time to start arranging a private wedding. It appears all of this conspiring of yours has paid off," Edgar said, winking at his brother.

"I really have no idea what you mean," Rupert said, offering Edgar and Marjorie a look of outrage. "I dare say that head injury has taken a toll."

"Seriously, brother," Edgar said, "don't you think tomorrow would be a good day for me to get married?"

Edgar smiled at Marjorie.

"A splendid idea, Edgar. Perhaps for something this important, I should handle the matter personally. Wouldn't want to bother the servants with all the details."

He backed out the door, then stopped his retreat. "By the by, do you still have that marriage license I gave you?"

"I entrusted Jones with it," Edgar said.

Marjorie tried not to laugh at Rupert's excited expression.

"Very good. Then I think I will just pop out and inform Sabeer that you are awake; I'm sure he will want to attend the wedding. Uh ...you two carry on."

That said, Rupert departed the room.

Left alone, Edgar and Marjorie stared at one another. After a short protracted silence, they both burst out laughing.

"Did you suspect?" Edgar asked.

"Not at first."

"He is my brother," Edgar said. "Growing up I always knew when Rupert was up to something. But playing Cupid; well, I'm surprised he actually pulled it off. In fact, have you considered that he might be better at this matchmaking business than you are, my dear?"

"Perhaps I should consider retiring, Your Grace." Marjorie said, frowning.

"I fear your full retirement may be detrimental to our sanity," Edgar said. "Also keep in mind I have two more unsuspecting, unmarried siblings: Which one do you suppose might be headed to the altar next, Pierce or Tiffany?"

After a short protracted silence, in unison they exclaimed, "Tiffany!"

Then they both burst out laughing.

~ ~ ~ ~ ~

"Life feels a whole lot better when

there are happy endings."

—V.H. Lunden

About the Author

Lunden's writing inspiration comes with an agenda, to write fun stories that encourage smiles. Be prepared to be transported to a time and place where love and laughter provide an easy distraction. Readers will also be introduced to characters who want to make a difference in the world, and by doing so become both unique and "incomparable!"

~ ~ ~

Grangefield Hall – The Series

Updates about upcoming books in the Grangefield Hall series are available via E-mail. Sign up at www.brightperformance.com.

www.ingramcontent.com/pod-product-compliance
Lightning Source LLC
Chambersburg PA
CBHW031939260626
47157CB00016B/89